ENRAPTURED

THE ROGUES SERIES BOOK 2

TRACIE DELANEY

Copyright © 2020 Tracie Delaney

Edited by StudioEnp

Proofreading by Katie Schmahl, Jean Bachen, and Jacqueline Beard

Cover art by *Tiffany @TEBlack Designs*

All rights reserved. No part of this publication may be reproduced, stored in any retrieval system, or transmitted, in uniform or by any means, electronic, mechanical, photocopying, recording or otherwise without prior written permission of the author.

This is a work of fiction. Names, characters, places, and incidents are either the products of the author's imagination or are used fictitiously, and any resemblance to actual persons, living or dead, business establishments, events, or locales is entirely coincidental.

Enraptured

BOOK TWO IN THE Rogues SERIES

What's your worst day ever? Mine is getting fired and discovering my boyfriend cheating on me in the same day.

At least I thought that was as bad as it could get.

Turns out I was wrong.

Only someone with my kind of luck could arrive at an interview for a job I desperately need and then discover my potential new boss is the guy I drunk-kissed the other night. An unsolicited—and unwanted—kiss if the way he recoiled is any indication.

I don't expect him to offer me the job as nanny to his seven-year-old daughter. I mean, who wants a drunken harlot taking care of something so precious? Except he does. And against my better judgement, I accept the position.

He's gorgeous and sexy and the kind of father that has my ovaries screaming. Yet to him, I might as well be invisible.

Until the night that everything changes.

Now, I'll do anything to keep him, especially when his past comes knocking.

A NOTE TO THE READER

~

Dear Reader,

Well, here we are at book 2 in the series already. Thank you so much for choosing to carry on with the ROGUES series. I have a lot more planned, so stay tuned.

Oliver is very different to Ryker. In fact, he's very different to any of the other ROGUES. Perhaps the fact he became a father at such a young age forced him to grow up whereas the other ROGUES were free to sow their oats a little more. Oliver is sweet and kind and Oh So Hot! His relationship with his daughter makes me swoon, and I hope you swoon, too.

And as for Harlow, well, she is the perfect woman for him, even if it takes him a little while to realize that. He's a bit broken, you see, and more than a little distrustful. You'll understand why as you read on.

I'd love to hear what you think about Enraptured once you're finished reading, either by leaving a review, or by joining my Facebook reader group Tracie's Racy Aces. See you there.

In the meantime, enjoy.

Love,
Tracie

BOOKS BY TRACIE DELANEY

The Winning Ace Series

Ace - A Winning Ace Novella

Winning Ace

Losing Game

Grand Slam

Winning Ace Boxset

Mismatch

Break Point - A Winning Ace Novella

Stand-alone

My Gift To You

Draven

The Brook Brothers Series

The Blame Game

Against All Odds

His To Protect

Web of Lies

The Brook Brothers Complete Boxset

Irresistibly Mine Series

Tempting Christa

Avenging Christa

Full Velocity Series

Friction

Gridlock

Inside Track

Full Velocity Boxset (Books 1-3)

ROGUES Series

Entranced

Enraptured

Entrapped

Enchanted

Enthralled

Enticed

1

Harlow

"Why are all men bastards?"

My best friend, Katie, arched her brows, her forehead wrinkling. "That's a bit of a generalization. What's happened?"

I tilted my phone toward me, the harsh lights overhead making it difficult to see her on the six-inch screen.

"What *hasn't* happened."

Tears pricked my eyes, but I refused to let them fall. "I got fired from my job, and when I arrived home, earlier than planned, obviously, I found Carter in bed with our neighbor." I laughed bitterly. "If you can count bending her over and doing her from behind as 'in bed'. And what's worse, he always told me he hated that position. Said it was degrading to women. Fucker."

Katie gasped and then gave me a sympathetic head tilt. "Oh, babes. I'm so sorry. Where are you?"

I sniffed, wiping my nose with the back of my hand. "McCory's."

"Hang tight. I'm on my way over."

"You're working tonight."

"I'm not due in until eight. Give me ten minutes. And don't empty the top shelf before I get there."

The screen went blank. I sighed, tossed my phone on the bar, and held up a finger at the bartender, pointing my chin at the empty glass in front of me that only five minutes ago had contained a "double gin and hold the tonic".

"Same again."

His lips flattened, his disapproval of my choice of drink clear. "How about a Coke?"

Fed up with men who thought they knew best, as if I didn't have a perfectly functioning mind of my own, I hit him with my fiercest glare. "I don't want a Coke," I said, crisply enunciating every syllable. "If I wanted a Coke, I'd have asked for one. Strangely enough, I'm a grown woman who knows what she wants. And I want a goddamn double gin. With ice."

He muttered something unintelligible under his breath, probably calling me a bitch. Just as well I didn't hear his undoubtedly barbed comment given my current black mood. A minute later, he returned and slammed down my gin, then snatched the check from the empty glass in front of me. He spun around and stabbed at the register, then shoved a new check in front of me.

"Thanks, dollface." I hit him with my sweetest smile.

A chuckle to my right drew my attention. I turned my head. "Something funny?" I growled at the guy sitting next to me nursing a scotch. His sharp suit and expensive watch caught my eye. Great. One of those Wall Street types who thought women were commodities, just like the stocks and shares they traded every day.

Before he could answer, Katie arrived, out of breath and red-faced. She must have run most of the way. She sat on my left-hand side and pulled me into a tight hug.

"Babes, I'm so sorry. If I see Carter, I'll stab him in the balls with a blunt needle. Water, please," she added as the bartender walked past.

He gave me a pointed look as if to say, "That's what you should have ordered."

I treated him to a cold glare, then picked up my drink and knocked the entire thing back, wincing as the alcohol burned its way down my throat. "And another double gin for me."

He jabbed a finger in my direction. "Last one."

"Fine," I spat. "Plenty of other bars in Manhattan."

"Take it easy, babes." Katie stroked a hand down my arm, a soothing gesture that usually worked.

Not today.

"I hope you kicked him out."

I nodded, my earlier tears threatening to return when I thought about how I would make rent this month. No job, no Carter. No hope.

"I suppose he had a pitiful excuse?"

"Yep." I pressed my hands together in prayer, imitating Carter's pathetic pleading. "I didn't mean to do it, baby. It was a mistake, baby. You're the one I love, baby. I told him to pack his things and leave before I get home, and then I came here." A tear clung to my lashes, then fell. I dashed a hand over my cheek, sweeping it away. "I don't know what I'm going to do, Katie. With no job and minus the safety net of Carter's salary propping me up, I can't make rent."

Her arms came around me again, and she put my head on her shoulder. "You can stay at my apartment until you get things situated."

I sat up straight. "You're an angel for offering, but your place isn't big enough for one, never mind two. I'll work something out. I'm paid up until the end of next week, so I won't worry just yet. Tomorrow, I'll call my recruitment consultant and see what she has on her books." I grimaced. "Although at such short notice, I'm unlikely to find anything close to ideal. I guess I can always flip burgers, right?"

Katie swept her hand down my arm once more, then squeezed my fingers. "You could temporarily move back in with your parents until you get back on your feet."

I shook my head violently, imagining the judgmental expression on my dad's face if I turned up jobless and broke. And Mom with her disappointed head tilt. *You wouldn't be in this mess if you'd worked harder at school, Harlow.* If only I *had* been gifted academically. Unfortunately for me, math and science were alien, beyond my comprehension, unlike my three brothers who excelled at school and then college, each one of them graduating medical school with honors and joining the long line of doctors in my family.

It didn't mean I was stupid, it just meant I had other skills like compassion and understanding, and patience. Those attributes had led me to a career in childcare, and I was good at it. Kids took to me. Sadly, looking after other people's children didn't pay very well.

"I'd rather sleep on the streets."

Katie studied my face, her eyes filled with sadness. She, of all people, understood the difficult relationship I had with my parents, having witnessed it since kindergarten.

"They love you, Harlow."

I threw my hands in the air. "I know. I know. But I can't, Katie. I just can't. I'm an adult, and I'm determined to stand on my own two feet. I won't go running back to Mommy and Daddy every time life dumps a pile of shit on me."

"I understand, babes. I do. You've always been stubborn and independent. But just think about it. Or at least call one of your brothers. They'd hate to think of you struggling."

I nodded, but both she and I knew I'd only call them as a very last resort. I *was* stubborn, *and* proud. Besides, my brothers would tell Dad, and that would be that. I couldn't stand another round of heavy sighing and miffed expressions. I'd find a way through this. I *had* to.

Katie sipped her water. "What's the skinny with the job, anyway? How come they fired you."

I bit my lip, regret swarming through me. If I'd kept my mouth shut, I'd still be in gainful employment. *And still dealing with that creep of a husband.*

"I finally told her. The wife. She didn't take it well."

Katie's jaw dropped to the floor. "Oh crap."

"That's one way of putting it. Goddamn!" I slammed a fist into my thigh. "I shouldn't have said anything."

Katie shook her head vehemently. "No, babes. That scumbag needed stopping, and the wife deserved to know. It's about time men realized that we're not their property, for them to paw at whenever they feel like it. Just because he paid your salary doesn't mean he can cop a feel." She shuddered. "You'd put up with that shit for long enough."

"Some good honesty did me," I said. "I bet she refuses to give me a reference, too."

"It's the rack," Katie said, giving me a playful nudge, her eyes twinkling in an effort to cheer me up. "Seriously, men lose their minds and only think with their dicks when presented with your girls."

"If I could afford the surgery, I'd get the damn things cut off," I grumbled. "She called me Harlot. Not Harlow. Harlot. On purpose."

Katie clasped a hand to her mouth in what I thought was empathy. Then I noticed the violent shake to her shoulders. "Oh dear," she managed to say through her emerging giggles.

For the first time all day, I found myself laughing. I held up my glass of gin. "Cheers, friend."

"You're welcome." She clinked her glass against mine. "Look, babes, you're terrific at what you do. Kids love you. And except for this latest family, your references are solid. You'll find yourself snapped up in no time. And for the record, I think you're better off without Carter."

"You're absolutely right on the latter, and I hope you're right on the former. Otherwise I'm fucked." I let out a heavy sigh. "That's it. From now on, no more guys. I'm done with men. And I'm going to insist my next role is for a single mother. I should be fine…" I waggled my eyebrows. "Unless she's a lesbian."

Katie laughed. "See, you're already looking on the bright side. And maybe a short break from relationships will do you some good."

"Yep," I said, setting my jaw. "I've definitely had enough. Men are all jerkoff useless bastards, and I'm done." I drew a finger across my throat to stress my point. "Done."

Katie rolled her eyes. "You're twenty-five, not seventy-five. Let's just say you're on a relationship sabbatical." She inclined her head. "Hmm, I might trademark that term."

I laughed. "Do it, before someone else does."

She glanced at her watch and jumped off the stool. "Damn, I'm late." She kissed my cheek. "Call me tomorrow and try not to worry."

"I will."

I finished my second—no, third—double gin. One look at the bartender told me I wouldn't get another. Screw him. I'd call into a liquor store on the way home.

"Not all men are bastards."

I turned my head which made the room spin. Yeah, I really had had too much to drink. I waited for everything to stop moving, then squinted at Mr. Wall Street. "Huh?"

"All men aren't bad. And all women aren't good."

"Well, aren't you a treat," I said, irritation heating my blood. Who did this guy think he was? "If this is a come-on, I'm not your girl."

"It isn't."

I suppressed a twinge of hurt. No woman liked to be told a

guy wasn't interested. *I'm such a dichotomy.* "Good. Because I'm done with men."

His lips curved up on one side in a faint smile. He had nice lips. And a nice smile. And gorgeous navy-blue come-to-bed eyes, and—

FFS, Harlow.

"Yes, I heard. I think the entire bar is aware of your newfound celibate status."

I narrowed my eyes and pursed my lips. "Are you for real?"

He patted himself down, then grinned. "It appears so."

I chuckled, my reaction surprising considering five seconds ago, I'd been on the verge of taking my anger and frustration out on him. "You're crazy."

He stuck out his hand. "Also known as Oliver."

I shook it. "Harlow."

"Did you say Harlot?" he asked with an arched brow.

I threw back my head and laughed—and it felt so good after the day I'd had. "You're as sharp as the suit you're wearing."

He gestured to the bartender, pushing his empty glass across the bar. "Another scotch. Single malt. And a glass of water for my friend."

Unlike my reaction to the bartender when he'd attempted to curtail my drinking, I meekly accepted Oliver's take-charge attitude, much to the surprise of the man serving the drinks if the flare in his eyes was any indication.

My gaze fell to Oliver's left hand. No wedding ring. How was that possible? He clearly had money. His watch alone probably cost more than my entire salary last year. He was funny, sexy, kind, had drown-in-me baby blues, and owned a body that filled his tailored suit in all the right places. Oh, and did I mention he was sexy? Yeah, I said that already.

I'm so wasted.

"Here, drink this," Oliver said, sliding the glass of iced water over to me. "It'll make you feel better—or at least minimize tomorrow's hangover."

I downed the whole glass in one, wiping my mouth with the back of my hand. The room spun again. I tried to focus on Oliver. There were two of him.

Time to go home, Harlow.

I unsteadily got down from the high bar stool, wavered, and almost fell. Strong hands gripped my arms, righting me.

"Sorry," I slurred. "It's been a horrible day."

Oliver reached for my purse and slid it diagonally across my body. "Let's get you a cab home, shall we?"

"I can manage."

He smirked. "I'm not saying you can't. However, my mother brought me up to be a gentleman. You're actually doing me a favor by letting me see you safely into a cab."

I peered up at him, then waggled my finger in his face. "Oh, you're good, mister. Very, very good."

He slipped his arm around my waist and eased me toward the door.

"Bye, dollface," I slung over my shoulder at the bartender. Then I giggled. "He hates me."

"I'm sure that's not true," Oliver replied.

The temperature outside had cooled considerably during the time I'd spent inside the bar. I shivered and wrapped my thin coat around me. Oliver held up his hand for a cab, and one instantly pulled over.

"Here we are." He opened the rear door. "Make sure this lady gets home safely," he added to the cab driver, handing him a fifty-dollar bill.

I should tell him I could afford my own cab fare home, except we both knew that was a lie.

I gripped the top of the door and tried to focus. "Look at you. A regular Prince Charming." And then I did something completely dumb. I stood on tiptoes and kissed him. Barely a kiss, really. More like a brush of lips.

Oliver reeled backward so fast anyone would think I'd shot him with a taser. "I'm sorry," he said. "I'm not... I mean, that's not... I have to go."

He hurried off and hurled himself into the back of a waiting limousine. It immediately filtered into the busy traffic.

I pressed the heels of my hands to my eyes.

I'm never drinking again.

2

Oliver

I touched my mouth with the tips of my fingers, still able to feel the unfamiliar sensation of Harlow's lips against my own. I should have dealt with that much better. She'd had a bad enough day as it was without my hang-ups adding to her misery. She wasn't the first woman I'd kissed since Sara left, but it was the first in a while.

Five years, to be precise.

When my wife walked out on me and our baby daughter, Annie, before she'd even celebrated her first birthday, I'd drowned my sorrows in other women. But all fucking anything with a pulse had done was make me feel even worse about myself. In the end, I'd simply given up trying to blot out the agony of Sara's betrayal and had poured all my energies into Annie instead. Her happiness was the only thing that mattered. She didn't deserve a string of dates—if I could even describe them as such—coming and going. And the last thing I wanted was for her to get attached to one of my brief flings, only for me to run a mile at the first sign of longevity.

I did my best to make up for the fact she didn't have a mother, but I had sleepless nights about the permanent damage Sara's abandonment might have caused. Annie wasn't short of love. She had me, my mom, my best friends and their families. But every day, I held my breath, waiting for her to ask why she only had a dad when all her school friends had two parents. And when that inevitable question arose, I worried that I didn't have a practiced answer.

I swept a hand over my face, exhaustion weighing heavily on me. I hadn't taken a full day off in over a month, and the long hours had begun to take their toll. I always made sure I had breakfast with Annie each morning, and waved her off to school, and in the evenings I never missed bath time or putting her to bed and reading her a story. Those were my favorite parts of the day. But in between those brief moments of joy, I filled the hours with work, work, and more work.

Maybe I should book a vacation. Take Annie down to Florida. A trip to Disney World might be the tonic I needed to find some purpose to life again. To let Annie's happiness wash over me, seep into my veins, and chase away the looming depression.

I closed my eyes, letting my head relax against the seat. Until I'd landed this latest deal, any dreams of a vacation would have to remain just that. Dreams. Besides, Annie had school. I couldn't remove her on a whim simply because I was feeling maudlin.

I can still smell her.

The woman from the bar.

She smelled clean, of soap and shampoo, and the barest hint of perfume.

I shook my head and pinched my nose between my thumb and forefinger. She was only in my thoughts because I felt sorry for her. From what I'd gleaned from her conversation with her friend, her sleazy employer had fired her because the husband had gotten a little too friendly, and then she'd returned home to find her boyfriend sticking it to the neighbor. That was a shitty day by anyone's standards. I didn't blame her for getting blind drunk. I'd have done the same.

Hell, I *had* done the same when my life had gone down the toilet six years ago.

The only person who'd saved me from myself? Annie. I'd do anything for that kid, and she would always, *always* come first with me.

I didn't matter. *She* did. Period.

My driver pulled up outside my apartment block that overlooked the Upper West side of Central Park. I'd bought the penthouse suite when ROGUES, the company I part owned with five of my best friends, hit the big time. We'd all met in college and, bored with the monotony of classes, began dabbling in gaming apps. One took off, sending us headlong into a life of riches beyond our wildest dreams. Now, all these years later, we were equal partners in a global brand, with a portfolio of diverse businesses from telecommunications to agriculture, a hotel chain, and even a string of exotic dance clubs.

I checked my watch. Five before seven, a little later than I usually arrived home. I wasn't in the habit of going to bars on the way home from work, but after the week I'd had, I'd craved five minutes to myself. It had done me good, not only for the few moments of peace, but because meeting Harlow had reminded me of how lucky I was. I had a mother who thought I was perfect, even though the reality was far from that, a daughter who was the light of my life, a fulfilling professional career, and five of the greatest friends a man could ask for.

The only blight in my otherwise perfect existence? An ex-wife who betrayed my trust so badly, I found it impossible to even consider dipping my toe into the water with anyone else. What kind of woman walked out on her husband and daughter without a backward glance? Even after I discovered she'd had a brief fling with our family doctor, I'd harbored slivers of hope that she'd come home. I'd have forgiven her anything back then, when I was young and stupid. But she'd ignored every olive branch I'd extended, every email begging her to reconsider, every text message where I'd attached pictures of Annie hoping to break through a seemingly impenetrable shell.

And in return, I'd received a letter from her lawyer ordering me to end the harassment.

Harassment?

That was the moment I'd filed for divorce. She didn't contest the application, but she did demand a large financial settlement. I'd paid without a murmur of dissent, just to end the torment once and for all.

I hadn't seen her since, and neither had Annie.

Fortunately, I had a selfless mother who'd provided rock-solid and unwavering support at a time of crisis in my life. She'd moved in to help me take care of my daughter. I honestly didn't know how I'd have coped without her.

I rode the private elevator up to the top floor and dropped my briefcase in the foyer before wandering into the main living area to find Annie and Mom. No doubt they'd be in the kitchen, clearing up after dinner. Sure enough, there they were, Annie standing on the step that allowed her to reach the sink, washing up her plate, and Mom beside her, ready with a towel to dry it. We had a dishwasher, but Mom liked to teach Annie that not everything came easy in life, and you had to know how to do the basics.

Christ, I loved my mom.

I leaned my shoulder against the entrance and folded my arms, watching the scene before me, love bursting from my chest. These people, right here, were my life.

Once Annie passed her plate to my mom, and the chances of her accidently dropping it passed, I crouched, then called out, "Hey, munchkin."

She wheeled around, a huge grin lighting up her face. "Daddy!" She leaped from the step and threw herself into my waiting arms. After a few seconds hugging, she drew back, then frowned.

"You're late. And you smell like whiskey."

Mom shot me a look, one eyebrow curved in query.

"How do you know what whiskey smells like?" I asked my daughter, who had now placed her hands on her hips and was giving me one of her impish looks.

"I know lots of things," she said.

I grinned at her sass. "Do you know that it's time for your bath?"

That made her pout. Annie was at the age where she wanted to stay up late for fear of missing out. I'd capitulated at the weekends, moving her bedtime to eight-thirty, but on a school night, I refused to budge from seven-thirty.

"Just five more minutes, Daddy, please," she begged. "I haven't seen you in forever."

I grinned again at her overexaggeration. "You saw me this morning."

"Daddy, do you have any idea how long ago that is?" She kicked out a hip.

My heart clenched. *Fucking adorable.*

"I do, munchkin. But there's only one more day of school, and then we have the whole weekend to look forward to." I waggled my eyebrows. "And who knows? We *might* take a trip to the zoo… if you're good."

"I'll be good," she expelled, running for the stairs. She stopped, then spun around and beckoned me. "Come on, Daddy!"

"That child gets more mischievous by the day," Mom said, her eyes filled with adoration.

"Tell me about it." I grinned and set off after her.

I bathed Annie, got her into bed, and read her a story. She insisted I leave her bedroom door ajar and the hallway light on. I did as she asked, blew her a kiss, then returned to the large open-plan living area that housed the kitchen, dining, and relaxation areas of my home. The hub of the place, really, and where we spent most of our time despite the penthouse having several other rooms, both formal and informal. This space had the best view of the park, though, as did Annie's bedroom. I liked that she woke up to greenery in a city full of concrete.

"I saved you some pasta," Mom said as she spooned spaghetti and meatballs into a bowl.

I sat at the kitchen table and loosened my tie. "What would I do without you?"

"Strange you should say that." She took a seat beside me and pushed the pasta and some grated parmesan in my direction. "I wanted to talk to you about something."

A twinge of anxiety twisted my gut. I shoveled a forkful of spaghetti into my mouth, chewed slowly to buy myself some time, then swallowed. "Oh, yeah?"

"Scott is taking a cruise around the world." She paused, took a deep breath, then hit me with it. "He's asked me to go with him, and I've said yes."

Scott was the man my mother had been seeing for the past few months. I liked the guy. Dad had died ten years ago, and Mom deserved to find happiness with someone else.

"For how long?"

"Three months, give or take. We leave a week from Saturday."

I didn't begrudge my mom anything. She'd basically given up her life for me and Annie. But how the hell would I cope without her?

I squeezed her hand, and, biting back my anxiety, I hit her with a broad smile. "It's wonderful, Mom. You'll have an amazing time."

"I know it's not ideal," she said. "But I've already contacted some very reputable agencies. I've told them we'll need someone who's willing to live in. And I'll handle the interviews, narrow them down to a short list. All you have to do is rubber-stamp the final choice."

"Whoa, back up," I said. "What agencies? Who's moving in?"

"Why, the nanny agencies, darling," Mom said, as though having an outsider in our home was the most natural thing in the world. Unlike most of my friends, I hadn't resorted to household staff, save a cleaner who came in twice a week to help Mom out, and I didn't intend for that to change.

I flexed my jaw. "I don't need a nanny."

"Correct, you don't," Mom said, chuckling. "The nanny is for Annie."

I bit the inside of my cheek. "Not funny, Mother."

"Come on, Oliver," she said. "You can't manage here alone, not with the hours you work."

"I'm not having a stranger living here."

Mom huffed, her arms coming across her chest in defensive mode. "Then give me an alternative."

I twirled spaghetti around my fork, my appetite waning as I racked my brain, trying to find a solution that didn't involve hiring outside help. Except there wasn't one. I couldn't take care of Annie alone and keep up with my other responsibilities. And I refused to stop Mom from going on this trip. She'd put her life on hold long enough. It was about time I took some of the weight off her shoulders.

"Fine," I said, my tone resigned. "When do we start the interviews?"

Mom smiled and leaned over to kiss my cheek. "Monday."

3

Harlow

Three days.

Three measly days, and then I'd find myself out on the streets, homeless. My rent was due Friday, and I didn't have the money to pay it. My hiring agency hadn't come up with any suitable opportunities. Strike that. They hadn't come up with *any* opportunities, suitable or otherwise. My drunken bravado last Thursday night that I'd only work for single women had melted away. If I placed too many conditions on my search, it'd cut my chances of finding work down even further.

I half-filled a bowl with cereal and sparingly added milk. I'd need to save every cent until I was earning again. Today, I would swallow my pride and look for any kind of work. And I'd go apartment hunting in the Bronx, or even farther out. I needed somewhere cheaper to live. Even if I found a job today, I couldn't afford this place without Carter.

One phone call to my parents or any one of my brothers

and a huge sum of money would be deposited in my bank account, along with a truckload of judgment.

I didn't need the cash that badly. Not yet, anyway.

I ate my meager breakfast, the food only taking the edge off my hunger rather than sating it, then went for a walk, dodging the rain the weather forecaster failed to predict. Even Mother Nature had it in for me. As I waited for the light to change, my head bowed against the driving wind, my phone rang. Ducking under the awning of a deli, I dug it out of my purse. My pulse jolted, and hope permeated my chest. My recruitment consultant.

"Tamara," I said, turning my back to the wind. "Please tell me this is good news."

"That depends on your performance at the interview I've secured for you," Tamara said.

I squealed, drawing an eye roll from a passing pedestrian. Who cared? I had an interview.

"That's fantastic. Where is it?"

"Upper West Side of Central Park. The lady's name is Liv Ellis, and she sounded so nice on the phone. It's a three-month contract, taking care of her seven-year-old granddaughter. I get the impression, though, that it could turn into a longer contract if she likes you. And it's live-in. She told me she's seen a few people, but none of them were quite what they're looking for. But you're a warm individual, Harlow, and kids adore you. Put your best foot forward, and this job could be yours."

Relief swamped me. This sounded like my dream job. Working for a woman, right here in Manhattan, and solving my accommodation challenges all in one fell swoop. There had to be a catch. I wasn't this lucky.

"Where are the parents?" I asked.

"She didn't mention any parents, and I didn't want to pry."

"Fair enough," I said, secretly thrilled with the idea of no male in the picture. "When's the interview?"

"This evening at six. I'll email you the details now. Call me immediately afterward."

"I will. You're the bomb, Tamara."

She chuckled. "Thank me when you're gainfully employed again."

She cut the call, and seconds later my mail service pinged with an incoming message. I opened it and scanned the details. I checked my watch. Eight hours until my interview. A whole day to fill where, with every passing minute, my hope would grow.

I could only pray this chance didn't turn to ashes.

At five-thirty that evening, I arrived at a towering apartment block that oozed money. Given the location, even a small apartment here probably cost millions. I checked the email Tamara had sent over once again. Liv Ellis lived in the penthouse. Christ only knew what the price ticket on that prime piece of real estate had been. Given my history with math, I probably couldn't count that high.

I entered the lobby. It exuded rich elegance with expensive artwork adorning the walls and luxurious rugs dotted about, breaking up the expanse of Italian marble flooring.

I crossed over to the reception desk.

"May I help you, miss?"

"I hope so. My name is Harlow Winter. I'm here to see a Mrs. Liv Ellis."

The receptionist smiled, then checked her computer screen. "Ah, yes, she's expecting you. The penthouse elevator is right over there." She pointed behind me, then handed me a card. "You'll need to enter this code into the keypad to gain access."

Wow. Heavy on the security. "Thank you."

On the way up to the penthouse, anxiety and nerves swarmed through my abdomen, and my palms were slicked with sweat. I wiped them on my coat. Slimy hands would not make for a good first impression.

Calm down, Harlow.

The elevator doors opened. Standing in the large foyer was a gray-haired, bespectacled woman, her hair pulled back into a neat bun. She greeted me with a warm smile. I immediately felt at ease, my pulse slowing to a more normal rhythm.

She thrust out her hand. "Harlow, how lovely to meet you. I'm Liv Ellis. Do come on in."

"Thank you, Mrs. Ellis."

We bypassed a wide open-plan living space that had an amazing view of Central Park, the sun just beginning to set over the trees, casting the green space in a lovely orange glow. Wow. Imagine waking up to that every day. For sure, that was a sight you'd never tire of.

We turned into a thickly carpeted hallway with doorways on either side. "You have a lovely home," I said, even though I'd barely seen it.

"Why, thank you," she said. "Although it isn't mine. It's my son's."

Before I could process the words, she ushered me into a high-ceilinged room with large picture windows that also opened out onto that fabulous view. But it wasn't the view that forced the air from my lungs and thickened my throat. It was the man standing beside a large fireplace.

Him.

Mr. Wall Street.

The man from the bar.

No. It couldn't be.

In a panic, I glanced over my shoulder, hoping for an escape route, only to find his mother standing directly behind me. She closed the door and gestured to a comfortable-looking sofa.

"This is my son, and Annie's father, Oliver. Sweetheart, this is Harlow Winter."

I almost blurted, "Sorry, there's been a terrible mistake",

except I caught the plea in his eyes, silently begging me to play along. No doubt if I left before the interview had taken place, he'd have to explain to his mother the reason why. Well, one thing was certain; they wouldn't offer me the position now. I rarely drank, but he wouldn't know that. If I wanted to hire someone to take care of my precious child, I wouldn't pick the girl who'd downed several gins, blabbed to an entire bar about her relationship and career troubles, then kissed a stranger.

Not that I could *ever* take this job, even if an offer was forthcoming.

"Nice to meet you," I said primly.

Relief that I'd decided to go along with the duplicity swarmed his dark-blue irises. "You, too," he murmured, walking over to shake my hand.

He sat across from me, joined by his mother. She opened a file and removed my résumé, scanning the neat, typewritten pages.

"So, Harlow, why don't you start with telling us why you left your last position."

I almost choked. My eyes darted to his. I expected to see my horror mirrored in his navy gaze. Instead, amusement played around his lips. I knew what those lips felt like. Firm, warm, inviting.

He leaned back and rested his right ankle over his left knee, his arms coming across his chest. Heat rushed to my face at the memory of how inappropriately I'd behaved. I'd thought last Thursday was the worst day ever, except this one was quickly taking the lead.

"I had a difference of opinion with my employers," I said, deciding I'd concentrate on his mother for the rest of the interview. Easier and far less embarrassing for both of us.

His mother's scrutinizing gaze locked on mine. "What kind of a difference of opinion?"

Fuck. I refused to lie, even if the truth wasn't something I particularly wanted to discuss in detail.

"I'd rather not be gratuitous, Mrs. Ellis," I said. "Let's just say that the male parent's conduct left a lot to be desired, and the duties he had in mind most certainly weren't in my employment contract."

Mrs. Ellis's eyes widened. "Oh my goodness." She clasped a hand to her chest and turned her attention to Oliver, then looked back at me. "Well, that isn't something of concern here. I brought up my son with manners, and to respect women."

Yes, I know.

She harrumphed. "Some people truly are foul individuals."

I nodded and offered a faint smile. "Yes, they are."

She scanned the papers in her lap. "Let's move on, shall we? Tell me, what made you want to work with children?"

The rest of the interview went off without a hitch. After I'd been questioned for forty-five minutes, Mrs. Ellis slotted my résumé into a folder and placed it beside her.

"Do you have any questions for us?"

I shook my head. "I don't believe so, no."

"Would you like to meet Annie?" she asked.

I smiled. "I'd love to," I said, partly because to give any other answer would come across as strange, and I had a genuine interest in what Oliver's daughter looked like. Would she have her father's dark, wavy hair and swoonworthy blue eyes, or had she inherited her mother's genes?

"I'll go fetch her," Oliver said.

His mother patted his hand. "No, no. I'll go. You chat with Harlow."

Oh god.

She left the room. An oppressive feeling descended, and I avoided Oliver's eyes while I nibbled on my bottom lip and picked at a piece of fluff on my best suit. Until today, I'd called it my lucky suit. That would change soon.

"I'm sorry," Oliver said.

I brought my head up, meeting his intense gaze. A fluttering set off in my belly, but I clamped down on it. Just because he seemed like a nice guy on the surface didn't make him one. My problem was I trusted too easily and always ended up on the receiving end of a steaming pile of shit. Well, no more. I was sticking by my mantra that all men were bastards, even if they came packaged as a stunningly handsome single dad.

"You have nothing to apologize for. If I'd known, I wouldn't have come. But my agency only mentioned a Liv Ellis." I glanced away. "I feel like such an idiot."

"Please don't," he said. "It's not a pro—"

The door burst open, and in came Annie, clutching her grandmother's hand. No denying Oliver was her father. She was like a miniature version, only with feminine features. Same dark, wavy hair, same navy-blue eyes. Same strong, determined jaw.

She wrenched free and ran over to me. "Are you going to be my new nanny?"

Blindsided by her directness, I widened my eyes. "Well, um—"

"I know Daddy and Nanan have been interviewing other people, but I didn't get to meet them. That must mean they like you." She sat beside me, staring up at me with beseeching eyes. "And if my daddy likes you, then I like you."

My chest tightened. What an absolute sweetheart.

"I'm going to miss Nanan a lot when she goes away," she continued, her declaration accompanied by a lip wobble. She peeked quickly at her grandmother. "But Nanan told me that she'd find me the bestest nanny in the world to take care of me and Daddy until she comes home."

I sneaked a peek at Oliver. He was watching me intently, his fingertips stroking his chin, deep in thought. I tore my gaze away.

"I'm sure you will miss your Nanan, Annie," I said, purposely ambiguous with my answer. It didn't matter whether they offered me the position. I couldn't take it. I'd always be the woman who drunkenly kissed a stranger, and he'd be on edge waiting for me to jump him again. No, it simply wouldn't work.

"But whoever gets to take care of you is so lucky." I put my arm around her and gave her a quick squeeze.

She grinned. "Do you want to see my bedroom?"

I cut my gaze to Oliver and his mother. He still had that intense look on his face, a direct contrast to his mother's beaming smile and encouraging nod.

"I'd love to," I said.

"Yay!" Annie grabbed my hand and tugged me to my feet.

After she'd excitedly shown me every single toy she owned and pulled all her favorite games out of an enormous stack in one of her closets, we headed back downstairs. My heart felt uncomfortable, sitting heavily in my chest. This job was perfect in every way, and I'd already connected with Annie.

If only I hadn't gotten drunk.

If only I hadn't made a fool of myself.

If only I hadn't kissed Oliver.

What a fuckup.

We returned to the formal living room to find Mrs. Ellis alone. *Where was Oliver?*

"Ah, there you are," she said. "Are you sure you don't need to ask me anything else?"

"No, Mrs. Ellis."

"Excellent," she said. "I'll see you out. Annie, say goodbye to Harlow, then go eat your dinner. Your father is in the kitchen preparing it."

I almost choked. *Jesus. He's man of the fucking year.*

I crouched to Annie's level. "Bye, sweetheart."

"Bye, Harlow. I will see you again soon, won't I?"

I refused to lie to her, so I pinched her nose instead, drawing an adorable giggle from her. "Be good."

"Okay," she said good-naturedly, skipping out of the room.

"She's beautiful," I said.

Mrs. Ellis nodded, pride oozing from every pore. "She certainly is. The center of our lives. I will miss her terribly."

"There's always FaceTime or Skype," I said.

She smiled. "How right you are."

We returned to the foyer where she shook my hand. "I'll be in touch very soon, Miss Winter."

The tone of her voice and the firmness of her grip showed she'd come to a decision, and no doubt, when she made the offer and I declined, it would leave her terribly confused. Still, I couldn't help that. *You reap what you sow.* That had been a favorite mantra of my mother's growing up when I'd come home with yet another disappointing report card from school.

For the first time, I understood what she meant.

I rode the elevator back to the lobby and exited onto the street. The sun had set while I'd been inside. I glanced up at the building, beyond frustrated at myself for screwing up such a wonderful opportunity.

Halfway to the subway, my cell rang. I tugged it out of my coat pocket and glanced at the screen. *Here we go.* "Hey, Tamara."

"Great news, Harlow. You nailed it," she enthused. "They *loved* you and want you to start as soon as possible. I'll get the paperwork sent over tonight. If you can get it back to me straight away, I'll work late to push it all through."

I gave a long, low sigh, my heart thudding dully against my ribs. "I'm so sorry, Tamara, but I can't take it," I said, my tone flat and dull.

Life sucked. *Sucked.*

"What the hell are you talking about?" Tamara demanded. "Of course you're taking it. It's perfect for you."

"It is absolutely perfect," I agreed. "I can't go into the details of why, but I can't accept the position. I'm sorry."

I cut the call and immediately switched my phone off. I knew Tamara. She wouldn't leave it there, but I needed time to think before I faced the ensuing interrogation.

What am I going to do now?

4

Oliver

"I don't believe it," Mom exclaimed, crazily waving her phone in the air.

"What don't you believe?" I asked, shoving Annie's plate closer to her. "Eat another sprig of broccoli and then you can get down."

Annie pouted. "I don't *want* any more."

I sighed. She'd been acting up ever since Harlow left. I still had reservations about Mom offering her the position, but Annie had been so taken with her that I'd put my own reticence to one side and gone with the right course of action for my daughter. And besides, it was clear to see the affinity Harlow had with kids. She had that intangible ability of being able to engage on a level kids understood. A rare and precious gift.

"You can go, Annie," my mother said.

I glared at her for overruling my decision as Annie beamed, scrambled off her chair, and skipped out of the kitchen, delighted at having gotten her own way.

"What the hell, Mother? I'm trying to teach her she can't always do what she wants."

Mom made a calming motion with her hands. "Normally I'd agree with you, but I didn't want her to hear this." She sat on the seat beside me and tossed her phone on the table. "Harlow declined our offer."

"She did? Why?" I played along, even though I knew the precise reason Harlow had declined a job she urgently needed.

Mom shrugged. "I have no idea. Her agency just called. When they rang to make the offer, she told them she couldn't take the job. No further explanation, just a straight no. It makes no sense. She didn't give me that impression at all." Mom rubbed her forehead. "I don't know what we're going to do, Oliver. None of the others were remotely suitable, and Annie took to Harlow. So did I." She narrowed her eyes. "Did you say anything to upset her when I went to fetch Annie?"

My forehead creased. "Like what?"

She patted my arm and let out a deep sigh. "Ignore me. She was so perfect, that's all."

An idea quickly took form. I needed to talk to Harlow. I agreed with Mom that we'd found the *best* candidate even if, from my perspective, she wasn't the *ideal* candidate. We'd always have that unsolicited kiss between us, but we were also both adults. I had to convince Harlow to accept our offer. The thought of starting from scratch, especially given some of the potential candidates a bunch of top agencies in New York had sent, filled me with dread.

"Mom, I need to go out for a couple of hours. Can you watch Annie?"

"Always, darling, but what's so urgent?"

I gestured dismissively. "A work thing I forgot about. I won't be long."

Mom gave me one of her looks. "And this is precisely why

we need to find a live-in nanny." Her lips pinched in at the sides. "I'll have to cancel my trip."

"You'll do no such thing," I said. "We'll figure it out."

I slipped my cell phone in my pocket and grabbed a set of car keys. I made a detour to my office and sorted through the résumés on my desk until I found Harlow's. I scanned the address, calculating it would take me about forty minutes to drive there providing I didn't get caught in heavy traffic.

I had to park a couple of blocks over from her place, and as I made my way to her apartment, I rehearsed my speech. Somehow, I had to convince her that our brief crossing of paths last Thursday shouldn't stop her from taking the position. I also knew she needed the money, and like any good businessman, I would use that knowledge to my advantage.

One thing I couldn't allow to happen was Mom canceling her trip. She deserved a life of her own, and by God, I wouldn't be the one to stand in her way.

Harlow's place was on the tenth floor. I checked the numbers on the doors as I walked along the hallway, locating the correct apartment about two-thirds down. I rapped twice and waited.

When she opened the door, her eyebrows almost disappeared into her hairline as she realized it was me standing outside.

"Can I speak with you for a moment?" I asked.

"Ah, um... sure." She rubbed her forehead, then stepped back, inviting me in. "Have a seat."

I glanced around. The apartment was small but neat and tidy with floral cushions dotted about and soft drapes at the window. I chose the chair, leaving the sofa free for her. She sat primly, her back pole-straight, her knitted hands resting in her lap.

"I believe you turned down our offer of employment," I said, deciding that cutting to the chase was the best course of action. She'd know the exact reason I was here anyway. No point skirting around the issue.

She pulled her bottom lip in, her teeth repeatedly grazing over the soft skin. "Yes."

I brushed my fingertips over my chin. "May I ask why?" I wanted her to tell me, rather than make an educated guess. I mean, I could be wrong and she had another, perfectly legitimate reason for turning down the job.

She laughed, the sound bitter and short. "You have to ask why?" She shook her head. "I'm so sorry about what happened last week. I feel like a klutz and an idiot. I want you to know that I'm not in the habit of getting drunk and throwing myself at strangers. It had been a very tough day."

"I'm aware." I quirked an eyebrow in an effort to put her at ease. Before she'd kissed me, we'd enjoyed some fun banter together. No reason why we couldn't have a perfectly good working relationship. And as I sat before her, my resolve hardened, despite my initial hesitancy. I *had* to find a way to convince her that her actions last week didn't matter.

Because they *didn't* matter.

She stroked the space between her eyebrows. "See, this is what I mean. Even if I accepted the job, every time you looked at me, you'd see the inebriated girl who told half the bar about her relationship and employment difficulties, and then kissed you without invitation."

"And that means we can bypass the 'getting to know you' stage."

She shook her head. "You really are crazy."

"I believe we established that as well."

A ghost of a smile appeared on her lips. "Yes, we did."

I leaned forward and dangled my hands loosely between my thighs. "What happened, happened. Forget it. What matters, to me at least, is that out of the ten potential candidates we saw, you were the only one we allowed Annie to meet.

And the fact she took to you so quickly is a huge comfort to me. Kids have a sixth sense about people, and if you're good enough for my daughter, then you're good enough for me."

She opened her mouth to speak, then closed it again. I took the opportunity to reassure her about something else that could be on her mind.

"I might not be a single mom, nor a lesbian." I waggled my eyebrows. She laughed, this time more naturally. "But I can one hundred percent reassure you that you will not have to deal with any kind of inappropriate behavior from me. I believe we can build a professional working relationship. Maybe even, over time, become friends."

I spoke the truth, too. After what Sara did, my trust in women had been well and truly erased. Betrayal would do that to a man.

Thanks for that, Sara.

Harlow lowered her head, her lips pressed tight, and then she expelled a long, drawn-out sigh. "I don't know."

"Well, I do. You're perfect for this role, and I'm in the habit of getting my own way. You wouldn't want to be the one to break my winning streak, would you?"

She grinned, shaking her head. "Crazy, crazy man."

I stuck out my hand. "That sounds remarkably like we have a deal, Miss Winter."

She stared at my outstretched hand for so long, I was convinced another decline was imminent. Then she nodded.

"I'd say we do, Mr. Ellis."

Her hand slipped inside mine, her skin cool and smooth. I suppressed a pleasurable shiver, my physical reaction to a woman's touch momentarily overriding the protective barriers I'd erected years before. I gave a brief, firm shake, then withdrew.

"I'll let your agent know you've reconsidered then." I got to my feet.

"Thank you," she replied.

She saw me out. I walked through the door, then glanced over my shoulder to find her watching me leave, a puzzled expression on her face as though she was having difficulty processing something. Then she held up a hand in greeting and disappeared inside.

A pang of loneliness squeezed inside my chest, its sudden appearance confusing me. I brushed it aside and sent a text to Mom.

Time to start packing.

5

Harlow

Two days after my interview, the cab driver dropped me outside Oliver's apartment building. I paid the fare, then hoisted my two suitcases from the trunk, their battered exteriors housing everything I owned. Not much to show for twenty-five years of life. But at least they belonged to me, paid for with money I earned, and they didn't come with unreasonable demands from my parents to conform to their way of life.

A twinge of regret pinched at my insides. I wished things were different, that I had a warm and loving family who couldn't go a day without speaking to each other, or texting. Even my brothers, who I knew loved me, also judged my lack of academic credentials. Every one of them truly believed it was a simple case of working harder or longer. With their big brains, they just couldn't understand that not everyone was made up of the same building blocks, that we had different skill sets, and not all of those commanded a large paycheck.

Shrugging off my melancholy mood, I tipped back my head

and gazed up at the imposing building that would be my home for the next three months. At least securing this position would buy me the time to look for a permanent, long-term job, and saved me from crawling to my parents with a begging bowl.

When I'd capitulated to the job offer after Oliver's visit, I'd carried out a little research into him. He part owned a large, multinational company called ROGUES which he ran with five friends from college. They had a diverse business portfolio with companies in construction, agriculture, and telecommunications. They even had a very successful and growing hotel chain across North America, as well as owning several exotic dance clubs under the brand name *Poles Apart.*

Didn't need to be a genius to work out what went on inside those particular establishments.

Apart from Oliver's extremely successful professional life, there were slim pickings on anything personal. His Wiki page mentioned he had a daughter, but no reference to a wife, either present or past. Maybe Annie was the result of a surrogate? After all, these days, you didn't have to be in a relationship to become a parent. Lots of people chose the surrogate route. And given the amount of financial backing Oliver had, I didn't imagine it would be hard to find a woman willing to carry a child for a rich billionaire—for an exorbitant fee, no doubt.

I gave my name at reception, hoping I didn't have to do that every single time. After handing me a small card with a code on it—same as last time—she pointed to the elevator. Nerves swarmed through my abdomen as I punched in the code and rode up to the top floor. I hated the first day of any job, but this one carried an additional influx of anxiety. Oliver might have reassured me I had nothing to fear from him, but once his mother left on her trip, I'd be all alone in the house with a young, virulent man. A man I'd already inappropriately made a pass at. A man who, despite the lies I liked to tell myself, I found attractive.

Not that it mattered. However nice Oliver appeared to be on the surface, I must not allow myself to fall back into bad habits, seeking validation and affection from the first guy who'd have me. That kind of behavior had led me to the likes of Carter, and look what a cheating asshole he turned out to be.

Then again, maybe Oliver was gay, and that was why he'd so vehemently stated that I wouldn't have to put up with any sexual advances the likes of which I'd suffered at my last placement.

Whatever the circumstances, in a strange way, I relished the idea of proving to myself that I didn't need a man in my life. That I could not only manage alone, but that I excelled at it.

Oliver's mother greeted me in the foyer. "Harlow, how wonderful to see you again," she said. "Do come on in."

I expected her to ask me why I'd declined the job offer and then done a complete about face and accepted it a couple of hours later. She didn't. Maybe Oliver had squared it with her, offering up a plausible explanation for my flip-flopping actions.

"Let me show you to your room and then I'll give you a tour of the apartment," she said.

"Is Mr. Ellis not here?" I asked, glancing around, both longing and dreading seeing him.

"No, he's at work. My son works very long hours. You won't see very much of him Monday through Friday. He'll leave right after you leave to take Annie to school in the morning and return in the evening in time for her bath and bed routine. After she's gone to sleep, he eats dinner, then usually retires to his office for the rest of the night." She sighed, her face darkening, her lips pinching at the edges. "I wish he'd take more time off, but there we are. I do hope it won't be too lonely for you here."

"I'm sure I'll be fine," I murmured, conflicting feelings of relief and disappointment at what she'd shared coursing through me.

"Now Saturday and Sunday, they're a different matter. Did your agent tell you that you'll have most weekends off?"

I nodded. "It surprised me, to be honest. Most families I've worked with, they want me around on the weekends."

"That saddens me." Her face softened. "Despite the hours my son works, he always makes sure he has time for Annie. It's important to him that she understands the central role she has in his life. Nothing is more important to my son than his daughter."

Jesus. This guy is definitely up for a Father of the Year award.

But no one was that perfect. There had to be a chink in his armor somewhere, a reason he lived as a single dad.

Mrs. Ellis took one of my suitcases from me, despite my assurance it wasn't necessary, then set off up the winding, contemporary staircase with its glass paneling and chrome handrails. At the top, it split off left and right. She turned left, heading in the same direction as Annie's room, drawing to a halt two doors down from the little girl's bedroom.

"Here we are." She opened the door and gestured for me to go inside. The room was large, fully furnished with a king-sized bed, a large dresser, and a walk-in closet. It also had its own en suite bathroom. I crossed over to the window.

"Oh, I can see the park from here," I exclaimed. The view wasn't as good as the one I'd seen from the living room and the room where I'd been interviewed, but damn, I wasn't complaining.

Mrs. Ellis joined me. "Beautiful, isn't it? The park is the reason my son bought the place. Oliver loved the idea of Annie having open green space right on her doorstep. It's difficult to find clean air in a city as overpopulated as Manhattan."

"It is," I agreed.

"Right, let's do a whistle-stop tour, and then we'll go through Annie's schedule, as well as touching on Oliver's, too."

It took her an hour to show me around the ten thousand

square foot penthouse. The place was enormous. I could fit my old apartment in a tiny corner of one room. As we arrived back in the main living area, panic took root in my chest. My parents were comfortably off, and I'd grown up in a nice five-bedroomed house, but nothing like this. What if I spilled coffee on the expensive rug in the living room, or Annie scrawled on the wall with a Sharpie? God forbid I'd drop a chocolate bar down the side of the cream sofa in the library.

This is wealth I couldn't even imagine before today. Sure, I'd worked for well-off families, but not *billionaire* wealthy families.

"You look a little perturbed if you don't mind me saying."

I turned my gaze to Mrs. Ellis. "It's pristine," I said. "How do you keep it so nice with a child around?"

She chuckled. "We don't."

I arched an eyebrow, drawing another chuckle from her.

"Wait until you've been here a while, then you'll start to notice things. Like over there." She pointed a perfectly manicured pink nail. "Oliver made that dent in the wall. He thought it would be a good idea to play soccer in here with Annie. He kicked the ball and knocked my favorite crystal vase off that table. It smashed and gouged out a large piece of drywall. Annie laughed so much, Oliver refused to have the wall mended." She smiled. "This isn't a home where you should be afraid to spill. We spill."

My nerves evaporated. "Thank God," I said, an image of Oliver playing with his daughter warming my insides. I'd worked with so many parents where the dads were absent most of the time, leaving all the parenting to the woman.

Which reminded me...

"I hope you don't think I'm being nosy, but where is Annie's mother?"

For the first time, a flash of pure rage crossed her face. Her lips flattened, and her eyes took on this hard glint that I have to say, I found more than a little scary. Mrs. Ellis was *fierce*.

"In Hell, I hope," she bit out, her hands making fists by her sides.

Taken aback, I waited for her to expand. She didn't. *Shit*. I'd well and truly fucked up. It answered one question, though: Oliver wasn't gay.

"I'm sorry," I said. "I didn't mean to pry."

Her features smoothed, and she unfurled her hands. "Please don't apologize. It's a perfectly reasonable question, but one I'd rather not answer."

"I understand," I said, even though I didn't understand a damned thing.

"Well, I have some things to attend to." She gestured around the room. "Please, make yourself at home. I'll come find you when it's time to pick up Annie from school."

She swept out of the room, leaving me alone in the huge, empty space.

With my curiosity raging, I trudged upstairs to unpack.

6

Oliver

The elevator doors closed, and I slumped against the back wall. My brain was operating on about five percent battery, and I felt exhausted and irritable. I'd had a shitty day at the office. The deal I'd been working on for months was on the edge of collapse despite the entire team putting in hundreds of hours trying to find common ground.

That wasn't the biggest reason for my malaise, though.

From now on, everything changed.

Today, Harlow had moved in.

Tomorrow, Mom would move out.

Not permanently, but enough to make me feel uneasy.

I left my briefcase in the foyer, ready to pick up again in the morning. I had no intention of working this evening. I was too damned tired, and I wanted to spend some time with my daughter, eat dinner, and crash.

Entering the main living room, I stopped dead, drinking in the scene that greeted me. Harlow and Annie were in the kitchen, baking. Annie was covered in flour, her hands buried deep in a bowl, but it was the way her face shone with sheer excitement, her smile open and wide, that had my heart squeezing in the most joyous of ways.

"Hey, munchkin," I called out.

Her head snapped up. "Daddy!" she exclaimed. She jumped off her step and ran over to me, trailing clouds of flour in her wake.

"Annie, no!" Harlow called out as my daughter flung herself at me, covering my suit in white dust and greasy butter.

I picked her up and swung her in the air, covering her face in kisses. "Are you having fun?"

"Oh, Daddy, the best fun. Simply the best. We're making cookies and cupcakes."

"Ooh, how marvelous," I said, grinning. "I can't wait to try them."

She wriggled, wanting me to set her down. "I haven't finished yet. You're home too early."

"Oh no." I put her on the floor. "Have I ruined the surprise?"

She planted her hands on her hips. "Yes, you have."

I pressed my fingertips to my lips. "Oops."

I turned my attention to Harlow, who looked horrified, her eyes wide as she hurriedly rinsed a damp cloth under the faucet.

"Don't sweat it. I have plenty of suits. I only have one daughter."

She dropped the cloth in the sink, flushed a deep shade of burgundy, and tucked her chin into her chest. "I'm sorry."

Hell, she thought I'd reprimanded her. *Off to a great start, dickhead.*

"Nothing to be sorry for." I strolled into the kitchen and scraped my finger along the edge of the mixing bowl, tasting the cake mixture. "Yum."

"Hands off," Harlow scolded, her embarrassed flush beating

a hasty retreat. She moved the bowl out of my reach.

"Yes, Daddy, hands off," Annie parroted, a girlish giggle spilling from her lips.

Harlow nudged Annie's shoulder and nodded as if to say, "That told him." Annie made a fist and bumped hers against Harlow's.

The tension that had been riding me for days melted away, replaced by immense relief. We'd made the right choice. Annie's obvious happiness was a testament to that, and it was only day one.

"Do you know where my mother is?" I asked Harlow.

She jerked her chin. "She's upstairs finishing packing."

"Right." I kissed the top of Annie's head. "You okay if I go see Nanan, munchkin?"

"Yeah," she replied, barely paying any attention to me. She was far too interested in watching Harlow spoon the mixture into the cupcake wrappers.

I jogged upstairs and found Mom in her room, several cases opened on the bed, and clothes strewn everywhere.

"Oh, Oliver," she exclaimed when she noticed me loitering by the door. "Thank goodness you're here. Tell me, how do I pack for three months away from home? What if I forget something?"

Chuckling, I walked inside and put my arms around her. "Then you buy it. Jeez, Mom. You're going on a cruise around the world, not being dumped in Siberia. There will be stores. You have credit cards. Stop stressing."

She patted my shoulder. "You're right. Of course you're right." She glanced at her watch. "You're home early?"

"Yeah. Challenging day at work. And I wanted to see how the new nanny had fared on her first day."

"Swimmingly," Mom said. "They're thick as thieves already. Have you seen what they're up to in the kitchen?"

I pointed to the flour and grease on the lapel of my suit.

"You could say that."

Mom smiled. "She's perfect, Oliver. You won't have any trouble with her at all."

"I think you're right." I kissed her cheek. "I'm off to shower before dinner. See you downstairs."

I stood under the hot spray, my head bent, and allowed the water to cascade over my back. Seeing Harlow interact with Annie had taken a load off my mind. Ever since Mom had dropped her bombshell, I'd felt jittery, on edge, worried about leaving my daughter with a stranger, even if it was only for a few hours each day. I'd still prefer my mom to be here, but Harlow would act as a wonderful substitute.

And I liked her.

The wayward thought crashed its way into my mind without warning.

I barely knew her.

Yet I had good instincts, ones I'd learned to trust over the last seven years of inhabiting the business world where everyone you met was trying to destroy you just so they could get ahead. Good people, *truly good*, were damned hard to find, yet I seemed to have stumbled on one by sheer good fortune.

And she smelled so fucking amazing. Like peaches. Ripe and sweet.

My cock twitched, surprising the hell out of me. Even more surprising was finding my hand wrapped around the shaft when I had no memory of putting it there.

I pulled once, twice, a third time. Groaning, I closed my eyes, recalling the memory of Harlow's soft lips that had so briefly pressed against mine outside the bar last week. Her wretched horror when she'd walked into my living room for her interview and seen me standing there. The guts and determination she'd drawn on to make it through, and then how she'd declined the position, even though she badly needed the work.

Then returning home this evening to find her teaching my daughter how to bake on her very first day on the job.

The speed of my orgasm shocked me. Thick ropes of semen spurted from the head of my cock, washed away by the punishing spray. I braced a hand on the tiled wall and rode out the exquisite pleasure.

Jesus Christ.

Did I really just jack off while thinking of the nanny? Talk about a fucking cliché.

I flicked off the shower and reached for a towel, wrapping it around my waist to hide my half-mast dick. It had meant nothing. I was a twenty-eight-year-old man who'd had a tough week. My actions were perfectly understandable. Show me a guy who insisted he didn't masturbate as a way of relieving tension, and I'd show you a fucking liar.

I changed into a T-shirt and a pair of sweatpants and went downstairs. In the time I'd been gone, Harlow had cleaned every speck of flour from the kitchen, and the aroma of cakes and cookies greeted me as I entered the living area. The memory of what I'd done in the shower while thinking of her a few minutes ago brought a tinge of red to my cheeks.

"Smells amazing." I peeked inside the oven to hide my embarrassment. "Looks amazing, too."

Harlow smiled. "I made parmesan chicken tenders with mixed peppers for dinner," she said. "Hope that's okay."

"Can I have cookies *and* cupcakes, Daddy?"

"You can't have either if you don't eat every bit of your dinner," I replied, earning a deep scowl and a pout for my troubles.

Annie turned her attention to Harlow. "Can I? Please?"

The little minx.

I opened my mouth to admonish her, but I didn't get to have my say. Harlow beat me to it.

"I agree with your dad. Dinner first. Then we'll see, but you can only have one cookie or one cupcake. Too much sugar is bad for your teeth."

I sent her a grateful smile. Kids loved to divide and conquer. Mom and I had worked out a system, but it had taken years of mistakes where we'd contradicted each other and Annie had taken full advantage before we figured it all out. Harlow had slipped right into her role without a ripple of turmoil.

"Ugh." Annie folded her arms over her chest. "I knew you'd side with him."

I picked her up and held her upside down. "Him? *Him*?" I said, grinning at her peals of laughter.

I caught Harlow watching us, her expression soft, a warm smile playing about her lips.

Yeah, not a good idea to think of her lips.

I cleared my throat and righted Annie. "Go wash your hands before dinner, young lady. And less of your sass."

She playfully stuck out her tongue, then hugged me tightly and kissed my cheek. "Love you, Daddy."

My heart filled to bursting point as she ran to the nearest bathroom to wash up, and a warm tingling sensation spread through my chest. For all the pain Sara had caused me, I'd never regret my relationship with her, because she gave me Annie.

"You're a great dad."

Harlow's interjection interrupted my musings. I turned to her with a frown. "Sorry, what?"

"I said you're a great dad. She's lucky to have you. I've worked with a lot of families, and the way you are with her isn't common."

"Thanks," I said gruffly, a little weirded out at how proud her compliment made me feel. I rubbed my hands together in an exaggerated fashion, eager to move the conversation into safer territory. "Let's eat."

7

Harlow

"Time for bed, Annie."

"Awww, five more minutes, please, Daddy," she begged. "It's Saturday tomorrow. Tell him, Harlow. You'll let me stay up, won't you? You did last Friday night when Daddy worked late."

Jeez. Way to throw me under the bus, kid.

Oliver arched an eyebrow. Heat flooded into my cheeks, and I nibbled my bottom lip.

"Um, that was a one-off, kiddo. Now do as your dad says. Scoot."

She pouted, muttered, "You're supposed to be on my side," and flounced off, her arms defensively crossed over her chest.

Oliver tossed his phone on the table and rose to his feet. I expected him to give me a lecture for overstepping the mark. It wasn't my place to flout the rules he'd laid down for his daughter, but we'd snuggled in front of the TV to watch *Frozen*, and rather than cut it short, I'd allowed her to stay up until the movie ended. I hadn't asked her to keep it from her father—I'd never do that—but after a week passed by without her mentioning it, I assumed she'd forgotten.

I should have known better. Kids had memories like elephants, especially when the event in question involved broken rules.

But instead of calling me out, he simply said, "There's wine in the fridge if you'd like a glass," then as I stood there with my mouth agape, he jogged upstairs to join Annie.

The more I saw of this guy, the more I liked him. He never acted the way I expected him to, which kept me on my toes for sure.

I took him up on his offer and helped myself to a glass of wine. My work week was effectively over. I had the entire weekend to myself—and I had no idea how to fill the time. I'd always spent my weekends with Carter before the cheating asshole wrecked our year-long relationship. Katie was working at the hospital, otherwise I'd ask her if she wanted to meet up. Maybe I'd go to the gym, do a little shopping. Read a book, perhaps.

Ugh. It all sounded so dull and boring. I tried to recall how I'd spent my weekends before Carter, then realized there'd simply been another Carter making my decisions for me.

Christ, I'm so lame.

With the entire night stretching ahead of me, and nothing to do, I decided I'd take a bath. A long soak with some bubbles and salts would give me time to reflect. I had to work out who I was without a man in my life, and I might as well start now.

I reached the top of the stairs, but as I passed Annie's room, I paused. I peeked around the door. Oliver was sitting on the edge of Annie's bed, his arm looped over her shoulder while he read to her. But he wasn't just reciting the words on the page. No, he'd gone into full-on dramatic mode, acting out all the voices while Annie giggled and urged him on.

He really was father of the goddamn year. I had yet to hear

him shout or yell at her or tell her he didn't have time or was too busy.

If only all dads were like that.

If only my father had been like that when I'd been growing up.

Would I still have this urge to always seek validation if my dad had made me feel like the most important person in his life? I shrugged it off. No point trying to find answers when they didn't exist. Dad was Dad, and Mom was Mom. Wishing we had a closer, more natural relationship wouldn't help anything. They were who they were, which was good people who happened to be extremely reserved and frugal with displays of affection.

How easy it would be to fall for a guy like Oliver. My ovaries ached just watching him with Annie. I shook my head in annoyance. Even if I was on the market for a guy—which I most certainly was not—he'd hardly stumble across the hall to fuck the nanny when he could have his pick of women. A man like that... filthy rich, uber-successful, drop-dead gorgeous. There wasn't a woman on the planet who'd walk away if he set his sights on them.

Once again, my mind turned to Annie's mother and what Liv had said before she'd left on her cruise. Her visible hatred for Annie's mother—Oliver's wife?—had my curiosity rocketing off the charts. Whatever had happened, I couldn't see it being his fault. Then again, what did I know?

But damn, I'd love to know the skinny.

"Harlow, is everything okay?"

I jerked my head up to find Oliver standing in front of me. I'd been so lost in my own thoughts I hadn't realized he'd finished with Annie's bedtime routine.

"Sorry, I was on my way to my room when I heard you reading to Annie. I hope you don't think I'm prying, but I love watching you with her."

"Oh." He ducked his head, apparently embarrassed by my lavish praise. "Well, don't let me keep you."

"Harlow?" Annie called out. "Will you tuck me in?"

"Annie, Harlow's finished with work now."

I touched his arm. "It's fine. Really." I smiled, then withdrew my hand in case he thought I was coming on to him. Ever since I'd moved in, I'd been careful to avoid any physical contact, accidental or otherwise.

"Thank you," he said. "She likes you enormously."

"The feeling's mutual."

He nodded. "Well, I'll see you in the morning."

I watched as he went downstairs, then slipped into Annie's room. I waggled my finger at her. "You're stalling, missy."

She put her hand over her mouth and giggled. "Busted."

I knelt beside her bed and tucked the covers underneath her mattress, then smoothed my hand over the comforter. "How's that?"

"It's good. Will you read me a story?"

I tipped my head to the side. "Another one?"

"Please," she begged, all wide-eyed and beseeching. A twinge tightened my chest. Kids and puppies. Both knew how to turn on that big-eyed stare that meant they'd get their own way.

"A quick one, then you go right to sleep. Deal?"

She grinned. "Yes."

I picked up a book and perched on her bed, then opened to the first page.

"Harlow?" she asked before I'd read a single word.

"Yes, sweet pea?"

"Will you be my mommy?"

I froze. *Oh, hell. How do I respond to that without crushing her?* I wasn't prepared for this line of questioning, especially when I didn't know the background.

"I'll be your friend," I settled on. "But, sweet pea, you already have a mommy."

Her eyes filled with tears, and her mouth turned down. "But she's not here, is she?"

God. This poor kid. With little experience on how to handle the situation, given all my other families had two parents in situ, I scrabbled around for the right thing to say.

"But if she came home, how would she feel if she found you'd replaced her with someone else?" I hugged her tightly.

She hitched a shoulder. "It doesn't matter. I don't know what it's like to have a mom, anyway."

My chest ached for her. I might not have worked here long, but Annie was such a terrific kid, bright, smart, funny, she'd wormed her way into my heart.

"Don't give up hope of seeing your mom again, Annie. Any day she could w—"

"Harlow!"

My head snapped up to find Oliver standing in the doorway, fury written all over his face. I swallowed. Dammit. I should have diverted Annie's attention, or made a joke, or tickled her. It wasn't my place to discuss her mom with her. That was Oliver's job.

"Yes," I said, my voice small and faint.

"A word, please. Annie, go to sleep."

"But Harlow's reading me a story," Annie whined.

"You've had a story," Oliver said, his voice softening as he spoke to his daughter. "Now be a good girl and I might take you to Bubby's for breakfast tomorrow."

Annie's face lit up. "Awesome," she exclaimed, then immediately snuggled under the covers, completely unaware of the political situation exploding right in front of her.

I tucked her in, kissed her temple, and by the time I'd straightened, Oliver had disappeared.

With dread circling my gut, I trudged into the hallway

where I found him hanging around a few feet from Annie's room. As soon as he saw me, he glowered, then pointed his chin toward the stairs and jogged down. I followed, feeling like I'd returned to my school days and the principal had summoned me to his office for a talking to.

He marched into his office, stood back for me to enter, then virtually slammed the door. I jumped. During my short tenure with this family, I'd never seen Oliver angry. He exuded calm no matter what the situation was. But I'd definitely pressed on a very sore point with my inappropriate conversation with Annie.

"Look," I began.

"No, *you* look." He planted his hands on his hips, his navy eyes burning with rage. "I will only say this once. If I have to repeat this statement at any time in the future, I will terminate your employment immediately. Don't you *ever* speak to my daughter about her mother again. Ever. You overstepped the line, so I'm redrawing it for you in thick, black ink. Do I make myself clear?"

I wanted to put up a defense, to explain that Annie broached the subject by asking me to be her mother, and while I could have handled it better, I hadn't intended to cause offense. Instead, I nodded glumly.

"Crystal," I muttered.

If I'd been told not to speak of the mother, I'd have known where I stood.

"Good." He raked a hand through his hair, his chest heaving as if he'd run a mile flat out. He turned his back, summarily dismissing me.

"Oliver," I said tentatively, not happy about leaving things this way. "I'm very sorry."

He grunted but remained staring out the window into the blackness beyond, his spine erect, his shoulders stiff.

"If you want me to leave, I will. First thing tomorrow."

I prayed he wouldn't accept my offer. I needed this job.

Badly. Standing on my own two feet and paying my way in the world was the only control I had, and I'd defend it fiercely.

"Goodnight, Harlow," he said firmly, a bite to his tone.

Even though he wasn't facing me, I nodded, acknowledging his approval to remain in my post, along with his cold dismissal and clear censure in relation to my conversation with Annie.

"Goodnight."

I opened the door and quietly left. I went straight to my room, half hoping, half dreading he'd come after me to apologize.

He didn't.

I'd thought Oliver was different, but he was just like all the rest. Well, from now on, I'd do my job to the very best of my ability, keep my distance from my employer, and never mention Annie's mother again.

I changed for bed and climbed under the covers, wishing I could turn the clock back on the last thirty minutes. One unwitting mistake from me and a few harsh words from Oliver, and the easy routine we'd fallen into had been annihilated.

8

O<small>LIVER</small>

I rose the next morning with a heaviness sitting on my chest. I recognized the sensation—remorse for the events of last night. I'd overreacted, my personal issues with Sara's disappearance rearing their ugly head when I heard Annie discussing them with Harlow rather than me. I'd only heard the tail end of their conversation, but that had been enough to make me react the way I had.

Harlow shouldn't have made a promise she had zero chance of keeping, albeit I'd stopped her before she could complete the sentence, and I didn't think Annie was any the wiser. But to threaten Harlow with the loss of her job was a step too far.

Harlow was a sweet, caring woman. She had an air about her, an aura of warmth, yet as soon as I'd uttered those cruel words last night, I'd felt her shut down, close me out, and that was all on me.

It was also on me to fix it.

Annie never asked me about her mother, and I took full

responsibility for that because I didn't encourage the conversation. Beneath the surface, though, she must have had so many questions running around her mind, and she'd chosen Harlow to broach them with.

Which meant she'd rejected me.

That hurt. Sliced through me as sharp as a scalpel. And I was to blame.

I would apologize to Harlow for my over-the-top behavior, and then I'd carefully raise the subject of her mother with Annie and see if I could get her to open up.

Trudging into my bathroom, I frowned at myself in the mirror. Beneath my eyes, dark circles told the story of the sleepless night I'd had. I heaved a sigh.

You're an idiot.

I had to stop reacting with barely contained anger every time the subject of Sara came up. Soon, I'd have to deal with the deep wound she'd caused by walking out that, like a martyr, I'd refused to allow to heal.

But not today. No, today I had a groveling apology to make to a woman who hadn't deserved my tirade.

I showered, dressed, and padded down the hallway. Poking my head around Annie's door, I smiled at the sight of my daughter sitting in the center of her room, legs curled behind her, playing with her toys.

"Morning, baby girl."

I wouldn't get away with that moniker for much longer, but for now, the term of endearment brought a huge smile to my daughter's face.

"Daddy!" She leaped to her feet and hugged me. "Are we still going to Bubby's this morning?"

Kids. In my experience they never forgot a promise, hence my response to Harlow virtually making out Annie's mother could walk through the door any minute.

I still didn't know what I'd do if that day ever arrived.

Put my hands around her throat and throttle her.

Hug the living daylights out of her.

React with an icy coldness that'd give her frostbite.

I kissed the top of Annie's head. "We are. Give me an hour, okay?"

She grinned. "Okay."

Such a good kid. *Thanks, Mom.*

Leaving my daughter happily playing, I carried on down the hallway, drawing to a halt outside Harlow's room. I cleared my throat, and, with a deep breath, I tapped on her door.

"Harlow, do you have a minute?"

Silence.

I knocked again, a little louder in case she was in the bathroom. Or maybe she was still asleep.

When a third attempt remained unanswered, I jogged downstairs in case she'd already risen. The living area was empty.

She could have either decided to ignore me, or she'd already gone out, pushed into walking the streets on her day off because I'd made her feel unwelcome.

Way to go, dickhead.

I made some coffee and sat at the dining table to read the newspaper, but I couldn't concentrate on world events, or the stock market. The way Harlow's face crumpled when I'd chastised her kept replaying inside my mind, like a movie reel on a continuous loop. Beneath her submissive employee facade, I knew a lion roared beneath. But I also knew she needed this job, our original meeting giving me information a normal employer wouldn't have. I'd bet that she'd been tempted to give it back to me as good as I'd given to her, but had held back out of necessity.

"Daddy, I'm ready."

Annie skipped into the kitchen wearing a Scottish kilt in red and green, pink tights, a white frilly blouse, and black patent leather shoes. I chuckled at my daughter's expression of style.

I arched a brow. "Where did you get that outfit?"

She grinned proudly. "Nanan bought it for me before she left." Her face briefly fell. "I miss Nanan." Then brightened. "But if Nanan hadn't gone away, I wouldn't have Harlow." She glanced around the room, the beginnings of a frown pulling her eyebrows together. "Where is Harlow?"

I cleared my throat and folded the newspaper to buy myself a few seconds. "Um, I think she's gone out."

Annie pouted. "Oh. I wanted to hug her good morning."

I stood and ruffled her hair, which earned me a furious scowl.

"Daddy!" she castigated, smoothing her dark tresses.

"Come on," I said, steering the conversation away from Harlow to benefit myself. Every time her name was mentioned, a twinge of guilt pinched at my insides. "I'm starved."

She slipped her hand inside mine, bouncing along beside me, and chattering about nothing as we made our way to Bubby's, one of her favorite places to eat breakfast.

The restaurant had been closed for a few weeks for renovations, and this was the first time we'd visited since they'd reopened. I liked what they'd done with the place. Same brick walls covered in pictures, but they'd added rustic oak flooring and finished off with a bright paint scheme. Annie chose a booth. I grinned and followed along. I liked to indulge my daughter now and then. For me, parenthood was a balance of discipline and allowing kids to express themselves, and between Mom and me, I liked to think we'd gotten it right. Everyone who met Annie always told me what a great kid she was, which made my chest puff with pride.

We ordered breakfast—Eggs Benedict for me and blueberry pancakes for Annie—and clinked our juice glasses as had become our tradition.

"So, how's school?" I asked.

Annie made a face. "Daddy, no school talk on the weekends." And then she sighed. "Polly Mason pulled my hair yesterday."

My forehead creased. "She did? Why?"

"Because Franco Ciccione likes me and not her."

What?

Boys?

Already?

She's only seven.

I was *not* ready for *this*.

"And do you like Franco?" I asked tentatively, holding my breath for the answer and watching her body language carefully.

She hitched her left shoulder. "He's okay, for a boy." She wrinkled her nose. "He smells a bit."

Immensely relieved at her first comment, I suppressed a chuckle at her second. "That's not a very nice thing to say."

She shrugged again. "It's true."

What can you say to that?

Our food arrived, and I listened as Annie chattered on while stuffing her face with the pancakes. I should tell her not to speak with her mouth full, but she was so animated, and I found myself enraptured by the excitement and energy with which she spoke, the way her eyes sparkled when she was being mischievous, the habit she'd formed in the last year of pushing her hair out of her face with a little huff of annoyance.

With half a pancake remaining, she dropped her fork and rubbed her stomach. "I'm full."

"I'm not surprised." I set my own silverware down. Nervous energy swirled in my gut as I contemplated how to approach the conversation Annie had with Harlow last night.

"Annie, I wanted to talk to you about something."

She instantly looked guilty in that way kids often did, their minds racing at what unwitting transgression they may have made that, now, they might find themselves reprimanded for.

"You're not in trouble, so don't give me that look."

Relief swarmed her face, and she shuffled in her seat.

I inclined my head. "But now I'm wondering if I should dig a little deeper." I accompanied my words with a broad smile so she'd know I was only teasing.

"Daddy, that's naughty," she said, her tone full of reproach.

I decided to plunge straight in. "I heard you talking to Harlow last night, and that's what I wanted to speak with you about."

"Oh." She nibbled her lip, sensibly waiting for me to lead the conversation.

"I'm sorry, baby girl. I should have realized you'd have questions about your mom." I reached for her tiny hand and folded it inside mine. "You can always talk to me, you know."

She took a deep breath, and her little chest expanded. The beginnings of a lip wobble had me preparing for tears. Then she seemed to steel herself.

"I know I can, Daddy. I'm a big girl. I don't have a mommy like the other girls in school, but I do have a Nanan and a Harlow." A huge grin almost split her face in half.

My chest constricted. I'd never wanted this for Annie. When Sara had given birth, I'd assumed having a child would enrich our lives and, soon, we'd add more kids to the brood and live a normal family life. Then Sara decided she wanted a different life, one that wasn't normal, one that was much more exciting than changing diapers and wiping up puke.

Yet, for me, the reward for going through the undoubtedly difficult baby stage sat right across from me. My beautiful, funny, kind, quirky, wonderful little girl who made me the proudest parent in the world.

"Do you like Harlow, then?" I asked.

"I love her," Annie expelled, giving me an odd look as

though my question was the weirdest one she'd heard from me today. "She helps me with my homework, and reads to me, and plays games. We sometimes go to the park after school and stroke the horses. I like doing that." She tilted her head to one side. "Do you like Harlow, Daddy?"

Out of the mouths of babes.

I smiled and squeezed her hand. "I do, baby girl," I said, realizing it was absolutely true. "I like her very much."

And if I didn't act fast, both Annie and I could lose that girl for good.

9

Harlow

Earlier that same morning.

I woke to a dark world, a pounding head, and a stomach full of regrets.

Straining my ears, I listened for any movement, but all seemed quiet. I folded back the covers and sat on the edge of the bed, raking my hands through my hair.

Suddenly my ideal job had turned into a living nightmare—and all at my own hands.

Oliver's harsh reprove from last night still stung. Every time I replayed it in my mind, I winced. I should have known he'd be protective of Annie, especially given both the physical absence of a mother, and the lack of evidence she even existed. Whatever had happened between a couple who, at least once, must have loved each other enough to create a baby, it had cut Oliver deep.

In Hell, I hope.

Once again, Liv's comments, her voice dripping with venom, came back to me. At the time, I'd assumed Annie's mother was still alive, but could I have been wrong? And if I was, that made the promise I almost gave to Annie that her mom might come home even more heinous. That would explain Oliver's incandescent, cold rage. For all I knew, they could have decided to keep the truth about her mother's early demise from Annie. And there I went, blundering in like a fool.

I scrubbed my hands over my face and got to my feet. I'd planned to meet Katie for lunch, and originally, I'd intended to hang around the penthouse, maybe play with Annie a little—even though it was my day off—or watch TV. But after last night, all I wanted to do was to slip out unnoticed and hope by the time I sidled home later this evening that Oliver might have forgotten about our disagreement. The last thing I wanted was to live under a cloud.

I showered, brushed my teeth and, hoping my blow-dryer didn't wake Oliver and spoil my plans, I dried my hair then pulled it back into a high ponytail. After dressing in jeans, a sweater, and walking boots—required footwear if I was to spend the entire day on my feet pounding the streets of Manhattan—I quietly opened my bedroom door and peeked into the hallway.

All quiet on the Western Front.

I slipped down the stairs, hoping they didn't creak. When I saw the main living space of the penthouse remained empty, I virtually ran to the elevator. Once inside, I pressed the button for the lobby level about fifteen times, as if that would make the doors close faster. As they edged together, I kept thinking Oliver might suddenly appear to stop me from leaving and give me another lecture on how to behave around his daughter.

He didn't, thankfully.

My stomach rumbled with hunger. I cut through Central Park, exiting opposite the Plaza. I jogged across the street, flipping off some asshole cab driver who honked his horn when he was nowhere fucking near me.

A normal Saturday morning in Manhattan.

Twenty-five minutes later, I arrived at one of my favorite coffee houses that, given the early hour, was still virtually empty. I took a seat in the window, ordered a coffee, a garden omelet, and a side of multi grain toast, but when the food arrived, I couldn't stomach it. Every mouthful tasted like regret. I downed three cups of strong java, though, which at least gave me an energy boost.

Walking the streets while waiting for one o'clock to arrive—the time I'd arranged to meet Katie—gave me an insight into how the homeless of this city must feel. I couldn't imagine having nowhere to be, nowhere to go to escape the cruel and biting snow of winter, the vicious and unbearable heat of summer. I made sure to drop a few dollars into the cup of a woman huddled in a threadbare blanket, sitting in a doorway that offered little protection from the chilly fall breeze. She smiled at me gratefully and said thank you.

Eventually, the time came to head to the restaurant. I strode out, grateful to have a destination, a purpose, somewhere to aim for. Even so, I arrived ten minutes early and had to hang around waiting for our table. They seated me a couple of minutes before my reservation time, but no sooner had I parked my butt than I spotted Katie giving her jacket to the greeter. I waved, and she waved back, then made her way over.

"Hey, babes," she said, enveloping me in a warm hug.

"You look amazing," I said. "I feel like I haven't seen you in forever."

"If three weeks counts as forever, then that's exactly what it's been."

Three weeks since I'd met Oliver in McCory's. If I closed my eyes, I could still feel my lips grazing his soft ones.

We ordered drinks—Coke for Katie and a glass of much-needed wine for me—and I listened as she told me about this patient she'd gotten close to who'd died just yesterday. Her eyes filled with tears as she recounted how they'd clung to her hand, then taken their last breath with no family around to comfort them.

"Anyway," she said, breezily waving her hand as if she wanted to make out it was no big deal, or maybe just change the subject to stem the pain. "How's the job? I want to hear everything."

My face must have given me away because she frowned, but before I could start to spill the whole sorry tale, our server came to take our order. When she retreated, I locked my gaze on Katie, nibbling my lip.

"The job is great, or rather it was… until last night."

She leaned forward, elbows on the table, giving me her full attention. "Go on."

I recounted every detail, from Annie asking me to read to her, to her fateful question that led to Oliver overhearing me seemingly gossiping about Annie's absent mother, and finally to the scolding he'd laid on me in his office. Katie listened without interruption save for the odd "Hmm". When I finished, I picked up my wineglass and took a huge slug.

"And what did he say this morning?" Katie asked.

I shrugged. "No idea. I left before he or Annie had risen."

Katie's eyebrows shot up. "So what have you been doing all morning?"

"Walking. Thinking. Wondering whether I've still got a job, and a home, to return to. Whether I'll find myself out on the streets by nightfall."

Katie snorted. "He'd be crazy to let you go." She pointed her finger in my direction. "And if he tries, tell him I'll kick his ass."

"He's six feet two."

"So?" She made a jabbing motion with her fist.

We laughed, and it felt good. I'd needed a catch-up with Katie to put things into perspective.

"If I were you, I'd go back to his place, sit him down, and calmly have a conversation about what happened. State your case, that all you did, in all innocence, was answer a question from his daughter. How were you to know you'd put your foot in it? He hasn't exactly been forthcoming about his domestic situation. If he had, all this could have been avoided. And after you've done that, demand the apology you are most certainly owed."

I nibbled the inside of my cheek. "You think I should? I did fuck up after all."

"Yes, I do," Katie insisted. "He has a right to feel annoyed, but to threaten you with the loss of your job was a step too far. And if he's too big of a prick to apologize." She hitched a shoulder. "At least you'll know you did the adult thing. But I do think you should have the conversation. The last thing you want is to spend the rest of your time there under a disagreeable cloud."

She had a point, a very valid one. Still, the thought of facing Oliver again flipped my stomach.

"Okay. I will."

"Good," Katie said, leaning back to allow the server to set down her plate of food. "Now let's eat. I'm starved."

By the time we'd paid our check and risen from the table to leave, I felt a lot better about the entire Oliver situation. Katie had helped me put what happened into perspective, and I vowed to speak with Oliver as soon as Annie went to bed this evening. Wiser to try to clear the air than live in a difficult atmosphere.

I hugged Katie and watched her dash down the street toward the subway, heading to another tough shift at the hospital. I struggled to understand how she maintained a sunny disposition when her days were filled with other people's sadness. She'd been born a nurse, though. To Katie, it wasn't a job, it was a vocation. An undeniable pull to care for others. I couldn't wish for a better friend.

The elevator up to Oliver's penthouse traveled faster than I would have liked, one of those strange time events where when you're looking forward to something, every second feels like an hour, but when you're dreading the upcoming experience, that pesky clock speeds up, taunting you.

The metal doors glided open, and I tentatively stepped forward, an invisible string pulling me back, urging me to give it a little more time. I peered into the living space.

No sign of either Oliver or Annie.

They must be out somewhere. I sighed. What did I do now? Rather than hang around waiting for the ax to fall—aka Oliver returning home—I remembered Liv telling me that the building had a gym that residents could use. Since taking this job, I'd allowed my exercise regime to slip, too busy trying to fit in with a new family and make a good impression.

Yeah, I'm rocking that goal.

I ran upstairs to pack a gym bag, and, on a whim, I threw in a bathing suit. A hard workout followed by a swim and maybe a sauna might be just the thing I needed to take my mind off the impending conversation.

Enjoying myself so much lazing about in the steam room, I didn't realize the passage of time, and before I knew it, two hours had gone by. I showered, dressed, and caught the elevator back up to the penthouse.

Distant sounds from the TV reached me as I entered the foyer. Steeling myself, I padded inside, gym bag flung over my shoulder. Oliver and Annie were watching the big screen in the living room, their dark heads pressed together. My heart did a weird flip. I might not like Oliver very much right now, but damn, as I'd said before, the man was a great father. The men of the world could learn a lot about parenting from this guy.

I walked inside. Neither of them acknowledged my presence. Hmm, maybe I'd be able to sneak on by without either of them see—

"Harlow!"

As if she had a sixth sense, Annie leaped from the couch and ran across the room, her arms outstretched. I dropped my bag and knelt to hug her.

"Hey, sweet pea. Good day?"

"The best. Where have you been?" she asked with a pout. "I haven't seen you all day."

"Annie." Oliver's smooth, deep voice reached me, a hint of warning to his tone. "Remember, I told you Harlow doesn't work weekends. She can come and go as she pleases."

I straightened, my gaze meeting his across the room. I went for a half smile. He answered in kind.

"Would you like to join us?" he asked. "I'm sure Annie would like that."

"I would," Annie said, her arms firmly wrapped around my waist.

I briefly flicked out my tongue to dampen my lips, and I swallowed thickly. "Thank you," I said politely. "But I have some personal things to catch up on."

I inwardly cringed at how formal I sounded.

"Aww," Annie moaned. "Just five, no ten, minutes."

I smiled at her attempt at negotiation and ruffled the top of her head. "How about tomorrow," I said, feeling cornered into making a promise. Not that I minded—as long as I didn't have to spend time with Oliver, too. No doubt he felt entirely the same.

"O-Kay," she pouted.

With a final glance at Oliver who was standing in front of

the TV scratching his cheek, his brows pulled into the hint of a frown, I took off upstairs. The second I entered what had become my sanctuary, my stomach unknotted itself, and the tingling in my limbs abated.

Tomorrow. I'll have that talk with him tomorrow.

10

Oliver

I watched Harlow spin on her heel and dash off, her rapid footsteps as she went upstairs telling me she wasn't taking them leisurely. *Dammit.* I'd hoped she'd hang around until after I'd put Annie to bed, and then I'd be able to talk to her in peace. Trying to have an adult conversation—particularly one where I intended to grovel—with a seven-year-old around was nigh on impossible.

I half considered going after her, but to chase her to her room right this second bordered too much on stalking for me to risk it, especially when she'd said she had things to do. I'd leave it a while and then go and see her. The passage of time would make it appear less stalker-ish—I hoped.

"Is Harlow all right?" Annie asked with the razor-sharp insightfulness that kids naturally possessed. Only as they grew into adults did society seem determined to knock it out of them, along with a carefree attitude to life, a lack of fear, and an ability to love unconditionally.

I beckoned to her to rejoin me on the couch. "She's fine, munchkin. I'm sure we'll see her later."

I wasn't sure of that—at all—but there seemed little to gain in sharing my concerns with Annie.

As she snuggled back into my side, my watch vibrated. I tapped the screen.

Buzz me up.

I groaned. Ryker. There could only be one reason for him to stop by on a weekend, and that was to discuss work. I had hoped that Ryker would take a step back from his twenty-four seven work ethic after finally growing a pair of balls and getting it on with Athena, the woman he'd been in love with since childhood, but no. Not even she seemed able to curtail his constant drive for success.

"Uncle Ryker's on his way up," I said to Annie, dislodging her. "Can you amuse yourself for a few minutes while I talk to him?"

Her gaze firmly fixed on the TV, she nodded. "Sure."

I sent him a onetime code for the elevator, and mere seconds later, he arrived in my apartment, fizzing with an energy few others on the ROGUES board possessed. We all worked hard, very hard, but Ryker just had that extra edge, stemmed no doubt from his poor upbringing. The other members of the ROGUES board had grown up in a more middle-class environment. We hadn't exactly had money to burn, but we'd lived in nice neighborhoods with enough money for an annual vacation, a nearly new car, and plentiful food. Ryker's childhood had been very different. Lucky for him, he was one of the smartest—if not *the* smartest—men I knew, and he'd won a scholarship to college, where we'd all met. From there, ROGUES was born, and now we all had more money than we'd ever manage to spend.

I sometimes wondered whether ROGUES would be as

successful as it was without Ryker's drive, ambition, determination, and vision. I doubted it.

"Hey, pumpkin." Ryker kissed the top of Annie's head. She greeted him with a distracted wave. "Huh? Too busy to give me a cuddle?"

She twisted around on the couch, raised up on her knees, and held out her arms. "Not for you, Uncle Ryker."

She gave him a cursory hug, then returned to her previous position and stared at the TV.

He grinned. "And just like that, she brings me back to earth."

"Kids." I cocked my head toward the kitchen. "Coffee?"

"Got anything stronger?"

Narrowing my eyes, I removed a bottle of scotch from the top cabinet where Annie couldn't reach, not even when on her step. Overcautious was the name of the game when it came to curious minds.

I poured two glasses, pushing one across the counter to him. "Anything I should worry about?"

He knocked back at least half. "I want your advice."

I smoothed my eyebrow with my thumb. "Now I *am* worried."

"It's Elliot." He blew out a slow breath and slid onto a stool at the breakfast bar, then downed the rest of his scotch.

I instantly knew what Ryker was referring to. Around five months ago, Elliot's sister—Ryker's girlfriend at the time and now his wife after they recently married in Paris—was snatched off the streets, drugged, and kept against her will. A ransom demand landed in Elliot's lap. He paid the ransom—or rather Ryker arranged for the payment—and Elliot's sister was returned unharmed, at least physically, but it had been a terrible time. Since then, Elliot had become almost obsessed with finding the person responsible.

"He won't let it go, huh?"

Ryker scraped a hand through his hair. "It's not about letting it go. I won't let it go, either. I want that bastard caught just as much as he does. The trauma Athena went through haunts me every fucking night. It's the way he's going about it that's concerning. It's like everything else in his life has taken a back seat. Nothing carries as much importance as uncovering the truth."

"How's Brie handling it?" I asked, referring to Elliot's girlfriend.

"Not well. That's why I'm here, actually. She came to me asking for my help, but I honestly don't know the best way to do that. Every time I broach the subject, he bites my head off." He went to take another drink of scotch, realized his glass was empty, then pushed it away. "It's getting out of hand."

I stood, grabbed the bottle, and refilled it for him. "What can I do that you can't? You're his closest friend, and Athena's partner. If anyone understands what he went through, it's you. Surely that gives you a common ground from which to discuss the best approach."

"I think that's the problem. I'm *too* close to what happened, too close to Elliot. If I ask him to calm down, to rein it in, he accuses me of not giving a shit about his sister, and then we get into a pointless argument."

I swirled my scotch, watching the amber liquid slosh up the sides of the glass. "What do you want from me?" I asked, already anticipating the answer.

"Will you speak with him? Just to see if he'll listen to you."

"Of course I will," I said. "I'll take him for a beer one night this week after work. I'm sure Harlow won't mind working a little later than normal."

"How's the nanny working out?"

"Yeah, good," I said. "Annie likes her."

"And what about you?" Ryker asked with that curve to his eyebrow that demanded a response.

I pulled my lips to one side. "She's nice enough. The important thing is that she's good with Annie."

Ryker narrowed his eyes. "What are you not telling me?"

I pressed my lips together in a slight grimace and lowered my voice so Annie wouldn't pick up on our discussion. "We had a bit of an argument. Last night. I think I might have overreacted."

"What was the argument about?"

Focusing on my drink rather than Ryker's insightful gaze, I sighed. "Sara."

I briefly told him what I'd overheard outside Annie's bedroom, and how I'd responded. Reciting it back had me wincing. I sounded like an arrogant prick.

"Jesus, Oliver," Ryker exclaimed in a too-loud voice. "When are you going to forget that woman ever existed?"

"Keep it down, for fuck's sake," I hissed, casting a glance at Annie. Fortunately, she was too engrossed in the TV to notice our heated exchange.

Ryker expelled a frustrated sigh. "You and Annie, you're so much better off without her," he whispered. "If you allow that woman to continue to have this kind of hold over you, you'll never move on. Is that what you want? You're twenty-fucking-eight, for Christ's sake. You really want to spend the rest of your life alone?"

I palmed the back of my neck. "Don't you think I've tried? I just don't trust women anymore, Ryker. Sara stole that ability from me. And what's a relationship without trust?"

"Maybe you haven't met the right woman yet." He faux punched my shoulder to lighten the heavy mood that had descended without either of us intending that consequence to our conversation. "I bet the perfect woman is right around the corner."

"Possibly," I murmured, disagreeing with his assessment but unwilling to expend the necessary energy to argue about it.

Ryker set down his glass, his drink half finished. "I'd better be off. Athena's reserved a table at the Rainbow Room tonight, and if I'm late, she'll be sure to let me know."

He rolled his eyes, but I could tell he loved it. Loved her. Envy pulled at my gut and tightened my chest.

"I'll talk to Elliot on Monday."

"Thanks, buddy. I owe you one."

After Ryker left, I cooked dinner for Annie and me, making enough for three in case Harlow decided to join us. She didn't. Annie's bedtime came around, and I put her to bed. We'd had such a busy, exciting day, she fell asleep almost as soon as her head hit the pillow. I closed her door, leaving it slightly ajar, and walked back along the hallway, stopping outside Harlow's room. I couldn't hear any movement from inside.

I took a breath. Time to make that apology.

I lightly knocked and waited. An interminable amount of time passed, and I was about to knock again when Harlow opened the door.

"Hi." I met her gaze. "Do you have a minute?"

She nibbled her lip. "Actually, I do. We need to talk."

"I agree. Would you like to join me for a glass of wine? And I bet you haven't eaten dinner either. There's leftover casserole if you're hungry." I smiled. "That sounds bad. I mean, there's a casserole. I made enough for three."

"I'm not hungry," she said. "But a small glass of wine sounds good."

She followed me downstairs. I removed the wine from the fridge while Harlow loitered by the window and stared out at the lights of Manhattan, twinkling in the darkness.

"Here you are," I said, joining her.

She took the drink from me and immediately walked away, as if I'd ruined her enjoyment of the view simply by standing next to her. I ran a hand down the back of my head and waited to see where she'd settle. She pulled out a chair at the dining table and sat, swirling her glass by the stem.

I chose a chair opposite, wanting to give her the space she so clearly desired.

"I'm sorry," I said.

Her head snapped up. "For what?"

I inclined my head. "I think you know, but you're entitled to make me work for it. I behaved atrociously last night. I'd like to say I didn't know what came over me, and pull out a few bullshit excuses, but dishonesty isn't really my thing. I know exactly what buttons you pressed that garnered that reaction."

"Your wife?" she asked, her full attention locked on me now that I'd begun to open up a little.

"Ex-wife," I clarified. "Sara walked out on me and Annie right before Annie turned one." The familiar stab to my chest brought up a curled fist that I rubbed against my sternum.

"Why?" Harlow asked, and then she shook her head. "Ignore that. It's none of my business."

"No, it's fine," I said, an urge to explain myself making me more forthcoming than normal. "Honestly, I'm not sure. One minute we were happy, and the next, we weren't."

I decided to refrain from telling Harlow about Sara's affair. I didn't know why. I guess it made me feel like a failure, and I didn't want her to see me in that light.

"After she walked out, she refused to talk to me, or see Annie. I tried everything. Emails, phone calls. And then out of the blue I received a letter from her lawyer saying if I didn't end the harassment, she'd apply for an injunction. That was when I filed for divorce. She didn't fight me, although she demanded a huge financial settlement, which I paid. I didn't have it in me to fight her over money when my daughter had just lost her mother. I haven't seen her since."

For the first time since I'd yelled at her last night, Harlow's face softened. "God, I'm sorry. I completely understand why you were angry, although the things you said did upset me. Annie asked me a question, and I answered as best I could have given the knowledge I had, which was zero by the way." She smiled. "Relationships are hard. People are complicated. Life is tough."

"How true," I mused at her perceptiveness.

"Shall we call a truce?" she asked. "Until last night's unfortunate incident, I really liked it here, and I kinda thought we had a good working relationship."

"We did," I said hurriedly, following up with, "We do."

"Then let's move on. Forget it ever happened."

"I will... on one condition."

She leaned away and defensively crossed her arms over her chest. "What's that?"

I smiled. "Eat something."

She chuckled. "If you insist."

Rising from my place at the table, I strolled over to the kitchen and fetched her a plate of chicken casserole. I set it in front of her, retaking my seat. She hungrily dug in.

"This is good. You can cook."

I laughed. "You sound surprised."

"I guess I am. I always imagined the super-rich would have oodles of staff catering to their every whim, but you don't. Why is that?"

I pulled my lips to the side. "I'm a private man. I don't like strangers in my home, and I don't want Annie thinking life is a breeze and her demands are instantly taken care of by a whole team of people. I want her to grow up with a desire to work hard and earn her place in the world."

"That's admirable." She ate another morsel of chicken. "I'm a stranger."

"Were," I corrected. "And I wasn't happy when I realized Mom's trip meant I had no choice but to hire someone to help me take care of Annie."

She grinned. "You hid it well."

I leaned back in my chair, sipping my wine, an overwhelming urge to spend more time with this perceptive, funny, smart woman coming over me. "What are your plans for tomorrow?"

She shrugged. "No idea. I'll stay out of your way, though. Probably hang around in my room and read or watch TV."

My spine stiffened. Did she really think she had to hide away in her room every weekend? "Would you like to spend the day with Annie and me?"

She dropped her fork, her eyes widening at my unexpected offer. Unexpected to her, and to me. I wouldn't take it back, though. The only fear I had right now was that she'd decline.

A beaming smile broke across her face. "I'd love to."

11

Harlow

I cast a glance around my bedroom at the clothes strewn everywhere. I'd tried on pretty much my entire wardrobe, yet still hadn't decided on a suitable outfit for my day out with Oliver and Annie. His offer last night had both stunned and thrilled me.

Careful, Harlow.

Oliver Ellis was a man it would be all too easy to fall for. Gorgeous, kind, funny, sexy, a brilliant dad, and he had quite a bit of money in the bank.

I had to remember that I'd sworn off men.

All men.

And that included Oliver.

Not that he'd shown an inkling of interest outside of his duty as my boss. Given what he told me last night about his ex, I wasn't surprised he kept a cool, polite distance. What a cow to just walk out like that on your husband and baby without a backward glance. What kind of person behaved in such a way?

Annie had only been in my life for a short while, and already I dreaded when the time came to leave her, and she wasn't even mine. It took a special type of woman to turn her back on a child she'd carried for nine months, given birth to, nurtured for that precious first year. And when I said 'special', it wasn't meant as a compliment.

Even if Sara had fallen out of love with Oliver, surely any normal mother would want to be with their child.

Still, I only had Oliver's side of the story. There were always two points of view in any disagreement. It wasn't fair of me to judge.

I did, though.

Because that woman walked out on her *child*.

Frustrated with my inability to decide what to wear, I snatched up a pair of faded jeans and, as the weather promised to be nice for this time in September, a frilly short-sleeved blouse in a smoky gray that went well with my hazel eyes. I paired the outfit with my comfy sneakers, added a touch of makeup, brushed my hair until it shone, and made my way downstairs.

Oliver and Annie were in the living room talking to Oliver's mom over Skype. Annie's excited voice as she regaled her grandmother with the events of the week brought a smile to my lips. Oliver spotted me and pointed to the pot of coffee, then held up five fingers. I nodded to show I understood, then poured a cup and wandered out onto the balcony, tilting my face up to the sun. The fall breeze blew my hair around my face. I tucked it behind my ears and leaned on the railing, the sounds of Manhattan on a Sunday morning unable to reach me this high up. I could just about make out people moving around on the street, though, and already it looked as if New Yorkers were up and about early, eager to make the most of what would undoubtedly be one of the last warm days until spring.

I loved everything about this city. The sights, the sounds, the smells, even the constant honking of car horns. On a day like today, I could just about tolerate Times Square. But seeing Oliver's mom reminded me that I might have to leave Manhattan once my tenure here came to an end. I had to go where the work was, especially as I'd be homeless *and* jobless, and although I'd fallen on my feet with this particular gig, lightning was unlikely to strike twice. I wasn't that fortunate.

My happy mood took a dip, but I pushed the sadness to one side. One day at a time. I still had over two months remaining on my contract and I was squirreling away every spare penny I could. In a few weeks, I'd give Tamara a call and remind her I would soon be back on the market, looking for opportunities. Recruitment consultants tended to need a firm nudge. Clients were easily forgotten.

"Sorry about that."

I glanced over my shoulder and smiled at Oliver. "How's your mom enjoying her trip?"

"She's loving every second. So much so, I asked her if she still intended to return home."

A false flicker of hope burned in my chest before it quickly withered and died. As if Oliver's mom would stay away forever. I wouldn't want that for Annie—or Oliver—even if it gave me a chance of a more permanent position here. Oliver was clearly very attached to his mom. And Annie… well, the love she had for her grandmother shone bright as a super moon.

"I'm glad she's having a nice time."

Oliver's steady blue gaze locked on mine. "She isn't the only one."

A flutter set off deep in my abdomen, a glimmer that maybe Oliver did like me—and not only because I was good at my job.

I plunged in. "Oliver, I—"

"Come on," he said, interrupting me. "Let's get going."

He spun on his heel and disappeared. I hung back, disappointed, trying to figure out if I'd imagined what just happened, or if there had been a brief connection between us, one that Oliver had quickly severed.

"Harlow." Annie ran over and hugged me. "Daddy says you're coming out with us today."

"If that's okay with you." I kissed the top of her head.

She wrinkled her nose as if what I'd asked struck her as strange. "Of course it is."

I chuckled and held out my palm for her to take. "Then let's get going."

"Duh," she said, planting her hands on her hips in a way that, on kids, was cute. On adults it appeared petulant. "We haven't had breakfast yet."

I slapped my forehead in an exaggerated manner. "Silly me."

Annie giggled, then ran inside. I followed her. Oliver shot me a friendly smile, a bowl resting in the crook of his arm as he beat pancake batter. Relieved that the awkward moment I'd sensed out on the balcony hadn't spoiled the day, I went to join him while Annie plunked herself down in front of the TV and turned on the Disney channel.

"Can I help?" I asked, feeling like a spare part.

"You can make a fresh pot of coffee if you like."

Glad to have something to do other than watch Oliver—which wasn't exactly a chore, but not the best idea either, given I'd begun imagining a glimmer of attraction in his midnight-blue gaze—I busied myself with grinding coffee beans.

Annie's constant chatter over breakfast filled the gaps in conversation between me and Oliver. Occasionally, our eyes met over Annie's head, and Oliver's would linger for a few seconds, then he'd look away.

When he focused his attention on his daughter, I stole an opportunity to get my fill of his stunning profile with that strong, determined jaw, perfectly straight nose, and high cheekbones. I could feel the pull of desire coaxing me into the disaster zone. Except, making a move on Oliver far exceeded a mere disaster. It would cause an apocalypse.

Biting back a groan when he used the pad of his thumb to swipe a crumb from the corner of his mouth, I scrambled to my feet, mumbling something about making sure I hadn't forgotten anything, and took off upstairs. Once inside the sanctuary of my bedroom, I leaned against the door, my heart bumping into my ribcage, and longing unfurled in my abdomen.

Face it, Harlow. You've got the hots for the guy.

This was a nightmare of epic proportions. And what a cliché. Nanny falls for captivating, charismatic, billionaire boss. Ugh. I could see the tabloid headlines now.

I slipped into the bathroom and dabbed a damp cloth to my forehead and neck. Time to pull myself together and behave professionally. This wasn't a date. Oliver had only invited me because he felt guilty for his behavior on Friday night. And to read anything more into today than that made me a fool.

A fool it is, then.

By the time I returned downstairs, Oliver had cleared away the breakfast dishes and was helping Annie tie her shoelaces. I paused at the entrance to the living area, watching him with her, my heart aching, and my ovaries screaming for me to "fucking do something!" If the women of the world ever banded together to design the perfect father for their children and a hot-as-sin husband for themselves, then I'd discovered the blueprint.

As he straightened, I moved forward in case he caught me lingering and wondered what the hell I was doing loitering and staring.

"Great sneakers, Annie," I said brightly.

She grinned and skipped over to give me a better look,

sticking out her leg and twisting her ankle from side to side. "Daddy bought them for me yesterday."

"Wow. You're a very lucky girl."

"She is indeed."

Oliver's smooth, deep voice wrapped around me like a cashmere scarf. Soft, warm, decadent. I craved more. It was as though something had clicked in my mind, forcing me to face up to my growing attraction to the man standing before me, and now, I couldn't turn it off. My body tingled all over from his proximity, and static energy sent goose bumps scattering down my arms.

"Right, let's go," I singsonged, holding out my arm for Annie to slip her hand inside.

We rode the elevator down to the lobby, the enclosed space making me hyper aware of Oliver. The way his jacket rustled when he moved, the hint of cologne mingled with his own manly scent that enveloped my nostrils, how his thighs so perfectly filled out his jeans.

Here's a man who doesn't skip leg day at the gym.

I tore my gaze away before he caught me ogling and fixed my attention on Annie. She'd be my safe haven, the one who got me through the day unscathed and without making a complete and utter idiot of myself.

Bright sunshine greeted us as we stepped onto the sidewalk. I dug my sunglasses out of my purse and put them on. "Where are we going?" I asked as it occurred to me Oliver hadn't mentioned our destination.

At that precise moment, a sleek black car drew up in front of us. A man stepped out and smiled at Oliver. "She's all gassed up and ready to roll, Mr. Ellis."

"Thanks," Oliver said, opening the rear door for Annie. "In you go, munchkin."

Annie climbed inside. Oliver reached in after her to help with her seat belt, giving me a perfect view of his ass.

What I wouldn't give to cop a feel. It looked as tight as the rest of his body.

Okay, Harlow. That's enough. You're bordering on inappropriate right now.

Oliver straightened, and I averted my gaze just in time. He gestured to me.

"You coming?"

I almost groaned. *I fucking wish.*

"Absolutely," I said, my voice far too cheery in an attempt to cover up my improper thoughts.

Oliver gave me an odd look, then strode around the hood to the driver's side. I recovered my composure and slid inside the plush leather interior.

"Wow, this is a nice car."

"It's not Daddy's favorite," Annie said. "But it has four seats. Daddy's favorite only has two seats." She shrugged.

"Well, it's very nice all the same."

I knew nothing about cars, and Oliver didn't offer any further details as he eased away from the curb. The engine scarcely made a noise, and the ride was smooth and even.

"Where are we going?" I asked again.

Oliver shot me an apologetic grin, then returned his attention to the road. "Coney Island. Annie loves it."

"Oh, so do I," I said. "It was one of my favorite places to go as a kid. I haven't been back in years."

I caught his sigh of relief. "You're a born and bred New Yorker, then?"

"Yep. From Queens originally, but when I was about twelve, my parents moved us upstate. What about you?"

"New York through and through. Born in Brooklyn, moved to Manhattan in my late teens after my father passed away. My grandparents lived in Manhattan, and Mom wanted us to be closer to them."

"I'm sorry. About your father."

His eyes briefly flicked to mine. "It was a long time ago." He cleared his throat. "Do your parents still live upstate, then, or have they moved back to Queens?"

"No, they're still upstate," I murmured, twisting my head to stare out of the window and make it more difficult for Oliver to read my pained expression. I hoped he didn't take my comments as a way in. I wasn't in the mood to share details of my place as the dumb one in my otherwise brilliant family.

"Sorry," Oliver said.

I turned to face him. "For what?"

He pulled his lips to the side. "Prying. It's clearly a touchy subject."

I hitched my right shoulder in what I hoped was a nonchalant manner. "It's fine. I have a difficult relationship with my parents, that's all. Very different from the one you have with your mother, and with Annie." The words came out bitter, in direct contrast to what I'd intended.

Oliver looked as if he might continue the conversation, then thought better of it.

Smart guy.

My hang-ups were best left well alone.

12

Oliver

By the time we stepped foot onto the pier at Coney Island, Harlow's smile had returned, and a warm glow spread through my chest as I watched her and Annie skip along the wooden boardwalk hand in hand. This was what Annie had missed out on when Sara left. My mom did her best, but she was in her sixties with her skipping days well and truly behind her.

A bitter taste flooded my tongue, and a black mood descended, chasing away the lightness I'd felt since Harlow and I patched things up. Thinking about Sara always lowered my mood. Why I still allowed her to get to me six years later was a matter I regularly examined and never concluded a reasonable answer to. Ryker had made a valid point yesterday. I had to find a way to put what Sara did behind me and move on with my life.

Her selfish actions had far-reaching consequences, but by living in the past, refusing to embrace the future with open arms, I was giving her all the control—control she didn't fucking deserve.

"Hurry up, Oliver," Harlow shouted over her shoulder, her grin broad, her eyes twinkling. "We're getting candy apples."

A vision of what my life could be like if I opened my heart punched me in the chest. My knees wavered, and I put out a hand to steady myself. I wanted that life, so badly I could taste it, but whenever I thought about moving on, an invisible force pulled me back, stopping me from taking that first, brave step. There'd been a moment, earlier, on the balcony at home where I'd almost reached for Harlow, driven by a potent desire to feel a woman's body against my own after such a long hiatus. And then my brain had kicked into gear, and I'd retreated.

Maybe the time had come to stop listening to my rational side and allow the crazy, idiotic side its turn in the limelight.

"Coming," I shouted, jogging to catch up to them.

Annie muscled in between us and grabbed both our hands. "Swing me," she insisted.

We did as she asked, her carefree giggles putting a smile on my face that nothing could wipe away. Not today.

We ate the sugary candy apples while we strolled the boardwalk, waiting for the rides to open. Soon, the crowds would arrive, and they'd jostle and bump us, and the magic of an early morning stroll would evaporate on the fall breeze. But for now, I lived in this moment, content for the first time in a very long while.

The day flew by. Annie dragged us onto the Trapeze, the Coney Tower—where Harlow's scream when the ride dropped almost burst my eardrum—to the much more sedate speed boat ride. Fortunately, she wasn't tall enough yet to ride the Cyclone, a fact that pleased me and Harlow—and annoyed Annie. We ate Nathan's hot dogs—a must at Coney—drank too much soda, and played Whac-A-Mole where Annie trounced us both.

At four o'clock, Annie's energy ran out. I lifted her into my arms and carried her back to the car. Before I'd even pulled onto the Belt Parkway, Annie had fallen asleep.

I grinned. "Peace at last."

"I could do with a nap myself," Harlow said, yawning. "Thank you, though, for inviting me. I've had a wonderful day. Far more exciting than the one I'd planned."

"You're welcome."

She closed her eyes, allowing me to steal a glance without the fear of getting caught. When Mom dropped her bombshell regarding her three-month trip, I railed against the idea of having a stranger in my home and now, I realized I'd gotten my wish. Harlow wasn't a stranger. Not to me. Not any longer. And certainly not to Annie.

But despite my growing attraction to her, and the revelation that I might be ready to dip my toe in the relationship pool, Harlow wasn't the right person to take that step with. She was my employee, my daughter's nanny. I refused to be that guy, the one that made a pass at the hired help. I recalled Harlow's conversation with her friend that night in the bar all too clearly. Her utter disgust with the guy who'd propositioned her still reverberated in my mind, and I didn't want her to think about me that way.

I rolled to a stop outside my building. Glancing in the rearview mirror, I saw Annie still fast asleep, and as I turned my attention to Harlow, I noticed she, too, was napping. I took the opportunity to cast my gaze over her face, and yeah, my eyes might have slipped south. Her breathing was slow and steady, each lungful of air pushing out her tits. My cock twitched, and I bit back a groan.

I needed to get laid.

Larry, the valet, made his way over, I gently shook Harlow's shoulder. She started awake, calming when she saw me. She rubbed her eyes.

"Are we home?"

My throat thickened, and a longing I didn't quite understand yet filled my chest. "Yes," I rasped.

"I can't believe I fell asleep." She removed her seat belt. "Let me help with Annie."

"It's okay, I've got her." I climbed out and passed the keys to Larry, then reached into the back. I flicked open Annie's belt, then lifted her into my arms. She stirred but didn't wake. I tried to remember the last time she'd needed an afternoon nap. Years ago, I thought. She'd been so excited when I told her I'd invited Harlow that I bet she hardly slept last night. That coupled with the adrenaline of the rides and all the sugary treats, no wonder she'd crashed. I'd let her sleep for an hour or so, but then I'd need to wake her. I didn't want her up half the night.

"Wait here for me," I said to Harlow as we walked into the living area of my home.

She appeared confused but nodded. I put Annie to bed, kissed her forehead, then set the alarm on my watch to remind me to wake her in an hour. Returning downstairs, I walked into the kitchen and removed a bottle of wine from the fridge. I felt myself crossing into dangerous territory, but I couldn't seem to pull back. I poured the cold Montrachet into two glasses and joined Harlow in the living room.

"I realize it's not quite five, but what the hell. One glass won't hurt."

She smiled and reached for one of the glasses. Our fingertips touched. I lingered, relishing the feel of her skin against mine, then withdrew. I went to sit across from her then changed my mind, settling on the couch beside her.

"Thank you for coming with us today. Annie adored having you along."

She gave me a soft smile that went right to my groin. I

hoped her eyes didn't lower. Or maybe I hoped that they did. My head spun at the dichotomy I found myself in.

"At the risk of repeating myself, she's such a great kid. A real credit to you. I've worked with a few families now, and I can honestly say she's the best by far."

"Best how?" I asked, shamelessly fishing for compliments on my daughter.

"She's smart, funny, well-mannered. I adore her."

"That's very good for my parenting ego," I said, grinning. "I'm glad you accepted the position. Annie has flourished under your care."

"Now *you're* being good for *my* ego." She nibbled her lip, blinking rapidly. "I'm really going to miss her."

The back of my neck prickled, and my insides quivered. "Why, where are you going?" The question came out sharper than I intended. Had she noticed me ogling her tits earlier, or found my lingering gazes on the creepy side?

Harlow gave me a puzzled look, her brows almost touching. "When your mom returns, I'll move on. My contract is only for three months, and I've been here almost three weeks already."

"Oh." I clasped a hand to my chest and breathed a sigh of relief. "I thought you meant you were leaving soon."

She dropped her gaze, thankfully not in the direction of my groin.

"Nine weeks is soon."

Silent moments stretched between us, Harlow staring at the floor, me staring at her. I rubbed my fingertips over my lips, struggling to find the right response. I didn't want to promise her something I couldn't stand by one hundred percent.

"A lot can happen in that length of time," I said softly, my intention to hint at possibilities rather than certainties.

She lifted her gaze, locking her hauntingly innocent eyes onto mine. "You're a good man, Oliver Ellis. One day, you'll make someone very happy, and they're going to be a very lucky lady indeed."

"My ex-wife would disagree. I'm damaged goods, remember." The bitter diatribe spilled from my lips before my brain had engaged into gear. I swiped my hand through the air, infuriated with myself, with Sara, with the whole damned shitty mess she'd left me with. "Forget I said that."

Harlow stared at me for a few seconds, then got to her feet and placed her half-finished wine on the coffee table.

"I think it's time I left you alone. Goodnight, Oliver."

I jerked myself into action. "But it's still early. And you haven't eaten dinner yet."

She smiled. "It's been a busy day, and I think I've eaten enough to last me a week. Tell Annie I had a wonderful time."

Before I could come up with the right words to persuade her to stay, she took off upstairs.

I pounded my fist into my thigh. *Fuck's sake.*

∽

Closing the lid on my laptop, I pinched my nose between my thumb and forefinger and glanced at the clock on the wall opposite my desk. Two a.m. My eyes stung from looking at the screen too long. After Harlow's swift exit, and Annie's brief appearance for dinner before she, too, preferred to play in her room and talk to her friends over Skype rather than put up with my progressively taciturn responses to her constant chattering, I'd taken myself off to my office to work.

After all, what else could a twenty-eight-year-old single man be doing on a Sunday night?

Kissing the nanny.

No.

Not going to happen.

My attraction toward Harlow might be growing, but it was

very one-sided, and I refused to behave like a creepy asshole, the likes of the last guy she'd worked for. On a positive note, maybe I could try dating again. I'd proven I could find a woman attractive once more. It didn't have to be Harlow.

Except no one else interested me.

I groaned and shoved a hand through my hair. Time for bed. Annie would be up in a few hours. She didn't deserve to awaken to a tired and cranky father. Tomorrow I'd put my best foot forward, paint a bright smile on my face for the sake of my daughter, and pretend everything was okay.

Pushing my chair beneath my desk, I flicked off the lamp and padded down the hallway toward the stairs. A buttery yellow glow coming from my left cast a triangular beam across the floor. I frowned. Had I forgotten to turn off the lights in the living area?

I turned in that direction—and hard-stopped. Harlow was standing over the stove, peering into a pan. My heart rate intensified, thumping against my ribcage, and my gaze traveled from her feet to her head. She was in a plum two-piece shorts and camisole set that showed off her slim, shapely legs to perfection. The thin strap on her top had fallen halfway down her arm, offering a glimpse of the top of her creamy breast.

I bit back a groan as my cock reacted accordingly, blood surging to my groin area. Her ass wiggled as she stirred the contents of the pan, and I almost shoved a hand inside my jeans, such was the urge to touch myself.

Fuck. I'm losing it.

Whether I made an inadvertent sound, or Harlow simply felt me watching her, she lifted her head, and our gazes met over the empty space between us.

Busted.

"Oh sorry, did I wake you?" She pushed a lock of hair out of her eyes. "I couldn't sleep, so I thought I'd make some warm milk. I hope that's okay."

I entered the living room when I probably should have walked in the other direction, left her to her milk, and gone to bed. My footsteps were tentative and wary. I was so turned on by the girl standing over my stove wearing virtually nothing that I didn't trust myself not to bend her over my dining table and fuck her into the middle of next week.

"You didn't wake me," I said, my voice raw and husky. "I've been working."

She arched a brow. "It's two in the morning."

I nodded in recognition of the time. "I often work late."

"You should relax more," she said, returning her attention to the pan. "From what I've seen these past few weeks, you work too hard."

I blinked slowly, knowing precisely what would relax me.

"Would you like some milk, too? I can easily heat up more."

I swept a tongue over my bottom lip. "No."

Her gaze lifted to mine, almost as though she'd heard something in my voice. I forced a swallow down a dry throat, my eyes roving over her face.

"Then what do you want?" she asked in a whisper.

The word "You" lodged in my throat. I dropped my gaze, recognizing the crossroads in front of me.

If I acted, and my advances weren't well received, I'd have a complex problem on my hands that I'd have to find a solution to, which would most likely result in Harlow leaving my employ. And that would upset Annie which, in turn, made me a shitty father.

If I walked away—the sensible course of action—then I'd never know what might have been.

"Oliver," Harlow said gently.

I raised my head. "Yeah?" I asked, barely recognizing the gruff rasp coming out of my mouth.

She turned off the heat and moved the pan of milk to one side. "Kiss me."

My eyes widened, and then I took two steps and my hands were in her hair, my mouth on hers, plundering, ravaging, taking all she had to offer and demanding more. God, she tasted so fucking sweet. Like ripe strawberries and summer rain.

Her tits flattened against my chest, her nipples hard points that begged for my tongue, but we weren't there. Nowhere close. A kiss was one thing. Yanking down her top and sucking her nipples would only lead us to one place, and though we'd both feel good while it lasted, the aftermath wouldn't be pretty.

She wound her arms around my neck, her nails dragging over the soft skin at my nape. She moaned softly, the sound a call sign that sent a signal right to my dick. I circled my hips, gaining light relief, but nowhere near what I needed. With the last ounce of mindfulness, I broke our connection but kept my hands around her face. I stared into her eyes, watching as a war swirled in her hazel irises, flecks of burnt orange surrounding her pupils.

"Have I just fucked up?" she asked.

"No. God no." I bent my head and brushed my lips over hers to demonstrate my point. "The exact opposite."

She smiled, relief infusing her expression. "It's just, after last time, you know, when I kissed you and you kind of freaked out on me, and then here I am begging you to kiss me again, except this time I'm your employee. Last time you were just some guy I met in a bar. You must think I'm very forward."

"You're rambling." I smirked. "Last time was different. Things change. And no, I don't think you're very forward. I think you're a woman who isn't afraid to ask for what she wants." I stole another brief kiss, then released her. "Would you have dinner with me tomorrow night? I can get a friend to watch Annie."

I'd ask Athena, Ryker's wife, to come over. She'd offered to look after Annie plenty of times, yet I'd always refused. And it'd be good practice for Ryker for when he and Athena had children of their own which, I expected, wouldn't be that far into the future.

A slow grin spread across her face. "I'd love that."

I smiled. "Then it's a date."

"It's a date," she murmured.

13

Oliver

With one hand buried in my pocket, I waved to Elliot, then watched as he climbed into his car and it drove away. Despair weighed heavily in my chest. This thing with Athena had become almost like an obsession for him. From what I could glean—because he'd kept his cards close to his chest—his determination to find the man responsible for what happened to his sister had overtaken his personal life in a big way. None of us could call him on his professionalism. Elliot was as committed to ROGUES as ever, delivering tons of value to the company every single day. But from the little he'd shared, his girlfriend, Brie, was having a tough time coping. I only got his side of the story, but he seemed to think she wasn't even trying to understand his point of view, resulting in several bitter arguments.

I hoped they worked it out. Brie was good for Elliot, the soothing salve to his fiery personality.

My car pulled up curbside. I got in the back, activated the privacy screen, then called Ryker.

"You on your way home?" Ryker asked when he answered.

"Yeah, leaving the bar now. Should be there in thirty. Is Annie okay?"

"She's having a ball," Ryker said, chuckling. "Athena and Harlow have kept her well entertained." His voice lowered. "I like her, Oliver. You chose well."

I snorted. "Getting ahead of yourself, buddy. Way, way ahead."

"It's a start," Ryker said. "I saw the glint in your eye when you asked me and Athena to watch over Annie this evening. Just try not to screw it up. Don't fucking mention Sara."

The mere mention of my ex-wife caused a dark cloud to settle over my head, but I refused to let it linger. Sara was in my past, and while Harlow might not be my future—it was far too early to make calls like that—she had at least shown me the way forward, out of the rut I'd lived in for the past six years.

"No success with Elliot," I said, diverting the conversation away from my love life. "While he understood and appreciated my concern, he told me, and I quote, to mind my own fucking business." I sighed and rubbed my forehead. "He mentioned Brie was struggling with the amount of time he's devoting to this search, though."

"Yeah, he gave me the same impression. Thanks for trying. I appreciate it. I guess we need to monitor the situation and intervene if Elliot's obsession gets any worse."

"Good luck with that."

Ryker laughed. "Yeah, he's always been a ticking time bomb, even when we were kids. He hasn't mellowed with age."

"Elliot would call it passion."

"I call it a pain in my fucking ass."

I chuckled. "See you shortly, bud."

Ending the call, I slipped my phone in my pocket and

closed my eyes. I let my head fall back. My mind turned to Harlow and our upcoming date. When I'd asked her out in the early hours of this morning, I'd momentarily forgotten my promise to Ryker to have a chat with Elliot, but the timing had worked out fine. I should be home by six-thirty. I'd made dinner reservations for seven. Plenty of time. The restaurant I'd chosen was literally five minutes away from home.

Nerves bit at my insides, leaving me with an empty feeling in the pit of my stomach, a dry mouth, and heart palpitations. The kiss we'd shared last night had been impulsive, in the moment, bursting with passion and longing and need. Even the day we'd spent at Coney Island had been full of ease with Annie providing the connection, and someone to fill any gaps in silence.

Tonight threw up a completely different challenge. It would be me and her. Alone. No one else to bounce off if the conversation dried up or things turned awkward.

My car coasted to a halt in front of my building. I instructed my driver to wait, then jogged inside.

"Daddy!" Annie greeted me with an enthusiastic hug, followed by a very adult, "How was your day?"

"Excellent. Thank you for asking." I swung her up into my arms and settled her on my hip. "How was school?"

Annie made a face. "All right, I suppose."

I kissed her cheek, then glanced around, looking for Harlow.

"She's finishing up getting dressed," Athena offered, correctly guessing my thoughts. "She'll be down in a couple of minutes."

"Aunty Athena told me you're going on a *date*, Daddy," Annie said with an impish grin. "With Harlow."

I glared at Athena and said, "Did she now?" then mouthed, "Thanks for that."

She mouthed back, "You're welcome."

I set Annie on the floor, then crouched down to her level. "And is that okay with you, munchkin? If Daddy takes Harlow out to dinner?"

Annie clapped her hands. "I *love* it." She skipped off and plunked herself on the couch to watch TV.

One potential disaster avoided.

Ryker wandered over with a glass of scotch. "Drink this before you puke. It's a date, not a trip to the gallows."

I took it gratefully. The first sip burned. The second went some way to settling my nerves. "It's been a long time."

"Too fucking long," Ryker agreed.

"I appreciate you doing this," I said, jerking my chin at Annie.

Ryker clapped me on the shoulder. "Anytime, buddy. Anytime."

The clacking of heels behind me drew my attention. I spun around, and my mouth fell open. Harlow had chosen a sleeveless fitted emerald-green cocktail dress paired with matching strappy sandals. The top half of the dress pushed up her tits and curved in at the waist, then snaked over her hips. It fell to mid-calf and split up the left-hand side, giving me a tantalizing glimpse of her smoking legs. She'd worn her hair loose but added soft curls that trailed over her shoulders. As always with Harlow, her makeup was light and fresh, adding to rather than detracting from her natural beauty.

"I hope this is okay for the restaurant," she said, her voice slightly wavering, a tell that she was as nervous as me. She smoothed her hands over her hips.

I wished they were my hands instead.

"You look..."

Like sex on a stick.

Hot. So fucking hot my balls ache.

Good enough to eat. In fact, let's forget the restaurant and dine on each other instead.

"Stunning," I finished, all the other thoughts running through my head rated R, and definitely not suitable for seven-year-old ears.

She broke into a wide grin. "Thank you."

"Okay, beautiful people," Ryker said, giving me a shove. "Off you go. Enjoy—and don't rush back."

He sniggered at his own joke.

I made sure Annie wasn't looking, then flipped him off.

His sniggers grew in volume.

Holding out my elbow for Harlow to slip her hand through, I said, "Shall we go and leave Athena to take care of the two children?"

Ryker's chortling followed us right into the elevator.

"He's funny," Harlow said.

"He *thinks* he's funny," I replied, conjuring up all the ways I'd pay him back for his unwelcome teasing.

The elevator doors closed, and silence followed. I couldn't take my eyes off Harlow. She, meanwhile, found a very interesting spot on the floor to give her attention to.

"How was your day?" I asked softly, my question bringing her head up. "Did Annie behave?"

She seemed relieved I'd steered the conversation on to common ground. "She always behaves. She's an angel."

"Not always, but I appreciate the sentiment," I said.

Once we reached the lobby level, I gestured for Harlow to walk ahead, pointing to where my driver stood by my car. I waited until Harlow had settled herself inside, then closed the door and strode to the other side. The privacy screen remained activated from my earlier journey, and I left it in place.

"I love that color on you," I said once the car started moving. Reaching for her hand, I pressed a kiss to her knuckles. "You look beautiful."

She ducked her head. "For someone who professes to have

been out of the dating game for a while, you're very good at this."

"Only with you," I murmured.

She dampened her lips with her tongue, then swallowed. "Oh god," she whispered, her eyes on my mouth. "I'm in so much trouble."

I snaked a hand around the back of her neck and drew her toward me. I meant the kiss to be soft and exploratory, but the second our lips touched, the intimate moment exploded into a passion that surprised us both. I licked inside her mouth, then wrapped my tongue around hers. The sound she made was one of the sexiest things I'd ever heard.

"We're here, Mr. Ellis."

My driver's voice came over the intercom, and Harlow stiffened, the intrusion into our private bubble unwelcome. I released her slowly, reluctant to break the connection. Her chest heaved, her breath coming in sharp little pants. Christ, if that was how enthusiastically she reacted to a simple kiss, what would happen when I got her into my bed?

Not that we were there—yet. But I'd accepted it would happen sometime.

Soon.

Very soon.

I pressed the flat of my palm to Harlow's lower back and eased her inside the restaurant, the warmth from her skin heating my hand.

"Oliver?"

"Yes?"

"After dinner, let's take the long route home."

14

Harlow

Talk about bold, Harlow. He might have asked you on a date, but he's still your boss.

More concerning, had my request sent a signal that taking the long route home meant I wanted more?

I mean, I did.

Just not yet.

Everything between us was still so new, so *unexplored,* so awkward. Jumping into bed with Oliver after two kisses—I refused to count the brief peck I'd given him the day we first met—albeit hot-as-fuck kisses, was a mistake.

I'd made enough of those to last two lifetimes.

Whatever we had going on—and I hadn't quite figured it out yet—sex was a big step, especially with the added complication of an employment contract. And in less than two months I'd have to start the search for a new job. If we took it too far, and it went sour, I didn't want that to ruin my chances of securing my next role. My industry, like most, thrived on gossip, and bad news traveled fast. Two strikes, and I'd definitely be out of the game.

"What are you thinking?" Oliver asked when we'd taken our seats and given our drinks orders. "Your face is very expressive, but I can't read you at all."

"I'm not having sex with you," I blurted.

My mouth popped open, while the woman at the next table flashed a shocked glance in my direction. Heat flooded my face, while Oliver looked highly entertained.

"Thank you for clearing that up. Frankly, that wasn't the response I expected to my question."

I picked up my menu and hid behind it. "Shit. I'm sorry. That came out wrong."

Oliver's fingers appeared over the top of my menu, and he eased it down, an amused grin curving his, frankly, sexy-as-fuck lips upward. I couldn't take my eyes off his mouth. I wanted to suck on his plump lower lip.

Jeez, what was happening to me?

No sex for more than four weeks. That's what's happening. And a delicious, fit, gorgeous man is sitting across from you not long after kissing you senseless in the back of his three million dollar limousine. No wonder my panties were soaked.

I almost shouted, "You're an ass, Harlow Winter", then remembered the conversation was inside my head and to yell such a thing out of the blue would no doubt see me expelled in disgrace from the fine-dining restaurant.

"Why don't we start again."

I nodded, thankful Oliver had such a forgiving personality. "That sounds good."

"I'm nervous, too, Harlow. This is a big step for me, and despite your kind words in the back of the car, I'm seriously out of practice. I haven't been on a date in over four years, and those I did go on after Sara walked out ended in complete disaster." He cursed. "Shit, Ryker told me not to mention Sara."

I wrinkled my forehead. "Why?"

He shrugged. "I guess mentioning one's ex-wife when on a date with another woman isn't the proper thing."

I gestured dismissively. "She's a part of your past, and Annie's mother. Can't wipe her from history."

"No."

His eyes slid away, pulling him into a place where I wasn't invited. To bring him back to the present, I traced a fingertip over the back of his hand.

"What are you thinking?" I asked, replicating his question of me earlier.

He refocused his attention on me, blinked twice, then smiled broadly. "I'm not having sex with you," he said, loud enough for the same woman at the next table to hear.

I hushed him. "Oliver."

His beaming grin widened. "Two can play at that game."

"You'll get us thrown out."

He shook his head. "Not a chance."

No, probably not. Rich people followed different rules than the rest of society. A man as powerful and wealthy as Oliver could ruin a reputation with a single tweet, or a brief conversation with some of their business associates. Not that I could imagine Oliver behaving in such a way, but the restaurant wouldn't know that, nor would they take the risk.

The server brought our drinks, a glass of red wine for Oliver and a pink gin and tonic for me. My one and only drink this evening. I didn't want a repeat of the first night we met. We might be on an official date, but I was still responsible for looking after Annie, and tomorrow was a workday.

"Talking of exes," Oliver said, sipping his wine. "Have you heard from yours? Carter, wasn't it?"

"Yeah," I said, surprised he'd remembered the asshole's name. Then again, I hadn't exactly hidden my wrath that night. Most of the bar could probably name the cheating bastard.

"And no, I haven't. Nor do I want to. I hope our neighbor gave him crabs."

Oliver arched a brow. "You're over it, then?" he teased.

I chuckled. "I am, yes," I replied honestly. "I still hope his dick falls off, though. It'd serve him right."

Oliver pretended to write on the palm of his hand. "Note to self. Don't piss off Harlow."

I narrowed my eyes. "You'd better believe it. Men, or women, who cheat are the pits, and they deserve everything coming to them."

A weird expression crossed his face, but he shut it down before I could fully assess what it might mean. He rested his elbow on the table and leaned his chin on his hand, his dark, vivid eyes locked on me. "You're magnificent. I love your indomitable spirit." His hand crept across the table, and he knitted his fingers through mine.

A shudder of pleasure reverberated up my spine. If this was Oliver out of practice, then I had no hope of resisting him. My *relationship sabbatical,* as Katie had put it, hadn't lasted long. But there was something unique about Oliver, and I wasn't referring to his insane wealth. I'd find him attractive even if he didn't have two cents to rub together. He had a vulnerability that called to me on a deep, emotional level.

"You're a dangerous man, Oliver Ellis," I said.

He brought my hand to his mouth, watching me as the tip of his tongue traced my knuckle. No one else would see what he was doing, but I felt it, right between my legs. I closed my eyes, giving in to the sensations rioting through my body. My chest tingled, and my breathing escalated.

"Ready to order, sir, madam?"

I tried to pull my hand away, resulting in Oliver gripping me tighter. He held my fingers, his thumb rhythmically tracing back and forth while he perused the menu.

"I'll have the monkfish. Harlow?"

I hadn't even looked at the menu, too busy controlling the urge to hitch up my dress, straddle Oliver's muscly thighs, and rub myself to a fast orgasm.

"Um, you order for me."

Oliver smiled. Closing the menu, he said, "Make that two."

"Certainly, sir." The server picked up the menus and backed away.

We slipped into easy conversation. I asked Oliver about his company, ROGUES, and he gave me a brief history of how it had started out. Nothing that I hadn't learned from Wikipedia, but it was nice to hear it directly from him.

"It must be extremely hard work juggling everything," I said.

"It is, but it's rewarding, too. Not many guys get to work with their best friends every day and make a very decent living at the same time."

"Are they all based in New York?" I asked.

"No. Three of us are. Myself, Ryker, and Elliot. Those two grew up together. The rest of us met in college. Garen is based in Vancouver, although he makes regular trips to Manhattan. Upton runs our West Coast offices, and Sebastian is based in London. He heads up the European arm of the business. We don't have anyone out east yet as we're still growing the business over there, but no doubt at some time, one of us will have to move, maybe somewhere like Japan."

I shook my head. All of this was so far outside of my comfort zone. "You must all be very clever." I nibbled on my lip and found myself sharing more than I expected. "I'm a huge disappointment to my mom and dad. Both of them work in medicine, as do my three brothers. As the youngest, they expected me to follow suit, except it turns out math and science were far beyond my capabilities." I barked a laugh. "I don't think they'll ever forgive me."

Oliver's eyebrows shot up. "Forgive you for what?"

I tucked my chin into my chest. "For not being smart."

He sucked in a breath, the air whistling through his teeth. I avoided looking at him, instead stirring my drink, the ice clinking against the side of the glass. He placed a finger underneath my chin and lifted my head.

"There's more to being smart than the ability to understand calculus or biophysics."

"Tell that to my parents," I said dully.

He squeezed my fingers. "Has it ever occurred to you that the skills you have are worth more than any college degree? Do you have any idea how hard it is to get a kid to like you? Kids have a sixth sense about people. They subconsciously know the good ones from the bad ones. I learn about people from my daughter every single day. I watch her reactions carefully. If I could take her to my business meetings, I would." He laughed. "Maybe in a few years, she'll be my secret weapon."

I smiled, but even though I couldn't see my expression, I knew it hadn't reached my eyes. "She'll be a great addition to your company. She's very smart."

He canted his head and brought my hand to his mouth. His soft, firm lips grazed my fingers. "You have more warmth, kindness, and integrity than ninety percent of people I know. And it doesn't matter what your academic background is, at least not to me. They can't teach the skills you have. They're either in you, or they're not."

"It's okay, Oliver. I'm used to living with my parents' disappointment. It's why I rarely visit them."

My mood had put a damper on the evening, and we ate our monkfish in virtual silence. When Oliver suggested dessert, and I declined, I could see the relief in his face.

Guess this will be our first and last date.

He paid the check and tapped something on his phone, then slid it into his pocket. As we weaved through the restaurant, Oliver captured my hand. A spark of hope lit within me.

Maybe I hadn't completely messed up the evening after all. His car idled at the curb. He had a quick conversation with his driver, which I couldn't hear, and then we climbed inside, but instead of heading back toward his apartment on the west side of the park, the car drove up the east side.

"Where are we going?"

"I want to show you something."

"The long way home, huh?" I said with a smile.

A flash of melancholy darkened his features, but in a microsecond, it had gone. He leaned over to my side of the car and touched his lips to my ear. "I'm going to show you your exact worth, Miss Winter."

I gave him a blank stare.

What on earth could he mean?

15

*O*LIVER

When Harlow realized she wasn't getting any further information from me, she stared out the window, her brow furrowed as she tried to work out our eventual location. I suppressed a smile. The unexpected turn of events and the way I'd decided to deal with them might cause a problem, meaning I'd have to delay the lesson I wanted to teach Harlow. It was late, after nine, and Debbie was extremely strict with the children in her care. Thankfully, she replied with a big thumbs-up to the message I'd sent her from the restaurant.

Excellent.

A short while later, the car turned off the main highway, stopping outside a familiar building. Familiar to me, but not to Harlow.

"Where are we?" she asked, wrinkling her brow and staring through the car window at the large eight-bedroom house.

"Come and see," I said, getting out.

I waited for her to join me, then captured her hand and

walked toward the house. Debbie opened the front door and smiled.

"You're lucky. Most of them are still awake, and you know they'd give me grief if they found out you wanted to come by, and I refused." She rolled her eyes. "Mind you, I'm in for a hell of a day tomorrow."

I laughed. "This is Harlow. Harlow, this is Debbie. She runs this place."

"Hi Debbie," Harlow said, confusion marring her features, although she didn't ask what I meant by 'this place'.

"Come on in, you guys."

I gestured for Harlow to go in first, then followed on behind.

Debbie pointed to the stairs. "You know where they are."

I held Harlow's elbow and guided her to the second floor. As soon as we were out of earshot, she halted.

"What is this place, Oliver?"

"It's a foster home for disadvantaged kids that I fund. We offer a safe environment for them to grow and develop. We provide education, healthcare, treatment for trauma which, in a lot of cases, is an absolute necessity. A couple of our kids have returned to their families, and we continue to support them and their parents after they leave. Most are adopted, providing we can find the right family. We're regulated by the city, but we provide a vital service. Debbie manages the facility and lives on-site."

Her mouth popped open. "You pay for this?"

"Yes. And I visit as often as I can. I also bring Annie. It's important for her to understand that not all kids are fortunate enough to have the kind of life she does."

"Wow." She tucked a stray strand of hair behind her ear. "What am I doing here?"

I grinned. "You'll see."

We continued up the stairs, and at the top, I pointed to the first room on the left. Rowan's room. Not that it made a difference where we began. As soon as the other kids got wind that we were here, they'd all come running.

My lesson for Harlow? These kids had been through a lot, and as such, they found it very difficult to trust or engage with strangers. I'd made a bet with myself that within an hour, Harlow would have them eating out of her hand.

That would be Harlow's lesson.

She beat my estimate by five minutes. Even Patsy, our most recent resident who'd only been with us for three months, and still hadn't spoken a single word, sidled up to Harlow after hovering in the corner watching as Harlow made every single kid fall in love with her. Harlow rewarded Patsy with a soft kiss to the top of her head but didn't push her. She simply let her watch and played with the others.

"Right, you guys," Debbie said, appearing in Rowan's doorway. "Time for bed."

Cries of "Aww, Debbieeee," and "Please, just five more minutes", rent the air. But Debbie was having none of it.

"Bed," she reiterated, herding the kids together. "It's after ten, and you all have school tomorrow."

We said goodnight to the kids and promised to return soon. Leaving Debbie to the fun of putting seven overexcited children to bed, we returned to the car. As soon as the door closed, and before the wheels had made a single rotation, Harlow turned to me, her eyes shining with elation.

"I'd like to visit again. Can I? Do you mind? I just… they have so much love to give." The words tumbled from her lips.

Lips I was desperate to kiss.

I reached a hand around the back of her neck and drew her to me, my mouth seeking hers in the dark, the car gently rocking us as we eased onto the road. I licked along the seam of her mouth, and when she opened for me, I wrapped my tongue around hers, almost lazily, wanting to take my time, to savor her, to taste the mint she'd slipped into her mouth after dinner when she thought I wasn't looking.

I wanted to worship her.

Drawing back, I dropped a peck on her lips, then rested my forehead against hers, waiting as our breathing slowly returned to normal.

"Yes, you can visit again. As often as you like. I'll text you Debbie's number, and you can arrange it directly with her." I cupped her cheeks, my thumbs brushing over her soft skin, I whispered, "Now do you understand how special you are?"

She ducked her head, but I wasn't having that. I pressed my thumbs underneath her chin until her hesitant gaze met mine.

"Do you?"

She shrugged. "I like kids. You don't have to pretend with them. You can be yourself. No agenda, no politics or stupid games. If they're happy, you know. If they're sad, you know. There's a wonderful..." she wrinkled her nose, "freedom to that."

I suppressed a sigh, holding back my disappointment. She'd grown up thinking she wasn't good enough. That kind of deep-seated belief would take time to break.

And I would. Eventually.

"You know Patsy?"

Her brows dipped. "Was she the girl with pigtails who didn't speak?"

I nodded. "Patsy came to us three months ago. She's..." I bowed my head. "She's had it very rough after witnessing her father beat her mother to death and then turn a gun on himself." Harlow gasped, but I continued. "So far, she still hasn't uttered a single word. Yet in less than an hour, she pressed herself into your side as if she craved your touch. *That's* the kind of power you have, Harlow. And while you probably won't believe me—yet—that is worth more than ten degrees from Harvard. That kind of power has the ability to change the world."

She nibbled on her lip. I wanted to do that, too.

"Thank you," she eventually said.

"For what?"

A ghost of a smile tugged at the corners of her mouth. "The list is long."

I caressed her face with the back of my hand. "What are you doing Saturday?"

She chuckled. "Apart from taking Annie to and from school, I barely know what I'm doing tomorrow, let alone five days from now."

"Excellent," I said, grinning. "Then you're free."

"No, I'm not free. Because if you're planning to go out, then someone needs to watch Annie."

"Annie is staying over at a friend's house on Saturday night."

Harlow tilted her head, suspicion prevalent in her gaze. "Okay Mr. 'I have all the bases covered'. What did you have in mind?"

I tapped the side of my nose. "Wait and see."

∼

"A business thing?" Harlow said as the car moved smoothly down Fifth, heading south. "If you'd told me that on Monday night, I'd have said I was washing my hair."

I laughed. "First lesson in negotiation. Don't show your hand too early."

"Noted," she grumbled. "Okay, bring me up to speed. Who are these people and what do they want?"

My insides warmed, and a freeing lightness filled my chest. It had been a while since I'd taken a date to dinner with business associates, and as we traveled toward the restaurant, I realized how lonely my life had been. It would be easy to blame Sara, but I couldn't lay this at her feet. She'd chosen to leave, but it had been my decision to allow her actions to take over my entire life, like a contagion dripping into my veins and poisoning every single thing it touched.

I'd ceded control to a woman who didn't deserve to be given such power.

Harlow was helping me regain that control.

"They're a consortium who've traveled from Europe in a bid to ingratiate themselves with ROGUES. They have an idea for a joint venture that I believe is a little too weighted in their favor in its current format. My job is to either rebalance the status quo or draw a line underneath their plans and end the association there. Either way, it will probably be an uncomfortable meeting. Both sides want to win."

Harlow clapped her hands. "You take me to all the best places," she said, a teasing note to her voice. "So, what's my role?"

I tucked a lock of her hair behind her ear, tracing the back of my hand over the soft skin of her neck. "To give me something to look forward to at the end."

Her gaze locked on mine, and I detected a slight shudder. "You're quite the smooth talker, Oliver Ellis. I think you're bullshitting me when you say you're out of practice."

"Come here," I murmured, palming the back of her neck and easing her toward me. Pausing with my lips a breath from hers, I drank her in, and then I kissed her. Softly, reverently, conveying a promise of something more. This week, we'd done nothing more than kiss, stealing the odd one here and there when both of us were sure Annie wouldn't burst in. Even though Annie had been delighted we'd gone on a date Monday, I didn't want to get her hopes up. Neither me nor Harlow knew what this was yet, and until we figured that out, Annie was my priority. Harlow was the first woman I'd brought into Annie's life since Sara walked out, and for now, I'd prefer her to see Harlow as her nanny rather than my girlfriend.

No complications.

No false promises.

No hopes that she might ultimately have dashed.

The car eased to a halt, and I drew back. "We're here."

Unfastening our seat belts, we exited the car, meeting on the sidewalk. I took her hand.

"Harlow?"

She gazed up at me, her hazel eyes wide and open. "Yes?"

"I'm glad you're here."

16

Harlow

With Oliver's words ringing in my ears, I walked into the restaurant with my chin up and shoulders back. I wasn't here as the family nanny or a pretty accessory. Oliver wanted me here, was glad to have me by his side, and that small fact gave me a confidence I'd badly needed. These weren't the circles I moved in. Sitting cross-legged on the floor playing with a bunch of kids was my happy place, where I was most comfortable. Having dinner with a horde of high-powered businessmen and women where most of what they spoke about would go right over my head wasn't my idea of fun, but I'd endure anything to spend time with Oliver.

Careful, Harlow.

I was falling. Fast. Too fast. We'd gone on one date and shared a handful of kisses. Hell, he hadn't even touched my boobs. We were a long way from anything more intimate happening. I was acutely aware of the scars Oliver's wife had left him with, and I refused to be the rebound girl, the one who acted as the carthorse for him to rebuild his confidence after taking a nasty tumble before he moved on to a more suitable thoroughbred.

Why am I thinking in horse analogies?

I vaguely heard the greeter ask for our names, Oliver's deep husky answer bringing me back to the present.

"Right this way, sir, madam."

"Are you okay?" Oliver whispered as we followed the chic woman who fit in to this high-class restaurant far better than I could ever hope to achieve.

I nodded, swallowing past an arid throat, my earlier confidence dissipating. All around me, smartly dressed men and women in outfits that probably cost more than a month's wages engaged in animated conversation, whereas I couldn't even muster a "Fine" in reply to Oliver's concern.

I wondered if anyone could tell I'd purchased my dress from a thrift shop. I'd splurged all my cash on the dress I'd worn on my date with Oliver Monday night, and I simply couldn't afford a second designer dress. Even so, this hand-me-down hadn't been cheap. I wasn't happy eating into my savings to buy clothes, but I didn't want to embarrass Oliver either.

"Relax," Oliver murmured. "You're stunning. Your beauty eclipses every single woman in this room."

I looked up at him gratefully. "Do you read minds?"

He slipped an arm around my waist and pressed a kiss to my temple. "I'm learning to read yours."

Oliver stopped beside a round table for eight, where six other people were already sitting. Four men. Two women. A moment of relief that it wasn't all men didn't last long when one of the women gave me a thorough head-to-toe once-over then whispered something to the other woman who glanced my way and then smiled kindly before shooting an irritated glare at her companion.

"Patrick." Oliver shook the hand of the man nearest to him

who'd stood to greet us. He urged me forward, his palm in the small of my back, the heat from his skin comforting. "This is Harlow."

I caught the note of pride in his voice, and when he snaked his arm around my waist and brushed over my hip with his thumb, I felt ten feet tall.

"Hi," I said with a smile. "Nice to meet you."

"And you," Patrick said.

We took our seats while the rest of the group introduced themselves. The women, I discovered, were Fiorella and Jasmine, and both worked in the marketing department.

"And what is it that you do, Harlow?" Jasmine, the mean girl, asked sweetly.

I fired a panicked look in Oliver's direction. We hadn't discussed this. Why hadn't we discussed what to say? I could hardly tell this bunch of high-fliers that I was the nanny. *Think fast, Harlow.*

"Um, I'm..."

"Harlow is my daughter's nanny."

Oliver's voice rang clear and true. I strained my ears to pick up any trace of embarrassment. No. Nothing, only the same hint of respect I'd caught in his earlier introduction.

"Oh." Jasmine's smug grin had my hands clenching into fists. "What a... worthy career."

"I agree," Oliver said brightly, turning a sharp gaze on Jasmine. "Far worthier than, oh, I don't know, say, a career in marketing." He finished off his barbed comment with an evil grin.

The entire table fell silent.

I shifted in my seat as an icy chill descended over the gathering. I hated silences, especially uncomfortable ones. When Oliver had mentioned tonight's dinner might be a little on the awkward side, I hadn't imagined this.

Reaching for the pitcher of iced water in the center of the

table, I scanned the sea of faces in front of me even though none were in focus. "Would anyone like water?"

Oliver laid his hand on my arm, preventing me from filling the glasses. "What *I* would like is for Jasmine to apologize to you or this will be an extremely short meeting."

Jasmine flushed beet red, and Fiorella gave her a hefty dig in the ribs to encourage her, while Patrick's face turned puce and he glared across the table at his coworker.

"I'm sorry," Jasmine said, her chin tucked into her chest. "That was totally uncalled for." She swallowed, hard, her throat bobbing from the effort of forcing her muscles to work. "I'm not usually such a bitch."

Fiorella laughed, except I couldn't identify any amusement in it. "Yes, you are."

I detected a European accent, possibly French, but it was faint.

"My niece graduated from college this summer where she achieved her qualification in childcare," Fiorella continued. "She's already secured a position with a wonderful family in London. I'm immensely proud of her. In her career, she'll make a difference, mold kids when they're still young enough for it to matter. Whereas us?" She gestured around the table. "We help our company sell stuff. That's it. We don't have any room to act in a superior manner."

Oliver clapped loudly. "Hear, hear. I couldn't agree more. My daughter is thriving since Harlow came into our lives." He slipped an arm around my shoulder and pulled me toward him, planting a kiss on my lips. "And so am I."

The relief on Patrick's face was almost comical. He either really wanted this business or desperately needed it. Both played into Oliver's hands, meaning this should make for a very interesting evening, and one I found myself looking forward to now that Jasmine had been put in her place.

"Okay," Oliver said. "Let's order, and then we'll begin."

I sipped my wine and watched with unveiled admiration as Oliver grilled the entire team on their proposal. He didn't miss a trick, but his insightful questioning highlighted the intellectual differences between us. I tried not to acknowledge how much the truth of that bothered me.

The best part, however, where I had to try damned hard to suppress a gleeful grin, was when he pressed Jasmine especially brutally, drilling into her ideas for developing the brand. She stumbled over a few answers, and like a predator with their prey on the run, Oliver pounced. Patrick did his best to cover up her fluffed responses, and over dinner, Jasmine grew quieter, retreating into herself. I couldn't even feel sorry for her. My friend Katie had a saying. "When someone shows you who they are, believe them." Well, Jasmine had shown me, and everyone else sitting around the table, exactly who she was. If ROGUES signed a deal with this company—and from what little I gleaned of the conversation, any deal was a long way into the future—I had the distinct impression Jasmine wouldn't be a part of any cross-party collaboration.

Dessert arrived, and with one look, my mouth watered. I dug into the lightest cheesecake I'd ever eaten, and, closing my eyes, I let the flavors explode on my tongue, then swallowed slowly.

"Jesus Christ," Oliver muttered.

My eyes sprang open, expecting to find him irked with a comment someone had made that I'd missed because I was too busy appreciating the tastiest thing I'd ever put in my mouth. Instead, his eyes were on me, the pupils dilated until they almost appeared black.

"What?" I asked, dabbing my mouth with a napkin in case I had cheesecake smeared on my face.

Instead of answering me, he beckoned to the server. "This cheesecake," he said. "Would you mind boxing up two portions for me to take home?"

The server nodded. "Certainly, sir."

"Thank you."

I gave Oliver a quizzical look.

He leaned close and, in a low voice, murmured in my ear. "Don't eat any more."

My forehead wrinkled. "Why not? I'm enjoying it."

"Because, when you slipped that fork between your lips, you looked as if you were having an orgasm. And the only person at this table who gets to watch that is me."

A raging fervor raced through my body. I almost reached for the pitcher of iced water to pour it over my head. I needed something to cool me down after Oliver's comments had heated me up to inferno levels. I pressed my thighs together, my breath hitching and my pulse thrumming out of control.

The server returned with a box and set it down in front of Oliver. He picked it up and stood. I followed.

"Thank you, Patrick. We still have a lot of work to do. Send me those reports next week and I'll set up a video conference to discuss them." He reached for my hand. "Goodnight all."

I squeaked out a goodnight, then Oliver swept me from the restaurant. His car idled at the curb. We climbed inside. I didn't even get as far as fastening my seat belt. Oliver pulled me astride his lap and drew my lips to his in an urgent kiss, full of longing and ardor. His erection pressed to my hot center, and on instinct, I rocked against him. He growled deeply, tilted his hips, and gave it back to me with interest.

I gasped into his mouth as his hard length connected directly with my clit. Something had happened tonight, and I couldn't quite figure out what, but hell, I wasn't complaining. Not with the way Oliver was making me feel.

Wanton.

Reckless.

Horny.

With a groan, he tore his mouth from mine. "Shit, Harlow. Sorry."

"No apologies," I panted, reaching for him again. This time I took charge of the pace, the potency, the fervor. I burrowed beneath his jacket, fumbling for his belt. I managed to unbuckle it, flip open the button, yank down the zipper, and slip my hand into his pants before he stopped me, his firm grip circling my wrist and putting a stop to my exploration.

"Not here," he rasped. "Not like this."

My eyes flared. "You're not rejecting me?"

He cupped my face. "Jesus, no. No. I want you in my bed, not to have our first time an uncomfortable fumble in the back of my car."

I rested my forehead on his. "I couldn't adore you more."

17

Harlow

Oliver's hand pressed to the small of my back and eased me into the elevator. The doors closed, trapping us inside the steel box. Electricity crackled through the air as our eyes met. I held my breath, anticipating Oliver's next move.

He didn't make one.

Instead, he stood with his back to the wall, one hand holding the box of cheesecake, the other hanging loosely by his side. His heated gaze burned a hole through my dress. I lowered my eyes, locking on the thick bulge in his groin, imagining the feel of him slipping through my folds and pushing inside.

I licked my lips.

"Fuck," he gritted out.

His hand curved around the back of my neck, and he yanked me to him, his mouth hot and urgent as he forced mine into submission. His tongue surged inside, scattering my senses until I couldn't think, couldn't breathe, could only feel.

The elevator coasted to a stop, and the doors glided open. Oliver clutched my hand and marched into the penthouse. He made a detour to the kitchen to drop off the box of cheesecake, then headed for the winding staircase that led to the upper floor. At the top, instead of turning toward my room, he led me to his.

Until now, I hadn't seen Oliver's room—why would I have? —But the dark wood furniture and pale-blue accessories suited him perfectly. Masculine with a hint of softness. Pictures of Annie, some alone, some with him, and others with people I didn't recognize, took up every available space on the dresser, and a large canvas of her as a baby, her eyes wide and inquisitive, took up most of one wall.

"That's beautiful," I said, freeing my hand from Oliver's and crossing the room to take a closer look at the black-and-white print.

He joined me, his arm coming around my waist. "She was six months old there. I love that picture. We had a professional photographer come by and take a bunch, but as soon as I saw that one, I knew I had to have it enlarged."

We.

One simple word, but a timely reminder that Oliver carried heavy baggage. As his head dipped to kiss me, I pressed a hand to his chest, stopping him.

"Convince me I'm not a rebound, that you're not using me as a way of proving you're over your wife, and then you'll move on to someone more fitting to your social circle."

His face transformed into a shock so intense, it couldn't be fake. His mouth parted in disbelief, his stare incredulous.

"Jesus. Is that what you think this is? Fuck." He palmed the back of his head, then stepped away. "Fuck, Harlow, no. No. That's not what this is. At all. And what the hell do you mean 'someone more fitting to my social circle'? Because if you're referring to cold, empty women like Jasmine…"

He broke off and glared at me as if he wanted to say more, but the words wouldn't come.

Shit. I've screwed this up.

He filled the space he'd created between us and cupped my face. His mouth closed over mine in a kiss that sent tingles down my spine. It wasn't rough or demanding. It was... apologetic.

Releasing me, he threaded his fingers through my hair. "However long it takes, I will show you your worth. I won't give up until you believe, truly believe deep in your soul, that you're worth ten, twenty, a million times more than women like Jasmine. You're a sparkling diamond. She's a lump of coal with a black heart to match."

I gasped. I actually gasped at the sincerity in his words. I touched a hand to his chest.

"Oliver."

The word came out husky, and a deepening ache grew in my core. This man... stole my breath and was well on his way to stealing my heart.

"Tell me you don't want me," he said, his eyes tracing my mouth. "Tell me and I'll let you go."

I shook my head. "I can't. It would be a lie."

A rumbling groan echoed through his chest and, in a move reminiscent of the hottest of movies, he slipped his hand down the front of my dress, hooked his fingers inside my bra, and jerked me to him.

"Last chance."

I tilted my head back and licked my lips. "Keep it."

His mouth crashed on mine, our teeth connecting, his tongue parting my lips with such authority and dominance, my panties soaked through in seconds. Gripping my zipper, he eased it down, one metal tooth at a time, unhurried and in control. For a man who claimed to be out of practice, he sure knew how to seduce a woman. He'd barely touched me, and already I'd give him anything he asked for.

My dress gathered around my feet, and I stepped out of it. Oliver still had three fingers inside my bra. I hoped that soon, he'd move them to a more intimate area, and I knew exactly how to make that happen.

I'd already unfastened his pants once this evening, and on the second run, I was even faster. As the material loosened, I snuck my hand inside his boxers to discover the prize underneath.

And what a fucking prize.

I curled my hand around his thick, hard shaft and squeezed. He wrenched his mouth from mine, his breathing coming in short, sharp gasps.

"Shit. More."

I tugged his pants down to his ankles. He helped me by kicking off his shoes and simultaneously shrugging out of his jacket. By the time I'd gotten his socks off, he'd discarded his shirt and tie, too.

"You work fast," I murmured.

"But I'll seduce you slowly. You're too special to rush."

My eyes closed, his words flowing over me like the finest silk. Despite the revolving door of boyfriends since high school, I'd only slept with three guys, and none of them had ever brought me to the cusp of orgasm using words alone.

I gripped his erection once more, the urge to taste him sending me to my knees. Oliver, though, had other ideas. He raised me. His hands caressed my hips, and he walked me backward. As the backs of my knees touched the cool cotton sheets, he maneuvered me onto the bed. I lay there, staring up at this incredible man, his body carved in muscle and sinew, the head of his erection jutting over the top of his boxers.

"Tonight is for you, Harlow. Let me worship every inch of you."

I'm close, and he hasn't even touched me yet.

He hooked his fingers inside my panties and slid them down my legs. Thank goodness I'd taken care of the lady garden. No one wanted an out-of-control bush when sleeping with a guy for the first time, especially if he was going to—

Oh god...

The heat from his mouth branded me, sending a surge of fire straight to my core. His thumbs parted my folds, and his tongue circled my clit, then slipped inside. My back bowed off the bed, my pelvis inching upward, seeking more of what he had to give.

Jesus, this man gives amazing head.

I lifted up onto my elbows, watching his dark head move as he licked inside my body. Threading my fingers into his hair, I pushed forward, urging him on.

A swell began in the lowest part of my abdomen. I forced my muscles to relax, eager to draw out the pleasure. He played my body to perfection, instinctively knowing when to apply pressure and when to ease off. In the end, though, I couldn't hold on. My calves cramped, and every muscle south of my belly button tightened. My insides swelled, then shattered into a toe-curling orgasm that had me screaming Oliver's name.

He kissed my mound, then my stomach, fluttering touches that left indelible marks on my skin. Not physical marks. Emotional ones. His lips glistened with evidence of where he'd spent the last few minutes and, with a smile that sent a fresh flood of wetness right to my core, he pressed his mouth to mine in the briefest of kisses.

"Oliver?"

"Yes?"

"Can we fuck now, please, before I lose my ever-loving mind."

His grin sent my heart fluttering. Rising from the bed, he

removed his boxers, allowing me to see him, for the first time, in all his magnificence.

I trailed my eyes over his defined pectoral muscles, the ridges of his abs, his firm thighs, that 'dreamed about but rarely seen in real life' V leading to a thick, beautiful cock that extended out a good eight inches from his hips.

He walked over to his nightstand, and I took a moment to slip off my bra. I didn't want any barriers between us, physically or mentally. He returned holding a square foil packet.

"Please don't think badly of me." He ripped the condom open with his teeth. "But after our date Monday, I bought a pack. Only in hope, not in expectation."

This guy. I'd never met anyone so thoughtful.

"I definitely don't mind," I said, watching as he rolled it down his impressive length. He crawled between my legs. I expected him to push straight inside. He didn't. I should have known by now that Oliver rarely behaved as I expected him to. His lips hovered over mine, and he gazed into my eyes. I read hesitation, a hint of worry swirling in his irises.

Of course.

Duh!

He'd told me it had been over four years since he'd had sex with a woman. And I wasn't just any woman; I was his employee. He probably feared a lawsuit. Especially in these weird times we lived in, where a guy could be sued for harassment for merely chatting a girl up in a bar.

It was up to me to take the lead. At least until we got the first time out of the way.

I curved one hand around his neck and pulled him in for a kiss. With my other, I gripped his erection, wrapped my legs around his waist, and coaxed him inside.

"I've got you," I murmured.

A deep groan eased from his chest, and he thrust his hips,

pushing all the way in. "Fuck, Harlow," he moaned. "Fuck, you feel good."

He pressed his lips to my neck, his breath hot against my skin, muttering unintelligible words, but whatever he said didn't matter. I could hear the raw pleasure through the rumble in his chest, the way he gasped when I clenched my muscles around him. I flexed my hips, driving him deeper, taking him all the way in.

"Tonight is for you, too," I said, replaying his earlier words to me.

He rolled back on his heels and lifted me until we were face-to-face, front-to-front. "Come here. I want to be closer to you."

He folded a strong arm around my waist, and his hand palmed my breast, his thumb brushing the stiff peak of my nipple, sending a bolt of pleasure sprinting down my spine. He rocked into me, using his hips to power him on. First times were weird. You never knew what it would be like. All mine had been huge disappointments, the anticipation of greatness often far outweighing the bruising reality. Usually good sex took a lot of practice, full of false starts and too-quick orgasms.

Not this time.

Not with Oliver.

The familiar wave of a pending climax built in my stomach. Too soon. Not yet. I didn't want this to be over yet. If I came, something told me Oliver wouldn't be far behind.

I cut off the visuals—Oliver looked too damn sexy—and shifted my weight slightly, which stopped my clit from rubbing against him.

Better.

"Look at me," he whispered.

So much for cutting off visuals.

My eyelids fluttered open.

He smiled, his gaze steady. "You're everything I dreamed and more, Harlow."

I didn't get to give a response before he bent his head and kissed me. His tongue slipped past my lips, stroking mine, while his erection slid in and out, massaging my insides, intensifying the ache rising within me. He increased his pace. Our bodies slapped together, and sweat trickled between my breasts. I wouldn't last much—

"Ohhhh shit," I expelled, my body detonating into pieces, slicing through my attempt at control with ease. I dug my nails into his shoulders, wishing this moment could last forever. We'd only ever have one first, but fuck me, what a first.

"So close," Oliver muttered. He thrust twice more, then stilled, his breath pushed out on a soft groan. "Jesus, Harlow. Jesus Christ."

We stayed in the same position, arms around each other, unwilling to break the connection, for what felt like minutes. He trailed his lips over my shoulder, soft, awed kisses, full of gratitude.

"That was…" He drew back wearing that beautiful smile I'd never tire of. "The best I've ever had."

18

OLIVER

"Wait there."

I threw back the covers and climbed out of bed. Removing the condom, I knotted the end, wrapped it in tissue, and threw it away. I picked up my boxers then, remembering Annie wasn't home, discarded them and crossed the room.

"Where are you going?" Harlow asked, rolling onto her side and slipping her hands beneath her head.

My heart panged as I looked at her. She belonged here. Right here, in my bed, in my home, in my life. I returned to her, leaned down, and kissed her forehead. "You'll see."

"Hang on," Harlow said as I turned away. "Don't move."

Pausing mid-step, I glanced over my shoulder. "Why?"

She grinned. "I like the view. You've got a great ass."

A lightness filled my chest, and I returned her smile with one of my own. "Back in two minutes."

I jogged downstairs and into the kitchen. Opening the box of cheesecakes, I peered inside. They'd survived the journey intact. I hoped Harlow was still hungry. I wanted a replay of her eating this dessert. I grabbed two plates, setting a slice of cheesecake on each one. I snatched a couple of forks and returned upstairs.

Nudging the door open with my hip, I entered my bedroom to find Harlow mid-stretch, her back arched, her gorgeous tits thrust upward, the nipples begging for my tongue. She made this satisfying keening sound that my cock approved of, given how quickly I hardened.

"You brought the cheesecake." She shuffled to a seated position and held out her hand for one of the plates. Her eyes drifted to my groin. "I see you brought me two gifts." She tapped her fingertip against her lips. "Now, which one should I eat first?"

I groaned. Setting my plate on my nightstand, I crawled into bed beside her. "I'm a man. There's only one answer to that question."

She inclined her head. "You're right. Cheesecake it is."

With an impish grin, she dug in. Her expression as she took the first bite almost brought me to orgasm. She'd given me a repeat performance all right, except this time, I didn't have to hold back.

I trailed my fingertips over her abdomen, creeping downward to the dampness between her legs. Gliding one finger inside, I bent my head and sucked on her nipple.

She gasped and widened her legs, giving me easier access. "Aren't you eating your dessert?"

Her nipple popped out of my mouth. I laved it with my tongue and glanced up at her. "You taste better than any cake."

She set down her half-finished cheesecake and threaded her fingers into my hair. "I'll finish that later. Or maybe I'll spread it over your cock and finish it that way."

"Oh, fuck," I muttered against her breast, my eyes closing, my imagination running riot. "Yes, please."

She pushed at my shoulders and flipped me onto my back, then straddled my legs. She leaned over to grab the plate. Her breasts brushed against my face, and I took the opportunity to flick out my tongue and taste her.

Returning to her previous position, this time holding the remnants of her cheesecake, she forked off a slice and held it out to me. I closed my lips over the prongs, getting my first bite. "That *is* good."

She looked at the remains of her slice, then at my cock, then over at my untouched piece on my nightstand. "I might need to borrow some of yours. You're not exactly small."

My chest puffed out. Every guy wanted the woman they were in bed with to think they were well-endowed. Harlow didn't disappoint on that score.

"It's yours," I said. "And if this is what you're going to do with it, I'll arrange for a regular delivery."

She set the fork to one side and dipped her finger into the creamy delight, then spread it over the head of my cock. It jerked in approval. She did it again, and then a third time, until the entire head was covered in pink cheesecake.

"Suck," she said, pressing her finger to my lips.

I obeyed, briefly acknowledging that this was the most erotic moment of my life. Sara had been my first, and although we'd fucked a lot in our college days, she hadn't been into experimentation. The women I'd torn through when Sara left in an attempt to get over her had provided nothing more than one- or two-night distractions. A release of pent-up frustration that had fleetingly allowed me to forget, only to wake up the next morning with a head full of regrets and a heavy guilt that, somehow, I'd cheated on my wife, even though she was the one who'd walked out on me and Annie.

With Harlow, I knew there wouldn't be a second of regret.

Keeping her eyes on mine, she licked around the head, her hand enveloping the base of my cock, firmly, confidently. She squeezed, not too hard but enough to garner a hiss of exhilaration.

And then she took me all the way in.

I fisted the sheets as she sucked, her cheeks hollowing, her throat working me, moans of enthusiasm tightening my balls. Christ, at this rate, I'd come in thirty seconds, and how lame would that appear?

I tried to think of other things to distract me from the feel of my cock in Harlow's mouth. Work, stocks and shares, that fancy new car I had my eye on.

Nothing worked.

"Shit, I'm coming," I gritted out, attempting to move away. Emptying my load in her mouth required a discussion we hadn't undertaken.

She tightened her grip and sucked harder.

I lost it.

Semen shot from the head of my cock, right down her throat.

And she swallowed.

Women *never* swallowed. At least the ones I'd been with hadn't.

I wrapped my hand around the back of her head and stroked, wanting to convey my gratitude but unable to speak yet. When I recovered, I cupped her chin until our eyes met.

"You didn't have to do that."

"I wanted to." She reached out and dipped her finger into the remains of the cheesecake, slipping the digit into her mouth, then she snuggled into my side where she rested her head on my chest and her palm on my stomach. "I told you tonight wasn't just for me. It was for us."

"Don't go," I blurted.

She looked up at me, confusion written in the creases around her mouth and the lowering of her brows. "I wasn't planning to go anywhere, unless you'd rather sleep alone."

"I'm not talking about tonight." I squeezed her tight. "I mean... don't go. When Mom comes back, I want you to stay." I shifted my position until we were eye to eye. "To stay with me."

Her lips parted, and she stroked my face. I leaned into her touch, craving more.

"Oliver, I'd advise you to not make decisions right after a blow job," she said, the beginnings of a teasing grin lifting her lips at the side.

I didn't return her smile. Instead, I pushed as much sincerity into my expression and my voice as I could. "I mean every word. I don't know about you, but this feels... right. Neither of us knows what this might turn into, but I'd like a chance to find out. Wouldn't you?"

She gazed at me, her eyes flitting across my face, looking for... oh, I don't know... hesitation or uncertainty, maybe. She could search all she liked. She'd only find commitment and determination.

"What about Annie?"

I tucked a lock of hair behind her ear. "What about her? She adores you, Harlow. Nothing's changed on that score, at least not for me. I'd still like you to take care of my daughter, be there for her. The only difference is..." I grinned. "I'd like you to take care of me, too. Just not in the same way, obviously."

"And there's Sara to consider, too."

My eyes narrowed. "There is *no* consideration needed regarding Sara. She's my ex-wife and a woman I haven't seen in six years. She's the past. You're the future."

She shook her head. "It all feels too soon to make a promise you might not want to keep in a week, a month, two months. And whatever you might say, I know Sara left scars that one night with me can't hope to heal."

She had a point. The damage Sara had done to me when she'd left ran deep, hence I'd hardly dated in years. But this time felt different, *was* different. I would have to find a way to convince Harlow.

"You're saying no?" I asked.

She cupped my face, the pad of her thumb brushing along my jaw. "I'm saying I want to explore whatever this is. I want to get to know you as your equal. But I think we should take it one day at a time. Wait until I've left my underwear scattered all over your bedroom floor for the eleventy-billionth time and then see if you feel the same," she said, joking and trying to lighten the mood.

It worked. I smiled broadly. "Scatter away. My space is your space."

"Let's revisit that comment in a couple of weeks."

I tucked her into my side and kissed the top of her head. "I can't wait for tomorrow."

"Why?"

"Because I get to wake up beside you."

19

Harlow

I rapidly blinked, trying to clear my vision and the grogginess from one of the deepest sleeps I'd had in a while. As the space around me came into focus, I frowned, confused.

This isn't my room.

And then my memory returned with an almighty crash.

Oliver.

Me and Oliver.

Me and Oliver fucking.

A lot.

Cheesecake.

Oh God.

I spread raspberry cheesecake on his dick and sucked it off.

Covering my face with my hands, I peeked through a gap in my fingers and turned my head to the side.

The bed beside me lay empty.

I placed my hand on the mattress. Warm. Which meant it had been occupied not that long ago.

And then the sound of running water coming from the bathroom reached me. I pulled the covers up to my chin, which felt a bit like locking the stable door after the horse had bolted. Oliver had seen me in all my naked glory. Too late to act coy now.

I hadn't even drunk very much wine at dinner last night—or had I? Whatever had taken place, hiding behind an excuse of "sorry, too much booze" wouldn't wash.

But there was something about waking up in my boss's bed with the cold light of day shining a beacon on my behavior that made me want to burrow beneath the covers and never show my face again.

The bathroom door opened.

"You're awake," Oliver said, his face softening. "How did you sleep?"

I slid my gaze over his naked form, my earlier embarrassment beating a hasty retreat when faced with a body carved of stone and a cock on the rise. Yeah, my memory hadn't let me down. The boss had muscles I wanted to lick.

Okay, stop thinking of him as 'The Boss'. It's just creepy. You've had his dick in your mouth, in your vagina. He's sucked on your boobs and given you head. No more boss-type shit, okay?

"Harlow?" Oliver's brows mashed together. "Is everything all right?"

I pulled my head out of my ass—not literally, obviously—and, riddled with doubt, I forced a smile. "Yeah... I mean, um... All's good."

Folding back the covers, he slipped into bed. He reached for my hand and linked our fingers together. "A little weirded out, huh? If it helps, so am I."

Relief rushed through me, and the smile I offered this time was real. "Oh, thank god. I started to think I was losing my mind. I mean, last night was great. Better than great. Awesome. But it's you, and it's me, and I'm your employee, and you're my employer, and there's Annie and..." I clasped a hand to my chest. "Okay, I think I'm hyperventilating."

Oliver chuckled. "You are seriously the hottest woman. Ever. I love your honesty."

He released my hand, slipped his arm around my waist, and tugged me on top of him where, yeah, I could feel his dick pressing against my center. As my body flooded with warmth, my instincts took over, and I rocked against him.

"Please tell me it's okay," I whispered.

He cradled my face, his eyes soft and holding so much emotion, my skin flushed as if I'd spent the last hour standing in front of a heat lamp.

"It's okay," he murmured, leaning up to brush his lips over mine.

I maneuvered myself until the head of his cock pressed against me, but before I could sink down onto that delicious length, he paused.

"Condom," he said.

I wanted to tell him "fuck it". Insist we didn't need a condom because I was clean and on the pill, and before last night, he hadn't had sex in forever. But Oliver struck me as the decent kind, and I wanted to honor him.

"Then move that fine ass, Oliver Ellis. It's mean to leave a girl hanging."

∼

"Here, let me do it," I said, plucking the bowl out of Oliver's hands. "At the rate you're going, you'll have pancake batter all over the ceiling."

Oliver grinned and allowed me to take over without making a fuss. He put some coffee on, then sidled up behind me and wrapped his arms around my waist. His chin rested on my shoulder.

"What do we tell Annie?" I mused as I beat the creamy mixture.

"Nothing," Oliver said. "She's a smart kid. She'll figure it out."

He kissed my neck, then moved on to my shoulder.

I shivered, my skin pebbled in goose bumps. "She'll have questions."

"And we'll answer them. Honestly. But I don't see the need to make a big thing of this. Annie absolutely adores you. She knows we're dating."

I set down the bowl and turned in his arms. "Is that what we're doing? Dating?"

He tongued his teeth and had a good peek down my top where an inch of cleavage showed. "Yes, we're dating. And fucking. I'll leave off the latter for Annie's benefit, though."

I struck his shoulder with my palm. "Oliver! I'm being serious."

"So am I."

He took my mouth in a searing kiss that left me tingly all over. When he withdrew, he hit me with a wicked smile. "I wonder if there's enough time for me to bend you over my dining table and—"

"Daddy!"

Annie sprinted across the living room and threw herself into Oliver's arms. After she'd thoroughly hugged him, it was my turn for an Annie special. Wrapping her in my arms, I still hoped she couldn't sense a shift in atmosphere, despite Oliver's nonchalance about the change in our relationship status. Kids were hellishly in tune with their environments, and while she wouldn't understand the sexual politics underlying the furtive glances between me and Oliver, I worried the change in circumstance would unsettle her.

"Next time," Oliver murmured in my ear before he smiled at

Sinead, the mother of Annie's best friend, Cara, and said, "Thanks for looking after her."

"You're welcome. The girls had a wonderful night. We'd be more than happy to have her over anytime."

Oliver cast a glance in my direction, winked, then returned his attention to Sinead. "I might just take you up on that."

I blushed, the meaning behind his comment clear considering what he'd suggested right before Annie arrived. Oliver saw Sinead out while I listened to Annie babbling about her night away from home. So far, she seemed none the wiser, and I breathed a sigh of relief. I wasn't ready to answer any difficult questions yet. I'd rather she remained oblivious, at least for the time being.

"Okay, munchkin." Oliver picked up Annie and swung her around, much to her delight. "What do you want to do today?"

"The zoo!" she announced.

Oliver looked over at me, his gaze hot and hungry. "I'd love it if you'd join us. Would you?" he asked in a husky tone that had my lady parts clenching.

I could have sworn my knees trembled.

"Oh, yes, please," Annie said, pressing her hands together in hope. "Please, Harlow. Me and Daddy will be so happy."

A feeling of breathlessness followed by a sense of belonging coursed through me, and my eyes filled with water. "You got it, sweet pea." I distracted myself by adding a spoonful of batter to the sizzling pan. "Pancakes first, then the zoo."

20

Harlow

Winter came early this year, and before we'd reached the end of the first week in November, a thick layer of snow lay on the ground, and cloudy skies cast a gray hue over New York. Today, mist hung low in the air, cutting off the tops of the high-rise buildings surrounding Central Park and giving the city an eerie air.

Pulling my coat around me, I burrowed the lower half of my face into my scarf, then tucked my hands inside my pockets. The bitter wind chapped my face, and leaves swirled around my ankles.

I miss summer.

Thinking about the warmth of the sun brought Oliver's mother to mind. She'd return from her vacation in five weeks' time, and Oliver still hadn't broken the news about us. He reassured me she'd be thrilled, and promised he'd tell her the next time she called.

"No agenda, Harlow," he'd declared when I'd challenged

him after her last call last weekend. "Just me being an idiot man and not thinking."

I wanted to believe him, but at the back of my mind, a niggle that wouldn't be silenced kept on and on that I was some sort of delayed rebound, a temporary salve for his battered soul, and once the scars his wife had caused healed, he'd realize we were terribly mismatched and decide to move on.

Except he still insisted that when his mother returned, I wouldn't be going anywhere. I'd all but moved into his bedroom, although I still made sure to set my alarm so I could rise long before Annie woke up. I didn't want her to catch me sneaking out of her dad's room or, worse, to burst in to find us in bed. Oliver thought I was crazy; I'd insisted they were my terms, like it or leave it.

I'd tentatively tested Oliver only a few days earlier by musing that I was thinking of giving Tamara, my recruitment consultant, a call. He'd vigorously shaken his head and told me I didn't need to find another job.

Yet I couldn't figure out how it would work when both his mother and I occupied the same space. Liv was lovely, but I worried I'd tread on her toes, or make her feel unwanted. I'd voiced my worries to Oliver, and he'd laughed and said his mom would welcome the ability to do her own thing. From what I could glean, she and her boyfriend—was boyfriend the right term when both parties were in their sixties?—had gotten even closer during their overseas trip. Maybe they'd want their own space. That would certainly make things a lot more straightforward and avoid any bad feelings on either side.

Annie still hadn't broached the subject of Oliver and me, despite Oliver showing me lots of affection in her presence. It was as though she simply accepted the change and didn't see the need to delve into the whys of it all. I loved that simplicity about kids, their adaptability and the ease with which they moved on in life without creating unnecessary waves. Adults could learn a lot from children, if they bothered to pay attention.

I waved to Debbie, my chest tightening at the sight of Patsy standing on the front step, fused to Debbie's side while sucking on her thumb. I visited the home Oliver funded as often as I could, and I'd fallen in love with all the kids here, but Patsy held a special place in my heart. Debbie was homeschooling her at the moment, Patsy's mental state too fragile to attend her local elementary school. She still hadn't spoken, although every time I stopped by, she would crawl into my lap and nestle her face in my neck—and I'd just melt.

I jogged down the steps to the subway—I still didn't like using Oliver's driver despite his repeated insistence that I should—and climbed aboard the first train heading to south Manhattan. Oliver had invited me to lunch, and I'd jumped at the chance to see him during the daytime, something I rarely did. Usually, he was far too busy, and often had a working lunch, or, on occasion, he didn't even stop to eat a sandwich. All the ROGUES directors seemed to work incredibly hard, although I'd only met Ryker and Elliot so far. Oliver assured me I'd meet the rest of the team at the ROGUES Christmas party that the company held in the third week of December each year. I acknowledged that his mother would have returned by then, yet he was still making plans for us. I wanted to believe in the future but was too damaged by the past.

Alighting from the train, I allowed the crowds of people to sweep me up to street level. I waited at the crosswalk, glancing up to the top floor of Oliver's building. I imagined him standing at the window, one hand in his pants pocket, watching me. Maybe even feeling a shiver of excitement at my imminent arrival as he thought about bending me over his desk and sliding his cock home.

Inwardly I chuckled. I'd always been a dreamer. In all likelihood, I'd find him sitting at his desk, a frown of concentration pulling his brows into a deep V as he stared at his computer screen, working on the next big deal, and when he saw me, he'd glance at his watch, astounded that the morning had passed by in a flash, his day so absorbing he hadn't given me a second thought.

I preferred the dream to the likely reality.

After signing in at reception, I rode the elevator up to the top floor. I'd only been here on one other occasion, two weeks earlier when Oliver had proudly shown me around, introducing me to everyone as his girlfriend.

Yet *still* I held back.

Still, I couldn't quite settle into that role, regardless of how often Oliver reassured me of my place in his life.

That damned niggle wouldn't quit.

"Hi, Harlow." Oliver's PA, Carly, greeted me with a wide, welcoming grin. "Go right on in." She gestured toward Oliver's closed office door. "Can I get you anything to drink?"

"No, thank you," I said. "I'm good."

That wasn't all together true. My mouth felt parched, but it wasn't due to dehydration. It had much more to do with excitement and adrenaline. Every time I laid eyes on Oliver, I'd get giddy, like a teenager experiencing her first crush. Last week, I met Katie for dinner, and right off the bat, I'd babbled on about Oliver for thirty minutes straight. When I finally shut up, she'd hit me with an enormous smile and said I was obsessed.

I couldn't deny it.

Whatever my feelings were for Oliver, they ran deep. Far deeper than they had with Carter, who I'd dated for a year before the cheating scumbag decided he'd rather stick his dick in the neighbor's pussy than mine. Whenever I thought back to him, I realized he'd been convenient instead of a conscious choice. A guy I'd liked, never loved, but who had at least provided me with company, someone to go to the movies with, and had given me a roof over my head. A roof I'd lost the minute I caught him with his bare ass in the air, wildly thrusting his hips as he threw away our entire relationship.

If I'd loved Carter, then I wouldn't have gotten over him so fast. I wouldn't have fallen for Oliver.

Wait... what?

I hadn't fallen for Oliver.

I was *not* in love with Oliver Ellis.

I liked him, that was all. And he was good in bed. Great, in fact. This was crazy talk brought on by regular, multiple orgasms. I barely knew the man. Except carnally. There, I knew him very well indeed.

"Harlow?"

I jerked out of my stupor and blinked at Carly. "Sorry, what?"

"Are you okay?" she asked, concern lacing her tone. "You kind of zoned out on me there."

"Yeah, I'm fine. Sorry. A lot on my mind. He's free, you say?"

She gave me a puzzled look. "Yes. You can go right in."

"Thanks," I mumbled, pulling myself together. I rapped once on the door and pushed it open.

Oliver wasn't sitting behind his desk staring at his computer screen as I'd expected. I found him standing with his back to the window, facing in my direction. He had one hand buried deep in his pants pocket, the other casually hanging by his side.

"Hey." I closed the door behind me. Maybe I was imagining it, but I could feel Carly's interested stare burning into the back of my head. "Is everything okay?"

He covered the space between us in four long strides and threaded his hand through my loose strands. He tipped back my head, then kissed me. Not a 'we're in the office, let's take it easy' kind of kiss, but one of those 'I don't give a fuck who sees us' kind.

"I missed you," he murmured against my mouth while

removing my coat. He tossed it over a nearby chair. "I watched you cross the street. I thought you'd never get here."

A thrill raced through me. He *had* watched me.

See... dreams can come true.

His lips feathered over my neck, and I tipped my head to the side to give him better access, biting back a groan in case Carly had her ear pressed to the door.

"Do you still have time for lunch?" I asked breathlessly.

"Can I eat you first?"

My stomach convulsed with wanton need. "We're in your office." I panted as he covered my right breast with his palm, his thumb sweeping over my erect nipple. "Anyone could walk in."

Oliver drew back with a wolfish grin. "I know."

He kissed my neck, and his hand burrowed beneath my clothes. I sighed. Skin to skin. There was nothing like it.

"Oliver," I gasped when he pinched my nipple, sending a flood of warmth between my legs. "Stop."

He paused, then raised his head. "Is that a real instruction, or one borne out of fear that someone might interrupt us?"

I flushed red. "The latter," I admitted.

He reached behind me where he turned the lock. "There," he said, returning to me. He tongued his top teeth and raked me in a full-on head-to-toe gaze. "Now you're mine."

21

OLIVER

I'm lost. I can't get enough.

Every sense I possessed felt on high alert. My fingertips tingled whenever they touched her skin, my nostrils filled with Harlow's unique scent, and her panting breaths were the sweetest sound. The taste of her filled my tongue as I thoroughly kissed her.

Carly would have heard the lock slide into place. By now, the PA gossip train would be in full flow, steam rising from the keyboards as emails flowed around the company, each one filled with salacious chatter.

I didn't care.

Sinking to my knees, I pushed up Harlow's skirt, bunching it around her waist. I hooked my thumbs into her panties and slid them slowly down her legs, my eyes fixed on hers. I watched her pupils dilate, the flare of desire eclipsing her hazel irises. She stepped out of her underwear, leaving her free for my fingers and tongue.

"You're soaked," I murmured, parting her folds with my thumbs. I licked along her opening, rewarded when she gasped and buried her fingers in my hair. I pressed down on her clit, then slipped my tongue inside her, purposely going slow, drawing out the pleasure, her soft little moans and sharp intakes of air giving me her blessing to carry on.

She tried to speed things up, to set the pace. I withdrew. She whimpered in frustration.

"Oliver, please," she pleaded.

"I love it when you beg." I nipped at her inner thigh.

She hissed through her teeth.

"Tell me what you want, Harlow."

"You. I want you. Your mouth, your tongue, your hands on me. I want to come, Oliver. And I want you to be the one giving it to me."

Man, this woman knows how to say all the right things.

"What's the rush?"

I lapped at her folds, then circled her clit with the tip of my tongue. In response, she dug her fingernails into my scalp, her head falling back.

"Yes. God, yes. Just like that."

"Pull up your shirt," I said. "Show me your tits. Tug on your nipples."

Okay, who am I?

I didn't recognize myself. This certainly wasn't the kind of sexual relationship I'd had with Sara, or my other brief flings. I felt myself changing, morphing into someone else.

A man I liked.

A man I respected.

A man who wanted to pleasure his woman far more than he sought pleasure for himself. One look at Harlow's flushed cheeks, swollen breasts, and stiff nipples, and I knew I'd never tire of watching her as she exploded into a shuddering climax.

"God help me," she moaned.

Her legs quivered, and her left shoulder twitched, a sign I'd noticed in the last couple of weeks when she orgasmed. Every day I learned something new about her, learned to read her body and adjust my actions to bring her the most satisfaction.

I rose to my feet and handed back her panties. She leaned into me for support as she pulled them on. Her eyes fell to my groin, my erection clearly visible through my pants. She reached for me. I stepped back.

"This isn't a tradeoff, Harlow. I didn't go down on you expecting you'd do the same for me." I bent my head and kissed her. "Let's go to lunch."

"Won't that be painful?" she asked. "I mean if I don't... help you."

I laughed. "Since getting with you, I've learned to live with it. Don't worry. I'll let you make it up to me tonight."

I picked up my cell phone and slipped it inside my jacket pocket, then helped Harlow back into her coat. I took her hand, unable to suppress a chuckle at her beet-red cheeks when we left the office, and Carly greeted her with a wink.

"I'm mortified," she said as I ushered her into the elevator and pressed the button for the lobby.

"You've made her day." I pulled her close. "And mine," I added in her ear.

My car was waiting right outside the ROGUES building. Harlow climbed in first, giving me a terrific view of her ass. She glanced over her shoulder and caught me ogling.

"You're insatiable," she said, grinning, her earlier embarrassment diminishing. "Where are you taking me, anyway?"

"JoJo's." I fastened my seatbelt. The car moved smoothly away.

Harlow frowned. "I don't think I know it."

"It's fairly new. Only been open a few weeks. I took a client there last week. The food is good, and the atmosphere is light and fun. Perfect for a flirty lunch." I picked up her hand and kissed her knuckles.

The journey to the restaurant took fifteen minutes. I'd called ahead to reserve a table. Just as well, considering how packed it was.

"What a great place," Harlow said after the greeter had shown us to our seats. She glanced around, taking in the art adorning the walls, the mismatched tables and chairs, and the colorful drapes adorning the windows.

"I believe all the artists are local," I said.

"The paintings are for sale?"

I nodded. "Yes." I gestured to the server. "Sorry to rush you, but I have to be back by two for a meeting."

"That's okay," Harlow said, scanning the menu. "I'll have the grouper with wild rice, and a water, please."

"Sounds great. Make that two."

"You should have canceled if you're busy," Harlow said when we were alone.

I took her hand and brushed my thumb over the back. "Never too busy to spend time with you."

"That sweet mouth of yours will turn this restaurant diabetic if you're not careful."

I chuckled. "This might surprise you, but my two o'clock appointment won't think I'm sweet."

"I can imagine. I've seen you in action, remember."

I traced the tip of my tongue over my bottom lip, and my gaze fell to her chest. "Yes. You have."

She giggled at my double entendre. "Can you turn anything into a sexual innuendo?"

"What can I say? It's a gift." I sipped my water. "I spoke to Mom about us," I added casually as the server brought our lunch order.

Harlow's eyes widened. She waited for the server to retreat, then leaned forward. Her hand went to her necklace, and she fiddled with it. "You did? Was she okay? I mean, what did she say? Is she fine with it all? With us?"

I grinned and reached across the table to still her zigzagging. "You'll break the chain if you carry on. And yes, she was fine. More than fine. Thrilled, actually. She likes you a lot."

I refrained from adding how relieved Mom had been, how she'd shared her worries and concerns that I'd allow what Sara did to ruin my entire life before I'd even reached thirty.

Harlow blew out a heavy breath between pursed lips. "Thank goodness for that. Is she still planning to return in a few weeks' time?"

I nodded. "I believe so, although I think her trip has given her the chance to reassess her life and what she wants from it. It wouldn't surprise me at all if she wants her own place when she returns to Manhattan."

She plucked at the skin at the base of her neck. "Not because of me, I hope."

"No," I said reassuringly. "I hope she does move out. She's given up enough of her life to help me through the last six years, and now..." I lowered my voice. "Now, well, I kind of hope you'll stick around for the next sixty or so."

"Oliver." Her voice came out breathy, a little hesitant. She set her fork down, her eyes glistening, that tempting little furrow appearing between her brows. The one I wanted to kiss every time it materialized. "You don't have to make promises to me. I'm not asking for commitment."

"And what if I am?" I asked. "What if I want to take the next step with you? Hell, Harlow, you've practically moved into my bedroom, even if you do leave before dawn breaks each morning. Which, by the way, you might as well drop. Annie knows exactly what's going on."

"Does she? How? She hasn't said a thing to me."

I chuckled as the conversation I'd had with Annie when I put her to bed last night came back to me. "She said that maybe now I wouldn't get so mad if she asked whether you could be her mommy."

Harlow covered her mouth with her palm. "Oh god," she said, her voice coming out muffled. "She knew about that?"

Fresh guilt raced through me at my behavior that night. It still surprised me that Harlow had forgiven me so easily for how cruel I'd been; for the terrible, cold, cutting words I'd used. Warmth rushed to my face.

"Yeah. Dad of the year, huh, not to mention the world's shittiest employer."

She inclined her head. "Oh, Oliver. You're an amazing father. Don't be so hard on yourself. That night is in the past. I could have, *should have* handled it better than I did, but what's the point in going over old ground? That was then, and this is now."

"I don't deserve you," I said.

She rubbed her forefinger over her bottom lip. "I think you've got that the wrong way around."

I ignored her self-deprecating comment. "Let's make a deal. I won't ever mention my appalling behavior that night, and you stop running out of my room at four in the morning, panicking in case Annie catches a glimpse of us lying next to each other. If you're that worried, I'll put a lock on the door."

"No, don't do that," she said hurriedly. "That's not fair to Annie. It's her home. She should be able to go where she pleases."

"It's our home, too," I said. "And Annie needs to learn that privacy is important. It won't be long before she's insisting I knock before entering her room."

Harlow grinned. "That's very true."

"We're in agreement then? No more sneaking out in the dead of night to return to a cold bed and leave me all alone." I pouted.

She laughed. "You're far too good at getting your own way."

I ran my tongue over my bottom lip. "I know."

Our flirty lunch relaxed my tense muscles, and by the time my driver dropped me back at the office, I was ready to take on my next appointment. I insisted Harlow take the car. I didn't need it until this evening. I hadn't a clue why she'd bothered riding the subway when I had a garage full of cars, but if it made her happy to continue, I wouldn't argue. I promised not to get home too late, and entered my building, giving her a little wave as the car pulled away.

22

Harlow

Sitting in the back of Oliver's luxurious limousine with the soft leather caressing every inch of me, I couldn't remove the beaming grin from my face. Occasionally the driver glanced in his rearview mirror, and his eyes crinkled as he looked at me.

I exuded happiness.

Oliver had basically asked me to move in.

Permanently.

Okay, not in so many words. He hadn't actually said "Move in with me, Harlow", but as good as. Oliver's actions always spoke louder, anyway. And he'd said "our home", not "my home".

I wrapped my arms around myself and squeezed, wishing they were his arms. Soon they would be. Tonight. I'd pick Annie up from school, then I'd prepare a delicious dinner for the three of us. He'd put Annie to bed, and then I planned to take him to bed—early—and show my gratitude.

I owed him, anyway, after his gift back at his office.

My face burned at the memory. No doubt, our *extra-curricular* activities would be all over the building by now. I mustn't let it bother me. It certainly didn't bother Oliver.

His driver stopped outside the building. I thanked him and exited the car, dashing into the apartment building and out of the cold. The lobby pumped out welcome heat. I unfastened my coat and headed for the elevators.

"Miss Winter?"

I glanced over my shoulder as I heard my name called. The receptionist beckoned to me.

"Miss Winter," she repeated. "You have a visitor."

I frowned, turning in the direction she pointed. Sitting on one of the sofa's scattered around the area was a woman with ash-blonde hair pulled into a high ponytail, a pair of sunglasses sitting on top of her head—no idea why she'd need those considering the dark-gray clouds stalking New York today—and a woolen knee-length dress that clung to her curvy body. So put together, she was the antithesis of me. She had one of those faces that made you think you'd seen her somewhere before, but I was fairly certain we'd never met.

I crossed over to her, and she rose from her seat as I approached.

"Hi," I said. "I'm Harlow Winter. Can I help you?"

She gave me a head-to-toe appraisal that reminded me of Jasmine, then smiled, one that didn't reach her cold, hard eyes.

"Yes, I rather think you can," she said, her New York accent prevalent, even though she tried to tone it down. "Tell me, Miss Winter, do you make a habit of stealing other women's husbands?"

She spoke so loudly, a few people nearby twisted their heads and openly stared.

Her identity came to me in a rush. *Fuck. This must be Sara. What the hell is she doing here?*

Despite the ice dripping through my veins and the painful

prickling creeping up my neck, I decided to play dumb and see how far she pushed it.

"I'm sorry," I said with as much grace as I could muster. "I don't know what you're talking about. You must have the wrong person."

I turned around. She gripped my wrist.

"I have exactly the right person," she bit out. "Tall, dark-haired, handsome guy with oodles of cash to buy anything... and anyone he likes."

I noticed she hadn't mentioned Annie, only Oliver. I glared at her until she released me.

"What do you want, Sara?"

She smiled. If a snake could smile, I imagined it would look exactly like Oliver's ex.

"Ah, so you *do* know who I am." She tapped her fingertip to her plum-colored lips. "What do I want, what do I want?" she chanted. "It's simple really, sweetheart. Now that I'm back, there's no need for you, is there."

She didn't frame it as a question, and I didn't answer it.

"Lucky for me, you're not my employer. Therefore, until I'm told otherwise, I shall continue to do the job I'm paid for."

Sara sneered. "There's a word for that, darling. Hooker."

I didn't remember hitting her. I did remember the sting in my palm, the gasp from the receptionist and several people still milling about watching the show. And I definitely remembered Sara clutching the side of her face, hiding the place where the outline of my fingers was clearly visible.

"I'm calling the police," she hissed. "That's assault, and I have witnesses."

"No, please don't," I begged. "I have to pick Annie up from school soon. Your daughter, Annie," I added. "Don't call the police. I'm sorry I hit you. I shouldn't have."

Sara remained quiet, allowing the silence to linger and my

panic to grow. Eventually, she said, "Okay, I won't call them. Yet. As long as you do one thing."

I don't like the sound of this.

"And what might that be?" I asked, dread circling in my gut.

"Call Oliver. Tell him I'm here, and I'm back to stay."

And with that, she wandered off toward the bank of elevators, trailing a cashmere scarf behind her. She stood by the private elevator, the only one that went up to the penthouse. The one you needed a code to access.

"Come, come, Harlow," she said, tapping her foot. "You surely don't expect me to wait in the lobby."

My palm itched to smack her other cheek. If I thought for one second I'd get away with it, she'd have a matching handprint on the other side of her face. But Annie needed me, and I had a feeling Oliver would, too. If I gave in to my baser instincts, the only thing I'd have to look forward to was a night in a cell.

But whatever Sara was doing back in New York, my Spidey sense told me it wasn't good—for any of us. Every nerve ending I possessed had jumped to full alert, and a semi-painful prickling sprung up over my entire body.

Adrenaline, I thought. *Fight or flight.*

I'd always been a fighter.

I strode across the lobby, pushing confidence into every step. Jabbing a finger at the call button, I waited for the doors to glide open, then moved past her and strode in first. The elevator swept us smoothly up to the top floor. I studiously ignored her, my gaze dead ahead, my heart pumping blood and oxygen around my body, each beat injecting more steel into my spine.

Oliver was *mine*. And I loved Annie as if she were my own. If Sara thought she could simply walk in here after six years and pick up where she left off, she'd better strap in for the fight of her life.

I had no idea how Oliver would react to her arrival. I hoped he'd throw her out on her ass and order her never to come back. I worried he'd hear her out, let her have access to Annie, and open the door for her to worm her way back into his and Annie's lives.

Which meant I'd be the one out on my ass.

As soon as we arrived at the penthouse, Sara swept her keen gaze around the living area, then crossed over to the windows and looked out at the view.

"He always dreamed of living in a place like this," she said, a tinge of nostalgia to her tone.

With no interest in speaking to her, I dropped my purse on the countertop, then removed my phone. I'd rather she didn't listen in to my call to Oliver, but equally, there wasn't a chance in hell I'd leave her here alone.

I moved as far away as I could while still able to keep an eye on Sara, and pressed the phone to my ear. Oliver answered on the third ring.

"Harlow, can I call you back? I'm in a meeting."

"I'm sorry," I said, keeping my voice low and watching Sara run her gaze over me, a smirk on her lips. She was loving every second of this. "But you need to come home, right now."

"Why?" Panic bled into his tone. "Is Annie okay?"

"Annie's fine." I took a breath. "Sara is here."

I heard his sharp intake of breath, the pause as he tried to process what I'd said, and then the whoosh of air as he emptied his lungs.

"I'm on my way."

23

OLIVER

"Hurry," I barked at Ryker's driver who was trying his best to navigate the Midtown traffic. I'd had to borrow Ryker's car as Harlow had taken mine. Usually, I enjoyed the forty-five-minute ride home as it gave me time to process the events of the day and empty my mind of everything to do with work, while looking forward to the evening ahead.

Not today.

I wished for the ability to teleport, to close my eyes and transport myself directly into my living room and find out what the fuck Sara thought she was doing showing up at my home after six years of silence.

I *had* to remain calm. Any other reaction would play right into Sara's hands. Adrenaline surged through my veins, and anger curled my hands into fists. The sound of blood pounded in my ears, drowning out the traffic noise from the busy streets.

"We should arrive in ten minutes, sir."

Powerless to part the lines of traffic, I sat back, running pointless scenarios through my mind. What had possessed Sara to return now? If she wanted more money, she could fuck off. I'd been overly generous in the divorce settlement based on the assets I had at the time. That I'd amassed a far greater wealth in the last six years was none of her goddamn business, and if that was her aim, she'd leave sorely disappointed.

Even so, I dropped an email to my lawyer, informing him of the situation and promising to call as soon as I'd gotten rid of her.

Harlow.

She mustn't have known what to do. Although I'd loved Sara, she had a vicious streak that the young me had taken for passion rather than meanness. If she'd turned her sharp tongue on Harlow...

Then again, Harlow was more than capable of defending herself.

It didn't make me worry any less.

I bailed out of Ryker's car before it had come to a complete stop and sprinted inside the building. On the ride in the elevator up to my penthouse, I took several deep, soothing breaths. I *must* remain detached. Cold, even. And businesslike. Treat this situation like any other. Discover the facts, assess, make the decision, move on.

Easy as that.

If only.

Entering my home, I found Harlow on one side of the living space, and Sara on the other, watching each other warily. Harlow spotted me first, and I offered her a reassuring smile.

"Sara," I said, my tone cold and dismissive. "What a surprise." I shrugged out of my jacket, tossed it over a nearby chair, and loosened my tie.

"Oliver."

She bestowed a familiar smile on me, the kind of warm, loving smile I used to treasure, and closed the space between us, her arms out in front as if she thought I'd greet her with a hug and tell her all was forgiven.

I reasserted control by moving around her and joining Harlow over by the kitchen. I slipped my arm around her waist and comfortingly brushed her hip with my thumb. "What do you want, Sara?"

She bowed her head, chin tucked into her chest, and fluttered those eyelashes at me in such a way that, at one time, would have had me striding toward her and carrying her up to bed.

"To talk." Her eyes slid to Harlow, then back to me. "Alone."

I nodded, my acquiescence to Sara's demands drawing a sharp inhale from Harlow. But my reasons were solid; I didn't want Harlow to witness this exchange, full of hurt and bitterness, and harsh words.

I squeezed Harlow's waist. "Would you go fetch Annie from school?" I asked. "Take her to her favorite place for something to eat. I'll call you."

Purposely speaking in code to avoid giving any unwitting information to Sara, I spoke with my eyes, praying Harlow got the message that I meant Bubby's restaurant.

"Got it." She reached up and kissed my cheek in a purely possessive move, one meant to send a very clear message to Sara.

I adored her for it.

She picked up her purse and, without even a glance in Sara's direction, left me alone with my ex-wife.

"What the fuck are you doing here?" I gritted out the second the sound of the elevator doors closing reached me. I could hear the confusion mingled with blind rage in my tone.

Sara inclined her head. "The nanny? Really, Oliver? Stereotypical, don't you think?"

I clenched my jaw tight. "Don't fucking judge me. You fucked off more than six years ago, leaving me alone with *our* baby. You're in no position to weigh in with opinions on how I conduct my life."

She winced, showing her emotions for the first time. Her expression softened, but my heart refused the concession. "No, you're right. I'm not."

She walked over to the nearest chair and sat.

I remained standing with my arms defensively folded over my chest. "Why don't you just tell me what you're doing here, and then you can go, and I can forget this ever happened."

Her eyes glistened with fake tears, and I raised my eyes to the heavens.

"Oh, please."

"When did you become so cruel?" she whispered, fiddling with the hem of her dress.

I choked out a laugh. "Are you for real?" I paced the floor in front of the kitchen. "You left, Sara. You made your choice six years ago. Have you forgotten how I *begged* you to come home, over and over? How I *pleaded* with you to reconsider? Annie needed you, *I* needed you, yet you walked out without giving us a second thought. And then, when I tried to make contact, you slapped a harassment order on me. Don't expect me to be happy that you're back. I'm not."

She covered her face with her hands, a quiet sob escaping. "I was young, Oliver. It was all too much. Us. The baby. I couldn't cope. So I ran. But I loved you both then, and I still do. And now that I'm older, I want to make amends."

I widened my eyes. "Oh, you are a piece of work. Either that, or you're a complete narcissist who has decided to rewrite history in your own fucked-up mind. Don't pull the 'I was young' card on me. We were *both* young." I glared at her. "Don't you even want to know how she is? This daughter you say you love? You haven't even asked about her."

"Of course I want to know," Sara cried. "I'm desperate for any tidbit you're willing to share with me. I'm not an idiot, Oliver. I know I've got a long road ahead of me. I did a terrible thing, one that destroyed your trust in me, and that isn't easily fixed. All I'm asking for is a chance. I want to get to know my daughter. I want to make up for all the missing years." She blinked up at me, and a tear rolled down her cheek. "I want you back."

Her words hit me like a battering ram to my chest. I stumbled back as if the words had the ability to physically impact me. A hundred responses sped through my mind, some harsh, most bitter.

I wanted to yell at her, to make her understand the pain and anguish she caused. Instead, I let out a resigned sigh. "What's changed?"

She pressed her hand to her chest. "Me. I've changed. I've had a long time to come to terms with what I've done. I'm not proud of my actions. I'm horrified at what I did, but I can't change the past. All I can do is try to be a better person, now and in the future."

I rarely drank in the daytime, but these were extenuating circumstances. It wasn't every day your ex showed up out of the blue after a six-year period of absence, during which time you went through a bitter divorce, only for them to inform you they'd made a terrible mistake, and that they wanted to wind back the clock and start over.

There was no starting over. Not for me.

Yet deep inside, my chest ached. I'd loved this woman so fiercely once. We'd made a baby together. We'd stayed awake through the night talking about our hopes and dreams for the future, planning the kind of life we wanted for ourselves and our children.

And still she'd cheated on me, then left without giving either me or Annie a second thought.

Sometimes I wondered if I'd ever truly known her. Could you ever really know a person, or did you only see the version they chose to share?

I poured a small scotch and knocked it back in one swallow, the burn welcome, the warmth the alcohol generated very much needed.

"Can I have one of those?" Sara asked.

I got a fresh glass and poured her one, pushing it across the counter. She stood and came to join me in the kitchen. Following my lead, she drank the amber liquid, then carefully set the glass back down.

"I'm happy, Sara. It took me a long time to get over you, but finally I'm happy. I'm with Harlow, and that isn't going to change. You say you want me back? You're wasting your time. I've moved on."

She shrugged, a faint smile touching her lips. "I didn't expect you to, even if I kept a flicker of hope alive that you might still love me. Annie is a different matter, though. I want a chance to get to know my daughter."

The words "over my dead body" were on the tip of my tongue, but until I obtained legal advice, I had to keep things on an even keel. There was no point riling her up. She'd only come out fighting.

"Give me some time," I said. "I need to think through the practicalities. She doesn't know you, and I won't have her confused or upset. This will have to be handled very delicately."

"Okay," she said in a small voice, gazing up at me from underneath her lashes. If she thought acting coy would win me over, she had another think coming.

"I'd like you to leave."

She nodded and picked up her purse from where she'd set it down on the coffee table. She slipped it over her shoulder.

"Why did you do it, Sara?" I blurted. The question had long

burned inside me, but until now, the chance to ask it hadn't arisen, and I hadn't expected it to come out now. "What possessed you to walk out on me and Annie? I forgave you for the affair. I poured all my love into you. I gave you everything, yet it wasn't enough. Why?"

She drew in a deep breath, her gaze slightly averted. "I've asked myself that question a hundred times, and the only conclusion I can come to is that I felt trapped. I was twenty-one years old with a new baby, a new husband, a life neither of us had foreseen during our college years. ROGUES exploded, and you simply... disappeared. The hours you spent at the office grew longer and longer. I barely saw you. And I was lonely, Oliver. That was why I had the affair in the first place."

"Why didn't you talk to me?" I asked.

"I tried," she cried. "So many times. But it was always, 'I'm too tired, Sara, let's do this tomorrow', or, 'I've just got to take this call', or the baby would cry and I'd be the one expected to see to her because you were too busy on your phone answering emails."

My mouth fell open. The picture she painted was far from my recollection. From my perspective, she cast aside our marriage without giving us a chance.

"If that's true, then you should have yelled, screamed, demanded I listen. One day you were here, the next you'd left, and insisting I only communicate through a fucking lawyer. Take one second to stand in my shoes and realize what that must have been like for me."

Her eyes lowered to the floor. "You do not understand the strength it took to walk away from you, from Annie. But I knew if I saw you again, you'd persuade me to return home, and I wouldn't be able to resist you. I never could resist you."

I scraped a hand through my hair. "Would that have been such a hardship?"

"Yes," she insisted. "Because nothing would have changed."

I thought back to the last few weeks with Harlow. I made sure I was home by six-thirty every night unless there were extenuating circumstances. I put Annie to bed and then Harlow and I spent the rest of the evening talking, kissing, fucking. Had things been different with Sara? I honestly couldn't recall. Sure, ROGUES took up a lot of time. Any new business that grew as fast as ours had needed a shit ton of care, but Sara talked as if I'd completely abandoned her.

I made a mental note to ask Garen for his recollection of that time. All the ROGUES guys had been around during the whole sorry mess, watching as my marriage, and then me, fell apart. But out of all of them, I was the closest to Garen. In college, we'd been the six amigos, but kind of paired up. Ryker and Elliot—best friends since forever—Sebastian and Upton who bonded over their love of Xbox online, and me and Garen, complete opposites who found we enjoyed the conflict our differing views on life brought to our many heated discussions.

"You didn't take Annie," I said, stating the obvious.

"No. I wouldn't have done that to you." She bit down on her lip. "She was better off with you, anyway."

Despite saying all the right things, I didn't trust her. Something rankled, and until I'd worked out what Sara's angle was, I'd be on my guard.

I removed my cell phone from the inside pocket of the jacket I'd discarded earlier. "What's your phone number?" Sara reeled off a bunch of numbers. I added her to my contacts. "I'll call you in a few days."

A few days. A week. Or how about never?

My internal thoughts were nothing more than a pipe dream. Sara wouldn't allow me to put her off. She'd demand to see Annie, and if I didn't handle my ex with kid gloves, previous experience told me she'd run straight to a lawyer.

"Thanks." She headed for the foyer, then paused in the entryway and glanced over her shoulder.

"You look good, Oliver."

She disappeared. Just as well. I didn't know how to respond.

24

HARLOW

My cell phone buzzed in my pocket. In my haste to retrieve it, I fumbled and dropped it on the floor.

"Shit," I bit out, picking it up and hoping the screen hadn't shattered.

Annie giggled. "You said a bad word."

I formed a fake smile solely for her benefit and pressed my fingertip to my lips. "Shhh. It'll be our secret."

She giggled again while I read the text from Oliver.

She's gone. Please come home. I miss you both.

Relief rushed through me at the speed of a freight train as I realized I'd internally prepared myself for rejection. Oliver and Sara had a history, albeit one fraught with bitterness and hurt. Three months ago, he and I hadn't even met. I'd never felt my temporary status more keenly than right now. It would be so easy for him to welcome Sara back into his life and make a family with Annie at the center. Sara's long-term absence had provided me with a veneer of security. Now... I no longer knew my place.

But Oliver's text had given me a taste of reassurance. I craved more.

Careful, Harlow. Don't turn into one of those clingy types who panics every time their man is out of sight.

I gestured to the server and asked for our check while Annie finished her bowl of chocolate ice cream. I leaned over and wiped away a smudge at the side of her mouth. My heart squeezed, and I struggled to get air into my lungs. It wasn't only Oliver I'd fallen for. Annie might not be mine biologically, but I'd gotten closer to her than any other child I'd ever looked after. She was *special*. If I had to leave her behind, it would break my heart.

This wasn't the outcome I'd expected when I took this job, and now, with Sara's return, my whole future could be snatched away in an instant.

"Ready, sweet pea?"

Annie nodded and jumped down from her chair, then rubbed her tummy. "I'm so full."

"I'm not surprised. You ate enough to last you a week."

Annie's chatter on the way home gave me something else to concentrate on. The last thing I needed was the chance for cynical voices to take over my mind, spreading their poison, and causing me even more stress.

Even though I knew Sara had left, as the elevator traveled upward, a knot formed in my stomach, and my throat felt dry and scratchy. I could still smell her lingering perfume.

Expensive, cloying, overpowering.

I held on to Annie's hand as we entered the living space to find Oliver standing in the kitchen, his gaze clouded, worry lines pulling his brows low and making his mouth turn down at the edges. He glanced up, and our eyes met. He shook his head, which I took to mean "Don't ask me yet" and "Act normal for Annie's sake".

Annie dashed across the space and gave him a hug, then proceeded to tell him all about her day, barely taking a breath between her stories of what she did in class, how she and another girl had a falling out over a slice of apple at lunch, ending with how full she felt after her impromptu dinner at Bubby's. Oliver listened with his usual intent expression, asking her questions and showing immense interest in her day. After she'd updated him on every detail, he sat with her at the dining table and helped her with her homework. Watching them with their dark heads pressed together, Annie oblivious to the momentous event that had put a huge crack right down the middle of our relationship, had tears pricking behind my eyes.

"Won't be a minute," I croaked, then sprinted for the stairs. I couldn't look at Oliver. I found myself standing outside Oliver's bedroom, our conversation from lunchtime today—God, it had only been a few hours ago—prevalent in my mind. He'd asked me to move in, properly, and I'd rushed to agree.

What a difference such a short amount of time made.

I reached for the door handle, then paused. Until Oliver and I had spoken about Sara, I couldn't go in there.

It wasn't my place.

Not now.

Spinning on my heel, I went to my bedroom. I closed the door and leaned against it. My mind raced, throwing up all kinds of dreadful scenarios where I lost the man I loved to someone I couldn't hope to compete with. And then the second I had those thoughts, I berated myself.

Give the man a chance, Harlow.

I jumped at a light tap on my door. There could only be one person on the other side. Annie wouldn't knock. She'd burst right in.

With a deep breath through my nose, I opened it.

"Hi," I said quietly, my gaze off-center, my teeth grazing my bottom lip.

"Give me a half hour," Oliver said, lightly touching my cheek with the back of his hand. "I'll finish Annie's homework with her, run her bath, and put her to bed. Then I'm yours."

I met his solemn navy-blue gaze. "Are you?"

His face crumpled. "Yes," he said earnestly. "And that's what I told Sara."

Hope spiked within me, but I tamped it down. Until we'd spoken properly, jumping to conclusions was a bad idea. "Go and see to Annie," I said.

He bent his head and brushed my lips with his, and then he was gone.

I closed the door, willing the time to pass. I thought about calling Katie and updating her, but what would I say? Oliver's wife had shown up to stake her claim on him and their daughter? I didn't know that for a fact. Before I vented to my best friend, I needed to understand the lay of the land.

Annie's chatter filtered through the closed door, and then the sound of running water filling the bathtub reached me. I slipped from my room and padded downstairs.

As I poured myself a glass of wine, it occurred to me how easily I'd started treating Oliver's home as my own. I didn't think about it as I used to. If I wanted a drink, or something to eat, or to kick back and watch a Netflix show, I did it without hesitation. Yet, now, it no longer felt like home. Whatever Oliver and I had become to each other, he still employed me as a nanny for his daughter.

And tonight, with the Sara complication raising its head, I'd never felt more like household staff.

I wandered over to the window and stared out at the view, my reflection in the glass gazing back at me, the despair I felt on the inside mirrored on the outside.

What made a woman who walked out on her family years

earlier suddenly return? Six years of silence—at least according to Oliver—and then boom! There had to be a catalyst, that one thing, or maybe a series of things, that drove a person into taking action.

Oliver's footsteps sounded on the stairs. I didn't turn around, instead choosing to keep my attention on the outside as though I could find the answers to my problems somewhere in the inky blackness.

"Want me to top that off?" he asked, referring to my half-finished glass of wine.

I shook my head. "I'm fine."

The fridge door opened, and Oliver poured himself a drink. He joined me by the window and slipped his arm around my waist, his thumb brushing over my hipbone. We stood in silence, neither of us quite knowing where to begin.

I began the conversation with the most burning question racing around my mind.

"Why has she come back?"

I sensed Oliver turn his head in my direction, yet still I gazed out of the window. If I looked at him and saw even a tinge of conflict in his navy-blue gaze, it would break my heart.

His breath hitched. The hairs on the back of my neck stood on end.

"She wants me to take her back."

I chewed the inside of my cheek. "I see."

Oliver gently cupped my chin, applying enough pressure that I had no choice but to lift my gaze to his.

"I don't think you do. She's not getting another chance, Harlow. I don't want her anymore. I want you."

I yearned to believe him. So much. But history had a way of shaping the person we were today, and mine was littered with men who'd let me down.

My father for whom I'd never quite been enough, no matter how hard I tried.

A high school fling who took my virginity then told all his friends about what a lousy lay I was.

My first proper boyfriend who had stolen from me to pay his gambling debts.

And then there was Carter, aka The Cheating Bastard.

"Harlow."

Oliver's tentative voice broke through the bad memories, his expression earnest as he waited for me to respond to his statement.

"I need you to be sure, Oliver. If there's even an inkling of a spark between you and your wife, then you owe it to Annie to try to patch things up. And if you're worried about hurting me, don't be. My feelings shouldn't come into it."

God, I'm a fucking saint. A dumb fucking saint.

Oliver plucked my glass of wine out of my hand and, along with his own, placed them on a nearby table. Then he returned to me, cupped my face, and kissed me with so much passion, my toes involuntarily curled inside my shoes, and my heart skipped a beat. Every nerve ending came alive, my body tingling with desire.

"There is no spark," he said, interjecting his words with soft kisses to my neck, knowing the feel of his lips there drove me wild. "At least not for me. But there's a fucking inferno between us. I burn for *you*, Harlow. Only you."

My throat tightened, and I drew in a ragged, shaky breath. I tried to swallow but couldn't, my throat too thick with emotion.

"Oliver," I said in a shaky voice.

"Yeah?"

"Please take me to bed."

His eyes smoldered as they traveled over my face, and then he swept me into his arms. I yelped, clasping on to his broad shoulders for security.

He kissed me once on the mouth. "Gladly."

25

OLIVER

I sat across the desk from my lawyer in his too-dark office surrounded by every law book ever written, and yet not a single one could stop Sara from strolling back into my life and demanding to see her daughter.

Not one.

That was the good news, he said.

Good news? If that's good, what's the fucking bad?

"Worst case, Oliver, after a period of time, she could apply for joint custody and, in all likelihood, a judge would award it."

My back stiffened, and the walls began to close in. I struggled to steady my breathing. "No. No, that's not possible. She left, Adam. *She* left *us*. Surely that negates her parental rights."

"I'm afraid it doesn't," he said, tapping his pen against a yellow legal pad sitting in front of him. "Unless you can prove she's a bad mother, that Annie would somehow be in danger in her mother's care, then the court will be sympathetic toward her. If you want my advice, I'd try to keep this between the two of you and out of the courts. That way you maintain control."

"An illusion of control," I said bitterly. *Why did I bother to pay five hundred dollars an hour for a lawyer who couldn't fucking help me?*

"It's better than the alternative," "It's better than the alternative." Adam leaned forward and put down his pen. "I know this is shitty, Oliver, but you're much better off keeping Sara placated than introducing conflict into an already difficult situation."

"Thanks," I muttered, getting to my feet. "I'll look forward to receiving your bill."

Normally Adam would grin at such a barbed comment and return the favor with interest. Instead, he appeared genuinely distraught.

"I'm so sorry. I wish there was more I could do. If anything comes up and you want to talk it over with me, call. Day or night."

I nodded, offering a faint smile when what I really wanted to do was to scream at the unfairness of the justice system.

Fucking justice, my ass.

I arrived at my office a little after ten to find Ryker sitting in my high-backed leather chair wearing a very strange expression.

"I tried calling." He fiddled with my Mont Blanc pen, his hooded gaze steady as he watched me hang my jacket on the coat stand by the door.

"You did?" I dug my cell phone out of my pocket and cursed. "It's on silent. Sorry. What's up?"

"You had a visitor earlier this morning. About an hour ago. I told her you weren't in, and then I told her to fuck off before I had her arrested for trespassing."

I blinked slowly. Goddammit. I'd wanted to break the news to the guys, but she just couldn't fucking wait.

"Sara," I said glumly, dropping my ass in the guest chair opposite my desk. I swept a hand down my face. "She showed up at my place on Friday. Accosted Harlow in the lobby."

"What does she want?"

"To see Annie." I decided not to disclose the rest of the conversation. No point consuming good oxygen with useless words. Last night wrapped in Harlow's arms was more than enough to acknowledge where my heart lay, and it wasn't with Sara.

"Fuck off," Ryker said, his tone incredulous. "That woman's got balls, I'll give her that."

"I'm late because I went to see my lawyer first thing this morning. Turns out if she wants to see Annie, I can't stop her."

Ryker's eyes widened. "Bullshit," he bit out. "He must have been smoking weed."

I shook my head. "The law is very much weighted in her favor. The only thing I can do is try to keep it out of court and minimize her visits as much as I'm able."

Ryker pinched the bridge of his nose. "Jesus Christ."

"Yeah, I don't think He'll help me either."

"Do you want to take some time off? I'll cover whatever you've got going on if you'd rather be at home."

"No, I'm good. It's better if I keep busy. Listen, though, if she comes here again and I'm not around, be civil. For my sake. If she's riled up, it'll only spur her on. You know what she's like."

Ryker snorted. "Unfortunately, yes, I do." He stood, came around the desk, and clapped me on the shoulder. "Athena and I are here if you need anything. *Anything.*"

"Thank you," I said. "I appreciate that."

I waited until he'd shut the door behind him, and then I called Garen. The jungle drums would start beating soon, and I didn't want my best friend to find out from anyone but me.

When Garen answered, I apprised him of the situation. He listened without interruption, but knowing him, he'd take it all in. Garen had an enviable memory, almost photographic. With most things, he could hear or see them once, and they stuck. No wonder the bastard had sailed through college, barely studying and still graduating *summa cum laude*. I should hate him. Instead, I loved him like a brother. More than a brother.

"Want me to put out a hit on her," he said, only half joking.

Garen hadn't liked Sara back in college. I distinctly remember on our wedding day, Garen had stood by my side and played his best man role to perfection, but I knew him almost as well as he knew himself. If he could have dragged me from the church to prevent me from making what he saw as the biggest mistake of my life, he would have. When I discovered her affair with our family doctor, I purposely kept it from Garen. When she walked out, I'd had no choice but to tell him the whole sorry tale. I'd dreaded it yet, as usual, he'd supported me through the entire mess without a single word of judgment. For Sara, though, his dislike turned into hatred and, instead of diminishing over the years, had only grown in intensity.

"No, but I do need another favor."

"Name it," Garen said.

"I can't shake the feeling she has an ulterior motive, and getting back together with me and reigniting her relationship with Annie isn't it."

"Sure she hasn't run out of cash?" Garen asked. "Sara always had expensive tastes."

"I don't know," I said, rubbing my forehead. *God, I'm tired.*

"Want me to see what I can uncover?"

"Yeah," I said. "I'd rather not bring in a private detective. I want to keep this to a small inner circle. I don't trust her, and I can't risk any investigation getting back to her somehow."

"Leave it to me. If there's dirt, I'll find it." He laughed. "What am I saying? It's Sara. Of course there's fucking dirt."

Despite the pressure I felt with her untimely and unwelcome return, I grinned. Talking to Garen always put me in a good mood.

"Thanks, man. I owe you one."

"You owe me nothing," he said. "Anyway, I need to come down to New York soon and meet the hot nanny keeping your bed warm."

I rolled my eyes. "Don't call her that."

"Why? I hear she's very hot, and she's a nanny. I'm just connecting words."

"You are such a dick, and Ryker has a big mouth."

"Wrong on the first count, right on the second. Although on this occasion I have to defend him. It was Elliot who said she was hot."

"He needs to focus more on his own love life and less on mine," I grunted.

Garen chuckled. "I'll be in touch, buddy. Try not to worry."

"Wait," I said, remembering the other thing I needed to discuss. "When Sara and I first married, do you remember me spending huge swaths of time at work, never going home, and when I did, always on my phone, answering emails late into the night?"

"No," he replied. "The complete opposite. Don't get me wrong, we all had to put in a decent shift. Working nine-to-five went out the window when ROGUES exploded, but you'd skip lunch, work like a demon, just so you could get home in time for Annie's bedtime routine. And while I saw the odd email after hours, you were normally an early morning guy. Why d'you ask?"

That was my recollection, too. I'd often wake early and go through my emails with Sara still asleep beside me, completely unaware. Why then, was her memory so different?

"Something Sara said. It doesn't matter."

"If Sara said it, then that makes me immediately suspicious. Lies fall too easily off that woman's tongue."

"Yeah, maybe," I murmured absentmindedly. "Thanks, man. Speak soon."

I hung up, opened my contacts, and stared for several minutes at Sara's number. I flexed my jaw. Might as well get it over with.

She answered immediately. "Hi," she said softly. "Thank you so much for calling."

"Ryker said you came by."

I predicted a gripe regarding his treatment of her. Instead, she giggled.

"He sure doesn't like me, does he?"

"Do you blame him?"

A heavy sigh. "No. No, I don't blame him. There is only one person to blame in all of this, and that's me. I take full responsibility."

Instead of finding reassurance in her words, the hackles rose on the back of my neck. This coy, contrite Sara wasn't the Sara I knew, and I firmly believed people didn't change their behavior, they simply learned to mask their true colors.

"About Annie," I said.

Her breath hitched. "Yes?"

"I need to talk to her, tell her you're back. She obviously won't remember you, and if she gets in any way upset at the idea of seeing you, it's not happening, got it?"

And fuck any court that gets in my way.

"Will you tell her I love her and that I've missed her so much?"

I almost choked on the little saliva I had left inside my mouth. My tongue felt twice its normal size, and I struggled to respond in a non-sarcastic manner.

"I'll let you know how it goes," I said.

"Oliver," she called out as I went to hang up.

"Yeah?"

"Thank you."

"Sure," I muttered, cutting the call.

I dropped my phone on my desk and let my head fall into my hands. Somehow, I had to find the words to reassure my little girl that her absent mother crashing back into her life wouldn't be a disaster.

Which meant I had to lie.

A knock at my door brought my head up. Carly peered inside.

"Oliver, sorry to disturb. Your eleven o'clock is here."

Pushing my dark thoughts away, and oddly grateful for the interruption, I gestured. "Send them in."

For the rest of the day, I hardly had time to take a breath. As I sat in the back of my car and made my way home at six that night, I called Harlow to let her know my plans to tell Annie this evening. I could hear the uncertainty and fear clogging her voice, and I felt exactly the same, but Sara had backed me into a corner and, right now, I didn't have anything to fight her with. I hoped Garen unearthed a pair of boxing gloves. At least then I'd have something with which to go into battle.

My legs were heavy as I trudged through the lobby and rode the elevator up to my home. I dropped my briefcase in the foyer and entered the living area. Annie and Harlow were in the kitchen, a place I often found them, cooking dinner. Or rather, Harlow was cooking dinner, and Annie was making a mess.

My heart squeezed. I loved this little girl more than my life, and I wanted nothing more than to keep her safe. Yet circumstances beyond my control forced me to risk her security and happiness on an unstable and unknown situation.

If Sara drew one tear from my baby, I'd fucking kill her.

"Daddy," Annie called out the second she spotted me, up to her wrists in flour. "We're making pizza."

"Ooh, amazing."

I kissed the top of her head, then brushed my lips over Harlow's. "Hi," I said softly, letting her know with my eyes how happy I was to see her. We still didn't go over the top with displays of affection around Annie, our reticence far more to do with Harlow than me.

"Hey, you," she said. "Go get changed before your suit gets covered in flour. Dinner won't be long."

I arched an eyebrow and cast a glance into Annie's bowl. "Are you sure?"

She pointed to some ready-made dough resting in another bowl and grinned. "Positive."

I adored how she let Annie spread her wings, make mistakes, try new things, yet always had a backup at the ready.

"Be right back," I said, heading for the stairs.

By the time I returned wearing a pair of scruffy, comfortable jeans and a T-shirt, Harlow and Annie were putting the finishing touches on the pizza. I poured us both a glass of wine and a juice for Annie as Harlow slid the pizza onto the stone warming in the oven.

"It'll be ready in about eight minutes," she said, sending me a silent message that waiting until we'd eaten was the better choice.

"Okay." I nodded to show her I understood.

I sliced the pizza while Harlow tossed the salad. We sat down to eat, and while I listened to Annie tell me about her day, a part of my mind was still trying to figure out how to start this difficult conversation.

By the time we sat on the couch after clearing away the dinner things, I still hadn't found a solution, but when Annie reached for the remote, I stopped her. This couldn't wait.

"I need to talk to you about something, munchkin."

She immediately looked worried in that way kids did when they either thought they were in trouble but didn't know what for, or they knew exactly what for and were wondering how they could lie their way out of the situation.

"What's the matter, Daddy?"

"Nothing, baby girl. It's just..."

I struggled to continue. Harlow pressed her palm to my back, the silent support worth more than a thousand words. I took a deep breath. "I had a visitor last Friday, someone who very much wants to see you."

She brightened considerably when she realized I wasn't about to chastise her for some unknown transgression. "Who, Daddy?"

I stroked her hair and tried to smile. I fell far short.

"Your mommy."

Confusion swirled in her eyes, eyes that were a replica of my own navy-blue. "My mommy," she whispered. "She's here?" She shot a glance at the doorway as if expecting to see Sara standing right there.

"She's in New York, yes," I explained. "She's desperate to see you, but I said no. Not until I had a chance to find out how you feel about that."

Her eyes lowered, and she nibbled her lip, a tiny frown drawing in her brows. When she lifted her head, bewilderment swirled in her eyes. "What do you think, Daddy?"

The muscles around my heart squeezed so tightly, I couldn't take a proper breath. My baby was worried about me. Not about herself. Seven years old, and faced with a momentous decision, and her first thoughts went to my feelings. Whatever my own frame of mind when it came to Sara, I couldn't let my loathing of my ex filter through to Annie.

"I think she's your mom, and she loves you, and I know that once you get to know her, that you'll love her, too."

Harlow's fingers curled against my back, and as I shot a glance in her direction, she gave me the smallest nod, an approval that I'd said the right thing.

"Will you be there, Daddy?"

I hugged her to me, breathing in the scent of her hair, my

chest filled with so much love for my amazing daughter. "Every step of the way, baby girl."

~

"What time is it?"

I checked my watch, even though it was the fifth occasion Annie had asked me the same question in as many minutes. "Four-twenty."

Annie bounced her foot and rubbed the hem of her dress—one she'd chosen especially for this occasion—between her thumb and forefinger. "What if she doesn't like me?"

I briefly closed my eyes to suppress the sharp stab of pain in my chest. I hated Annie's uncertainty, created through Sara's abandonment of the one person a woman was supposed to love and protect above all others: her daughter.

"She loves you, Annie. How could she not?"

She peeked at me from under her lashes, her expression hesitant. "I hope so."

My cell phone buzzed, and I checked the screen. A message from reception, asking me to approve an access code for a Sara Ellis.

"She's here," I said, wishing I had Harlow beside me. We'd jointly decided it'd be better if Harlow wasn't here for their first visit, but I felt her absence keenly. She always knew the right thing to say, and I desperately missed her counsel. She'd hidden her own agony at being cut out of this unwelcome family reunion. I'd known how deeply it hurt her, though.

Annie jumped to her feet, as did I. Taking her hand, I walked to the foyer. The ding of the elevator signaled Sara's arrival and, as much as I tried not to hold my breath, my body had other ideas.

The doors parted, and Sara stood there holding an enormous teddy bear and a helium balloon.

Over the top much?

I berated myself for such an uncharitable thought. Sara would be as nervous as we were, and as I'd made the decision to let her see Annie, I had to cut her some slack.

She stepped out of the elevator and crouched. "Hi, Annie," she said. "I'm... your mommy."

I felt the tension in Annie's shoulders, but when Sara held out her arms, Annie didn't hesitate, throwing herself into her mother's embrace.

I wanted to be happy.

It was the worst day of my life.

26

HARLOW

Two painful weeks.
 Fourteen torturous days.
 Three hundred and thirty-six agonizing hours.
 That was how much time had elapsed since Sara burst back into our lives. Oliver professed to find it as difficult as I did, but with each passing day, his ex-wife burrowed her feet farther beneath the table, and I found myself sidelined with Oliver determined to play the long game. What that meant in reality was that he pandered to Sara, unwilling to rock the boat in case she chose to get the courts involved. He was doing exactly as his lawyer recommended.
 Didn't mean I had to like it.
 Annie had accepted her mother's return so easily. Kids had such forgiving natures, something we lost as we moved into adulthood. She didn't question where her mother had been or why she'd left in the first place, or how she'd managed to

breathe without hugging her baby every day. She simply basked in the happiness of having a mom again.

I wanted answers to all those questions and more. While Sara was nothing but charming to me, especially if in the presence of Oliver or Annie, I recalled with vivid clarity our first meeting when she'd shown me her true colors. All she was doing now was painting over them in bright pink and hoping I couldn't see through to the murky brown beneath.

I conversed with the other nannies and the occasional mom while I waited for Annie after school, but I only half listened to their chatter, envious of their easy lives.

Still, no one had held a gun to my head and ordered me to fall in love with my boss.

"Hi, Harlow," Annie cried, running to me, her braids flying behind her as she ran from the building. "Is Mommy coming over tonight?"

I suppressed a wince, pain darting through my chest. Annie wasn't even aware of it, but in the last few days, I'd noticed how she'd begun to treat me more and more like a nanny now that her mom was back in her life. Those little things we used to do together were activities she now wanted to do with her mom. Like cycling in the park when the weather permitted, stroking the horses lined up in front of the Plaza as their owners waited to fleece unsuspecting tourists, eating pancakes at Bubby's on a rainy Saturday. Or snuggling up on the sofa watching a Disney movie, hiding behind our hands when the wicked witch appeared on screen.

"I don't know, sweet pea. We'll have to ask your daddy."

"Can we ask him now?" Annie pleaded, her big eyes—so like Oliver's it physically hurt to look into them—beseeching me to agree.

"We'll see," I murmured, capturing her hand.

I strapped her into the car, and it set off, smoothly filtering into the traffic. Picking Annie up from school was the only time

I ever used Oliver's chauffeur-driven car without him, despite his insistence it was mine to use whenever I needed. It still didn't feel right, although I couldn't put my finger on precisely why.

Annie appeared to have forgotten her request to call Oliver, her excited chattering as she told me all about her day filling the silence. One of the great things about kids was their ability to talk and talk without requiring an answer beyond the occasional, "Mm-hmm", or "Oh, that's nice".

When we returned home, Annie burst from the elevator, dropping her school bag in the foyer. A couple of books spilled out, and I grinned and bent down to pick them up.

"Mommy!" Annie's excited exclamation rent the air.

Dread curled in my gut. Great. Sara was here.

Hang on...

How the hell did she get in?

I followed Annie into the main living area to find Sara in the kitchen hugging her daughter. She spotted me and offered up one of her false smiles.

"Hi, Harlow. Thank you for picking Annie up from school."

"It's my job," I responded, setting Annie's bag on a nearby chair. "Sorry, how did you get in?"

She pressed three fingers to her lips. "Oops," she said with an impish grin. "Busted."

Annie giggled.

I scowled. "Annie, go get changed out of your school things, and then we'll get started on your homework before Daddy gets home."

Annie pouted and clung tighter to her mother. "Aww, Harlow."

I arched a brow. "Now, please."

She stood her ground, hands planted on her hips. "I want to stay with Mommy."

Sara tried to hide the look of triumph. She failed.

"Go on, Annie." Sara gave her a nudge. "Do as your nanny tells you."

I ground my teeth at her not-so-subtle putdown. Annie, none the wiser, immediately obeyed, scampering upstairs.

I waited until she was out of sight, then returned my attention to Sara.

"I'd like to know how you got in here."

Her mask slipped, and she let out an exasperated sigh. "For goodness' sake. It's not an issue. What do you think I'm going to do? Steal from my own family?"

I folded my arms across my chest, irked that this woman had the gall to call Oliver and Annie her family. "You can't just come and go as you please. This isn't your home."

"It isn't *your* home, either," Sara stated. "And out of the two of us, I'd say I have more right to be here than you."

A prickling sensation crept up my neck, and my muscles quivered as I tried to hold on to my temper. "Oh yeah? I beg to differ. I'd say you relinquished your rights six years ago when you walked out on Oliver and Annie."

My barb hit its target. A flush of red crept over her jaw, bleeding into her cheeks. "Haven't you ever made a mistake?"

I raised my eyebrows. "A mistake is forgetting to turn off the oven or leaving the butter out in the sun. I hardly think abandoning your baby daughter and husband counts as a mistake."

I was way overstepping the mark, but something about Sara got to me. Maybe it was the smug expression that she saved only for me, or how she honestly thought she could wipe the slate clean, pretend the last six years hadn't happened, and walk right back into Oliver and Annie's lives.

Or maybe it was the jealousy spreading through my gut driving me on.

"He isn't yours," Sara hissed, taking a step toward me.

I stepped back. Sara had a few inches on me, and I didn't want to find out how good her right hook was. I'd had the element of surprise on my side when I'd slapped her in the lobby when she showed up out of the blue, and other people had been around.

"Really?" I pushed as much sarcasm as possible into my voice. "Funny you mention that since I'm the one sleeping with him."

I *hated* this version of myself, the clichéd envious harpy going toe to toe with the ex-wife, but I refused to back down. If I did, Sara would take over, and I'd lose the man I'd fallen in love with.

"You don't even know him," Sara bit out. "Not like I do. I know what he needs."

"I love him," I said, conscious I probably should say those words to Oliver at some point, and certainly should have said them to him before I blurted them out to Sara. I didn't know why I'd told her at all, especially when her smile built, and stayed there, fixed to her face as if the wind had changed and she'd frozen in place.

"Oh dear." She shook her head. "So, you have made a mistake. A big one. He isn't yours to love."

"Well, he certainly isn't yours."

Sara's haughty expression sent a shiver running through me. "Yes, he is. He's always been mine. And he will be again. Now run along, you little tramp. I'm sure there is some menial household task that needs doing."

My fingers twitched, but I wouldn't allow her to draw me into hitting her. If I gave in to my baser instincts, she'd win. "Fuck you," I bit out. "Fuck you right back to hell where you belong, you evil witch."

"Harlow?"

Annie's tentative voice had me wheeling around. She hovered at the foot of the stairs, her face white, her knuckles almost translucent where her clenched fists rested by her sides.

And right behind her, his expression unreadable, stood Oliver.

Shit.

Why was he home so early? And how much had he heard of our bitter exchange? *God, please don't let him have heard my declaration of love.*

"Oliver—"

He ignored me, instead cutting his gaze to Sara.

"I'd like you to leave, please, Sara. Next time you want to drop by, arrange it with me beforehand."

A rush of relief sent me lightheaded, until he continued.

"Harlow, if you wouldn't mind giving Annie and I some space. I want to spend some alone time with my daughter."

I felt his brush-off keenly, a painful tightness in my throat making it difficult to swallow.

"Sure," I said glumly.

"Oliver," Sara said. "I came by to talk to you."

"Not tonight," he said firmly.

"But—"

"I said not tonight, Sara. Now go."

"Of course," she said, gathering her things. She laid her coat over her arm and walked toward them. Bending to kiss Annie, she straightened and brushed a hand down Oliver's suited arm.

She was lucky I didn't rip it off.

"Call me," she said, then left.

Oliver ignored her. Instead, he picked Annie up and swung her around, peals of laughter spilling from her lips. I trudged by, my tail thoroughly between my legs, and headed up to my room. I rarely came in here anymore, and as I closed the door behind me, it felt like the end of a fairy tale.

27

Oliver

I tucked Annie into bed, squished her latest favorite teddy bear next to her—one of the many gifts from Sara—then kissed her forehead.

"Sleep tight, munchkin."

"Daddy," she called out as I straightened.

"Yeah, baby girl."

"Don't be mad at Harlow."

I crouched to her level again, plucking at a strand of hair that had caught on her eyelash. "I'm not mad at Harlow," I said. Disappointed was much more like it. And confused. I didn't know what had gone on between her and Sara, but the acrimony spilling over into Annie's world was something I wouldn't tolerate.

"Good," Annie stated. "I love Harlow. Will you tell her for me? I love Mommy, too, but you can love lots of people. Isn't that right, Daddy?"

My chest felt tight. "Yes, baby girl. Your heart always

expands to fit more love inside." I gave her another kiss. "Go to sleep. I'll see you in the morning."

I closed her door and padded down the hallway to Harlow's room. Instinctively, I knew she wouldn't be in my—our—bedroom. Her insecurity had grown in the last couple of weeks, and I understood why. Our relationship was still very new, and Sara showing up out of the blue had shaken the ground beneath her feet. Hell, it had shaken the ground beneath mine, too.

It was up to me to reassure her, to show her with my actions and my words that she played a pivotal role in my life.

I tapped on her door. "Harlow, let's talk."

A few seconds passed, then she opened the door. Her face showed signs of tear tracks, and a rim of red circled her almond eyes.

"Can I come in?"

She jerked her shoulder and turned around. "It's your home, Oliver," she said dully.

I stepped inside. "It's your home, too."

She barked a laugh. "Not according to your wife."

"Ex-wife."

She spun to face me. "Have you told her that?"

I frowned, then sat on the bed, tugging her down beside me. I caressed her face, then tucked a lock of hair behind her ear. "Talk to me. Tell me what happened tonight."

Her resigned, almost defeated expression sent a dart of worry through me. "She wants you back, Oliver, and she won't rest until she gets her way."

"I don't want her, Harlow. I want you." I'd said the same thing several times, but no matter how I phrased it, Harlow didn't seem to hear me—or maybe she didn't believe me.

"She's clever, Oliver. Much cleverer than me. And sneaky, too. She'll gradually worm her way into your life. You won't even see it coming."

I sighed. "What would you have me do, Harlow? Annie is thrilled to have her mother back in her life. If Annie had rejected her, I'd have thrown her out on her ass. But I'm backed into a corner here."

"Just be careful," she warned. "She's sweetness and light with you and Annie, but trust me, when it's me and her, she punches straight and true, leaving me in no doubt about what she wants."

I frowned. "What exactly did she say to make you respond the way you did?"

Harlow shook her head, lowering her gaze to the floor. "It doesn't matter."

I lifted her chin back up with my finger. "It does to me."

She drew her teeth over her bottom lip and rubbed the space between her eyebrows. "She treats me like the hired help which, I guess, is exactly what I am."

"You are *not* hired help," I gritted out. Fucking Sara and her vicious tongue.

"Then what am I, Oliver?"

I cupped her face, tilting her head back. Her eyes swirled with hurt and a tinge of anger. The latter caused by Sara, the former, all me.

"You're the woman I love," I said, my declaration long overdue. I should have told her weeks ago, but I'd held back for fear she might think it too soon or, worse, that she wouldn't say it back. But life was full of risks. Each day we put ourselves out there where danger lurked around every corner, both physical and emotional. I'd spent six years shielding my heart from hurt, and now it was time to open myself up.

She blinked rapidly, her brow furrowing. "What did you say?"

I smiled, bent my head, and pressed a hard kiss to her lips. "I love you."

She touched her fingertips to her mouth. "Oh God, Oliver. Do you mean it?"

I covered my heart with my palm. "Every word."

Her eyes glistened, and for the first time since Sara burst into our lives, she looked at me, her face alight with hope. "I love you, too. You know that, right?"

"I do now," I said, easing her back onto the mattress.

Slowly I began to undress her, taking my time with each piece of clothing, savoring the feel of her soft skin beneath my fingertips. I explored her with my mouth, my hands, every touch meant to convey my feelings for her. I didn't want her to feel second best to Sara, and as soon as I got her alone, I'd tell her straight up that Harlow was the woman in my life and whatever fantasies she'd harbored before returning were just that. She was Annie's mother, but to me, she meant nothing.

I discarded my clothes and caged Harlow with my body. She wrapped her legs around my waist and clamped her hands on my ass.

"I need you," she murmured into my ear.

I pushed forward, slipping inside the heat of her body, her velvet walls sheathing my cock. We'd stopped using condoms a few days ago, a sign of our mutual trust in each other. Having no barriers between us heightened the sensations, and long before I'd had my fill of her, my balls tensed. I bent my head, sucking her nipple into my mouth and shifted the angle of my lower body, each thrust brushing against her clit.

She came quietly, the speed of her breathing and the way her muscles clenched around me the only sign of her climax. She touched her lips to my neck and held me close. My own climax followed, our quiet orgasms somehow a testament to the poignancy of tonight.

This wasn't fucking. This was love.

I held her in my arms, her back to my front until the shift in her breathing to a steady rhythm meant she'd dozed off. Slipping out of bed, I pulled on my boxers, and, gathering my clothes, I crept out of the room. After changing into sweats and a T-shirt, I tiptoed downstairs and padded to my office.

I had a few missed calls, work related. They could wait until morning. Then I noticed a text from Sara.

I'm sorry about before. I do hope I didn't cause any trouble.

I began typing a reply, then deleted it. I'd deal with her tomorrow, face-to-face, not via an instant message. Instead, I called Garen. I hadn't heard from him in a while, and I wanted to see if he had news.

"Hey," he said, answering immediately. "I was going to call you tomorrow."

"Saved you the trouble. Have you uncovered anything yet?"

"Not yet," he said, a hint of hesitation in his tone which made me think that comment wasn't all together true. "There are a few leads, but I'd rather ride them to the end than jump to conclusions. How's she been?"

"With Annie, model behavior. Annie's thrilled to have her back, so who am I to get in the middle of that. With Harlow, however..."

"She's a complete bitch," Garen finished for me.

"You could say that, although Harlow's no shrinking violet." I apprised him of the scene I returned home to this evening.

Garen laughed. "Evil witch? I gotta meet this girl, and soon. It's good she's willing to stand up for herself. Can't be easy."

"No."

"Listen, man, don't let Sara come between you two. The way you talk about Harlow shows me you think she's special. You've been to some very dark places these past few years, and the last thing I want is for Sara to destroy you all over again. If you find yourself weakening, remember the hell she put you through. And if you still need a reminder, call me."

"I feel nothing for her beyond the fact that she's Annie's mother."

"Keep it that way," Garen said. "Give that woman the hint of an opening and she'll slither back into your lives and fuck you up all over again."

"Not a chance."

"Buddy, I gotta go," Garen said. "Eliza just arrived."

Eliza was his latest girlfriend, if four dates could be counted as such. Garen always had a line of females vying for his attention, but he suffered from a short attention span and the lowest boredom threshold I'd ever seen. For him, the thrill was all in the chase. The problem he had was that very few women ran.

"I'll call if anything changes."

"Thanks. Enjoy your night."

"Oh, I will, buddy. I will."

I chuckled and ended the call. My stomach growled, and only then did I realize I hadn't eaten dinner, too caught up in the drama of the evening. And then it occurred to me that Harlow wouldn't have eaten either, unless she kept a stash of snacks in her room, which I doubted.

I headed to the kitchen and opened the fridge. I removed a couple pieces of chicken and rubbed in some spices, set them to cook on the stove, and rustled up a quick salad. As I thought about going to wake Harlow, she appeared at the foot of the stairs wearing my shirt, the tails skimming her soft, creamy thighs.

"That smells good," she said, drawing my attention back to her from where my eyes had locked on to her legs.

"It's only chicken and salad."

"Works for me." She slid onto a stool and rested her elbows on the counter and watched me cook. "Oliver?"

"Yeah?"

"Don't hurt me."

I set down the cooking implements and moved around the counter, taking her in my arms. "Never."

28

*H*ARLOW

Whatever Oliver said to Sara must have worked because there were no more unexpected visits. In fact, I barely saw her unless she came to pick up Annie or when she dropped her off, and during those times, she made a conscious, albeit fake, effort to be nice to me.

I didn't buy it for a second.

Oliver, though, was a different story. He made a point of regularly asking me if I'd had any further issues with Sara which, of course, I had to tell him that no, I hadn't. How could I begin to explain the niggling doubts clawing at me, or describe the feminine intuition that Sara was playing a far smarter game?

I thought I'd feel more secure since we'd declared our love for one another, and at times I did. Then something innocuous would happen, and my inner voice would start a whole series of what-ifs, leaving me floundering and exhausted.

And so here I sat waiting for Katie to arrive for a long

overdue catch-up over dinner and drinks on a cold Saturday night. Oliver had been the one to encourage me to go, reminding me with an impish grin that I didn't work weekends, and that, as Annie was staying over at her best friend's house, he'd arranged to go for a drink with Ryker and Elliot.

At first, I'd declined, citing tiredness, but then the more I thought about it, the keener I grew to see her. I needed someone with a little perspective to tell me if I was mad and simply looking for problems in my relationship where none existed.

I needed my best friend.

I'd always assumed when you found The One, you'd be happier than you thought possible, yet my days were filled waiting for the other shoe to drop, for Oliver to confess his love for Sara and confirm they were getting back together.

It would destroy me.

I spotted Katie shrugging out of her winter coat and a long scarf she'd wrapped around her neck multiple times. She hung them on a hook by the door and waved, then made her way over to our table. We hugged and then ordered a bottle of wine.

"You look awful, by the way," was Katie's opening gambit.

"Gee, thanks," I drawled. "You're full of compliments."

She peered closer, her eyes scanning my face. "Babes, if this is what being in love looks like, you can keep it." She grinned, but her smile didn't hold as she realized I wasn't joining in with her teasing. She reached for my hand.

"Tell me everything."

Words swirled around my mind, all vying for first place, the sound too loud for me to organize my thoughts.

"I don't know where to begin."

She tilted her head to the right. "Anywhere you want, babes."

Katie knew Sara had returned to New York, but I'd kept the details scant. I didn't like talking on the phone all that much, and conveying how I felt over text wouldn't cut it. With Katie pulling double shifts at the hospital, tonight was the first time our calendars had aligned in weeks.

"She wants him back," I settled on, plunging right in with fear number one. "Sara, I mean."

"How do you know?"

"Because she flat-out told me right to my face."

Our server brought the wine and, after I'd assured her we could manage, she caught the atmosphere at the table and beat a hasty retreat. I unscrewed the top and poured healthy servings for me and Katie. Picking mine up, I swallowed a large mouthful.

"Did you tell Oliver?"

I nodded. "He assures me it doesn't make a difference because his feelings for her are nonexistent, but I can't help worrying. She's everything I'm not. Smart, sophisticated, in a word, perfect."

"As well as hard-nosed, cold, and lacking in empathy." Katie sipped at her wine. "The woman walked out on her young husband and baby daughter and didn't get in touch for six years. Who does that? So, yeah, you're right. She's everything you're not—thank fuck."

I loved Katie. She always had my back, and me hers.

"So, what do I do?"

"Sit it out. Sooner or later she'll slip up. I mean, come on, there has to be a reason she's returned now, and I don't think it's because she woke up one morning after more than half a decade away and realized she missed her husband and kid. Mark my words, there's more to this than meets the eye."

Inclined to agree—I'd had very similar thoughts myself—I nodded.

"Have you thought about calling his mom?" Katie asked. "I remember you telling me she didn't seem all that keen on the ex."

An understatement if ever there was one. Liv's remark came back to me when I'd asked where Oliver's wife was. "In Hell, I hope," she'd said.

"I admit I briefly thought about it, but that is way overstepping the mark. It's not up to me to tell Liv that her son's ex has breezed in wanting to pick up where she left off. That's Oliver's decision."

Katie pursed her lips. "Yeah, I guess you're right."

"I'm glad we got to do this tonight," I said. "I've missed you."

She picked up her wineglass and held it toward me. "Cheers, babes. Right back atcha. Now, let's get shit-faced."

We finished the first bottle of wine over the appetizers, then ordered a second one to accompany the entrée. Well on my way to drunkenness, Katie announced she'd purchased tickets to a comedy show on Broadway.

"It's that guy who recently landed his own TV show on cable. Simon Caldwell."

I beamed. "Oh, I love him. He's hilarious. But that show sold out months ago. How did you get tickets?"

She grinned. "I fucked half the hospital."

I arched a brow.

She held up her hands. "Joke. A guy at work was selling them half price because he got dumped by his girlfriend last night." She shrugged. "I took advantage of his situation. Sue me."

I laughed. "You're a wicked woman."

Riffling in her purse, she withdrew two tickets and waved them in my face. "A wicked woman who has front row seats to the hottest show in town."

"Front row? Jesus, he must have wanted to impress the heck out of his girlfriend."

"Yeah, or he used them to barter for sexual favors and she told him to fuck off." Katie grinned. "He looks the type. A bit shifty."

I laughed again. Already I felt lighter. Spending time with my best friend and getting to watch one of the country's up-and-coming comedic geniuses was exactly what I needed to lift my spirits.

Neither of us could manage dessert and so, slightly inebriated, we weaved our way down Broadway, occasionally stumbling, laughing the whole way, eventually taking our seats in the theater.

The show was awesome. Katie made the mistake of heckling, and Caldwell's comebacks had me bent over double, my stomach in agony from laughing so hard. I couldn't remember the last time I'd enjoyed an evening this much, and by the time the show ended at just after eleven, all my worries had dissolved.

"How about a nightcap?" Katie suggested. "There's a great little Irish place not far from here."

"Sounds great," I said, not wanting the night to end.

I linked my arm through hers as we dodged the crowds on Broadway. It had begun to sleet, and I zipped up my coat to chin level, burying my mouth to avoid breathing in the freezing air. Passing by a cozy café, I glanced in the window.

My heart stopped.

"Oh God," I whispered.

At a table inside the café was Oliver, and sitting across from him was Sara. She was talking, her hands gesticulating as she made her point, Oliver leaning forward, listening intently. And then he reached out a hand, taking hers.

I spun away. "He told me he was meeting Ryker and Elliot," I said, a lump forming in my throat.

"Is that her?" Katie asked.

I nodded, tears pricking the backs of my eyes.

"I'll kill him."

I tugged on the sleeve of her coat, yanking her away. "Leave it. I'll deal with this in my own way."

"You're not thinking of leaving him in there with her."

"I'm sure there's a plausible explanation," I said, disbelieving each word even as they spilled from my lips.

"He *lied* to you," Katie bluntly stated.

"I think I'll pass on that drink." I set off at a clipped pace.

Katie jogged to catch up to me. "Do you want me to come back to his place with you?"

"No." I smiled weakly. "You go home. I'll call you."

"I'm not happy leaving you like this."

"I'll be fine," I said, unsure whether I'd ever be 'fine' again. Oliver had insisted Sara had killed his feelings for her when she walked out, yet if that were true, why would he even entertain her request to see him? I realized then that Oliver had unfinished business with his ex, and until he properly closed that door, we'd always have that lingering between us, ever-present, dripping poison onto our relationship.

By the time I walked inside the empty apartment, I'd reached a decision. I'd ask Oliver to explain and hear him out, but whatever his excuses, real or imagined, I couldn't stay here until he resolved the Sara situation. The time had come to give him the space he needed to work out whether his feelings for his ex-wife truly were dead.

I didn't have to wait long for Oliver to arrive home, maybe ten minutes or so. He greeted me with a warm smile.

"You're home." He crossed the room, bent his head, and pecked my lips. "Did you have a good time?"

He shrugged out of his coat while I sat in silence, his question remaining unanswered. He caught the mood, a frown pulling his eyebrows down and inward.

"Is everything okay?"

"How was your evening?" I countered. "Ryker and Elliot okay?"

"Yeah, they're good." He flopped down beside me and kicked off his shoes.

"And what about Sara?" I asked, my tone dripping ice. "How is she?"

He paled as the reason for my coolness became apparent. "It's not what it looks like."

I barked a laugh, shuffling out of his reach when he extended his hand toward me. "Wow, and I thought the nanny getting it on with the boss was a fucking cliché. I'm clearly an amateur." I folded my arms over my chest. "Did you actually see Ryker and Elliot tonight, or was that a ruse so you could spend the night with your wife."

"*Ex*-wife. And yes, I did. Sara called when I was on my way home asking if I could meet for a quick drink. She wanted to talk to me about something."

"I'll bet she did," I said bitterly.

"Harlow, please."

He tried to touch me again. I stood, moving out of his reach.

"You have to believe me. There is nothing between me and Sara."

"That's bullshit, Oliver, and you know it. She's made no secret of the fact she wants you back."

"And I've made it very clear, to her *and* you, I'm not interested in any kind of a relationship, other than one as civil as we can create for Annie's sake."

"Is that why you were so keen for Annie to spend the night at her friend's house again? And why you were so encouraging when I mentioned meeting Katie? Because that left you free to see Sara?"

He shook his head despondently. "That's not it at all. You're blowing this out of all proportion."

"Oh, am I?" I scoffed.

"Sara received some bad news. A friend of hers has been diagnosed with stage four cancer, and she was upset. She needed someone to talk to, that's all."

"And that had to be you?" I asked, internally cringing that

my first thought wasn't for the poor soul who'd received such terrible news.

"She doesn't have anyone else."

I lowered my head, shaking it. And there it was. There'd always be something. A sick friend, a bad day at work, a snag in her pantyhose. Sara would find ways to draw Oliver to her, and he was too nice to say no.

"Harlow, you have to believe me. There's nothing going on between us."

"I do believe you," I said truthfully. "But don't you see? She'll always come between us. I'm sorry, Oliver. I can't do this. I won't be a third wheel."

Panic crossed his face, and he got to his feet. "What are you saying?"

I sighed, sadness weighing on my chest. "We need some time away from each other. You have to work out how you can square this circle, and I need a break from it all."

He strode toward me, gripping my upper arms. "Please don't do this. Don't leave me."

"I-I'm not leaving," I said, although I wasn't sure whether that were true. "I'm taking some time away to think things through."

"Don't. Stay. Please, I don't want you to go."

His expression, so dejected and desperate, cut me deeply. I nearly gave in, but I steeled my spine and hardened my resolve. I had to buy myself a few days to figure out if I was strong enough to handle a relationship with a man whose ex refused to accept their affiliation was over.

"I can't. Give me a couple of days. And please, don't try to call me. Allow me the head space to work this through."

I stepped backward. His arms fell to his sides.

"What will I tell Annie?"

Tears I'd tried so hard to hold back streamed down my cheeks. "Tell her I love her."

29

OLIVER

"Earth to Oliver."

I raised my head and narrowed my eyes at Elliot. "What?"

"Precisely." He aimed a paperclip at my head. "You're not in the game, man."

I batted it away, then swept a hand down my face and tried to focus on the thick wad of papers in front of me. The words blurred and swam. "Sorry. I didn't sleep very well last night."

"No word from Harlow, huh?"

I shook my head. "It's been the longest three days of my life. Annie's devastated. I told her it's only temporary, but she's a smart kid. She knows I'm stretching the truth."

"And what about Sara?" Elliot asked.

I pinched the bridge of my nose, exhaustion swamping me. "She said she feels partially responsible for coming between us."

Elliot snorted. "Try *wholly responsible*," he said. "If she'd stayed the fuck away, none of this would have happened."

"Mom is due back next week," I said. "Just as well, although when I tell her Sara's back she'll go ape shit."

Elliot's eyes widened. "You haven't told her?" He let out a low whistle. "I hope Sara is prepared. Your mom is fearsome."

He wasn't wrong. Mom had felt equally betrayed by Sara absconding. She'd loved her like a daughter, and her leaving had hurt Mom deeply. I had no idea how she'd react when I broke the news, hence I'd put it off until now. One thing I couldn't do was allow her to return unprepared.

"Preach," I said, the faintest grin touching my lips. "I guess I hoped to have all this in hand before she landed. I thought Garen might have discovered Sara's angle by now."

"You still think there's more to it than the weight of guilt pressuring her into returning?"

I pulled my lips to one side. "No idea. I might be way off track, and Sara's intentions are entirely honorable."

Elliot arched a brow. "You believe that?"

I blew out a slow breath. "I honestly don't know what to think anymore."

"You're not falling for her again, are you?"

I shook my head. "No. I love Harlow, and I will fight with everything I have to get her back. But I think that over the last six years, I've built Sara up to be a monster, a terrible human being who is self-serving and selfish, only thinking about themselves, their wants and needs. Since coming back into our lives, she's tested my beliefs. Sure, she was bitchy to Harlow in the beginning, but she made no secret of the fact she hoped we'd get back together. Ever since I made it abundantly clear that wasn't going to happen, she's accepted it and moved on. And I can't fault her commitment to Annie."

"I don't envy you, man," Elliot said. "It's a toughie."

"Yeah." I stared out the window, then returned my attention to him. "Let's finish reviewing this contract. I have to pick Annie up from school in an hour."

∼

I watched my daughter run out of the school building and lock her gaze on me, then immediately look around for Harlow. Her crestfallen face when she realized I was alone bore a fucking great hole in my chest. She'd had the same response yesterday, too.

"Hey, munchkin," I said, swinging her up in the air. "How was school?"

"Okay."

She mumbled where she usually giggled. I set her on the ground. "How about dinner at Bubby's?"

"Can we ask Harlow to come?" she asked, a brief flicker of hope lighting her eyes.

"I don't think so, baby girl." I clasped her hand. As a compromise, I found myself saying, "But we could ask Mommy if you like," then immediately cursed the idea. Too late now, Annie's face lit up, and she beamed.

"Can we?"

I didn't want to play happy families with Sara, but I also knew I'd do anything for my little girl. So I nodded. "Absolutely. I'll call her on the way and ask her to meet us there."

Annie clapped. "Excellent."

I strapped her into her car seat, jogged around to the driver's side—I'd driven myself today—then put in a call to Sara. She answered so fast, it was almost as if she was waiting for my call.

"Oliver, how lovely to hear from you."

"Ah, yeah. You've got Annie to thank for that," I said, keen to distance myself from this conversation. "We're going to Bubby's for an early dinner. Annie would love it if you joined us."

"And what about you?" Sara asked. "Would you love it if I joined you?"

I almost groaned aloud. Sara wasn't going to give up on this crusade to stitch back together the family she tore apart.

"Whatever makes Annie happy is good with me," I said, sidestepping her question.

She chuckled, knowing I was avoiding the question. "I'll make my way over there right now. See you both soon."

I hung up, dread circling in my gut. I felt so torn between wanting to make Annie happy and desperate to win back Harlow. Spending any time with Sara in public made me nervous. What if Harlow happened to pass by and see the three of us acting like a happy family, even if the reality from my perspective was far from that? She'd jump to even more conclusions, the result being she'd edge farther away from me.

Talk about a rock and a fucking hard place.

I parked a block away from Bubby's. Annie skipped the whole way to the restaurant, her earlier despondency a distant memory. I envied the simplicity of kids.

I opened the door to the restaurant and couldn't help glancing around, worried about bumping into Harlow. Sara must have been close when I called her because she'd already secured a table and waved madly when she saw us. Annie dashed across the room and threw herself into her mother's arms.

Sara urged Annie to sit beside her. "I got us a table. I hope you don't mind."

"Why would I mind?" I bit out, harsher than I intended.

Sara raised her eyebrows. "Are you all right?"

I blew out a slow breath and yanked the chair from underneath the table. "I'm fine. Busy day, that's all."

"You work too hard, always did," Sara said.

I picked up the menu and pointlessly scanned it. We came here so often, I knew the food offering by heart, but focusing on the choices printed on the page was preferable to sitting here with Sara when I should be working on ways to win Harlow back.

We ordered our food, and I played with a paper napkin, feeding it through my fingers while Annie, oblivious to my darkening mood, chattered away happily. Sara shot the odd glance my way, her brow furrowed.

"What's the matter, Oliver?" Sara asked when Annie's attention was diverted by the arrival of her dinner.

"Nothing," I muttered, pushing my food around my plate.

"Then at least try to engage, for Annie's sake," she hissed.

I widened my eyes. "Excuse me?"

Sara rapidly backtracked. "Sorry. That came out all wrong."

"Did it?" The iciness to my tone had Sara blushing.

"Is it Harlow?" she asked in a low voice. "Can I help?"

I laughed bitterly. "Somehow I don't think a woman-to-woman chat with you will aid the situation."

Her eyes held the gentle concern that had drawn me to her in the first place. She slid her hand across the table and squeezed my fingers. "I'm so sorry, Oliver. I haven't handled the situation with Harlow well at all. I guess I was jealous of her. She had you. I wanted you back. I still want you back."

"Sara," I said, my voice holding a warning.

Releasing me, she raised her hands in surrender. "I know. I know." She smiled. "But we can still be friends, can't we? We have a child together, a history. I take full responsibility for my actions, but people change, Oliver. *I've* changed. I won't lie that getting back together with you would be wonderful, but I accept you're not there. What I can't accept is that you'll *never* be there. The love we had for each other doesn't just disappear. I hurt you, and I'm sorry. All I ask is that you give it some time."

My cell phone rang, saving me from answering. I fished it out of the inside pocket of my jacket. *Garen.* Standing to take the call, I moved away from the table.

"Hey," I said. "What's up?"

"Where are you?" he asked.

"At Bubby's," I replied. He knew the restaurant was Annie's favorite. "As a treat for Annie. She's still hurt over Harlow, so I let her invite Sara."

"Well, un-invite the bitch and get your ass home. I'm here."

My eyebrows shot up. "In New York?"

"No, in fucking Hell, which is where you'll be as soon as I share what I've discovered about your delightful ex. Now fucking move it."

He hung up without giving me the chance to respond. The hairs on the back of my neck stood up, and my skin prickled, a sure sign of a sudden spike in adrenaline. I slid my gaze over to our table, watching as Sara whispered something to Annie which made her laugh. My jaw flexed.

What the fuck had Garen uncovered?

30

Oliver

I returned my phone to my pocket and sat back down. "Hurry up, Annie." I jerked my chin at her almost-finished plate of food. "I have work to do this evening."

I wasn't happy rushing her, but with Garen waiting at my penthouse, no doubt pacing, his impatience increasing with each passing second—along with my own—I was anxious to get going.

"Aww, Daddy, I wanted ice cream."

She pouted. I always let her have ice cream when we came to Bubby's—but not tonight.

"There's ice cream at home," I said, gesturing to the server to bring the check.

"What's the hurry?" Sara asked, her eyes narrowing as she tried to figure out what had changed in the last few seconds. "Who was on the phone?"

"None of your business." I set my credit card on the table.

Sara rose from her chair and snatched up her purse. "There

is no need to be rude, Oliver." Bending down, she kissed the top of Annie's head. "I'll see you soon, my sweet girl."

She swept out of the restaurant, her long black coat trailing behind her like a scene out of Van Helsing.

"Daddy, what's the matter?" Annie asked. "You seem angry."

I scrawled my name on the check, then stood and waited for Annie to scramble to her feet. "I'm not angry, munchkin." I fixed a warm smile to my face for her benefit when inside an icy chill filled my veins. "There's just something urgent I have to deal with." I crouched to her level and kissed her forehead. "And I have a surprise for you."

"You do?" she said, her confusion at my odd behavior vanishing, no doubt as fast as the ice cream would when we returned home.

"Uncle Garen is here. He's waiting for us at home."

He hated it when I laid the Uncle moniker on him which, of course, meant I did it all the more.

"He is?" She clapped her hands. "Has he brought me a present."

"Annie," I warned. "That's not very polite."

She dipped her chin into her chest. "Sorry," she mumbled.

I ruffled her hair. "Come on. Shall we go see?"

Her despondency didn't last long. "Yes!" she said excitedly.

Annie barely waited for the elevator doors to open into the foyer of my penthouse. As soon as they'd parted far enough, she squeezed through yelling, "Uncle Garen" at the top of her voice. By the time I'd caught up to her, Garen had her upside down by her ankles, demanding penance for calling him Uncle. It was a game they'd played ever since Annie first uttered the word—heavily coached by me—and she loved it.

"Call me that again and I'm returning your gift to the store."

"I won't, I promise," Annie giggled, except, of course, she would.

"Okay then." Garen set her on her feet then rummaged

through his bag, producing a gift-wrapped box. "For you, sweet Annie."

She reached for it, eyes wide, bursting with excitement.

"What do you say to Uncle Garen, Annie?" I asked, earning a fierce glare from my best friend and a sneaky one-fingered salute behind Annie's back. I grinned and winked.

"Thank you!" she gushed.

"You don't know what it is yet," Garen said. "It might be an empty box."

Her face fell, and then she inclined her head and grinned. "You'd never do that to me."

She tore off the paper to reveal a plain brown box. Opening the flap on the top, she reached inside and removed the latest top-of-the-range tablet for kids.

"It's loaded with all the latest games," Garen explained. "Or so the lady at the store told me."

Annie squealed with delight, then threw her arms around him. "Oh, Uncle Garen. I love it. I love you."

She smothered him in kisses, and while he tried to hold her at arm's length, I could tell that on the inside, he couldn't be more pleased with her animated reaction to his gift. Garen tried to act as if he didn't care, but I knew the real man behind the mask.

"All right, all right, that's enough," he said, making a big show of wiping his face.

Annie giggled, then turned to me. "Daddy, can I go play with it in my room?"

I opened my mouth to say, "Homework first", then changed my mind. Garen had done this on purpose. Homework wouldn't have absorbed Annie's attention to the same extent that an electronic gift with all her favorite games to play would. This way, we'd get to talk in peace, and while I was usually strict when it came to her schoolwork, I figured missing one night wouldn't hurt. If necessary, I'd write a note for her teacher.

"You can, munchkin."

She squealed again, darting up the stairs and disappearing from sight. Garen sauntered over and shook my hand, then pulled me into a rough hug, clapping me on the back.

"It's great to see you, man," he said. "Been too long."

I laughed. "You see me on Skype at our weekly catch-ups," I said, referring to every Friday when the ROGUES team had an hour-long meeting over video conference. Sebastian had suggested it, and we'd all embraced it, especially as we only got to see each other in person every couple of months.

"It's not the same," Garen grumbled.

"Jeez, sweetheart, you'll have me gushing in a minute."

Garen smiled, but he couldn't hold it.

"What did you find?" I asked.

He pointed to the couch, indicating I should sit, then crossed over to the kitchen. He removed two crystal tumblers from the cabinet and poured us each a healthy serving of scotch. Returning to the living room, he handed one to me.

"Cheers." He knocked back half the glass in one swallow.

I sipped mine. "Can we get to it?"

He set his glass on the coffee table and unzipped the front pocket of his carry-on bag, removing a sheath of papers. He handed them to me.

"These are for later when you're craving more details, but in the meantime, I'll sum it up for you.

"Sara had an elderly aunt on her father's side who, long before Sara was born, had a falling out with the family. She ended up meeting and later marrying the Earl of Montgomery, a member of the British aristocracy. Despite trying for children of their own, they were unable to conceive but, by all accounts, they had a happy marriage.

"The earl died over a decade ago, and then, last month, the

aunt died, too. She left her entire fortune and, just as important, her title of Countess to Sara. Unusual, but not unheard of in special circumstances to bequeath titles through an estate, even when they were inherited through marriage."

He paused to take a drink, a more moderate sip this time.

"Does Sara know?" I asked.

Garen snorted. "Oh yeah. She fucking knows."

I twisted my lips to the side. "Strange she didn't mention it."

"Not strange at all when you know what I know."

I arched a brow. "Which is?"

"There's a condition attached to the bequest. Sara's aunt was old-school, and so she added a proviso. To inherit the money, the title, all of it, Sara has to marry."

"So? She's a beautiful woman. She won't find it that difficult to meet and marry someone, even if she goes through with it for money rather than love. She can always break it off afterward."

"Ah," Garen said, "but there's a rather large problem with that scenario. When I said the aunt was old-school, I wasn't joking. She was a devout Catholic who believed wholeheartedly in the sanctity of marriage and, therefore, deemed it only possible to have one husband in the eyes of God. And, well..."

Realization slammed into me, and a sudden coldness hit me in the gut. "Sara's already had a husband. Me."

Garen theatrically threw his hands in the air. "Bingo. Poor, poor Sara. What *is* a girl to do? And then a lightbulb goes on. She'll simply remarry her ex. You," he added pointlessly. "That would satisfy the requirements. After all, according to the aunt's beliefs, you can't actually get divorced. She married you, and therefore, she's married to you forever. Unfortunately for Sara, the law doesn't work that way. She needs the bit of paper to claim her inheritance."

I nibbled on my thumbnail, my mind racing, trying to take in the enormity of Garen's news. "And that's the only reason she came back?" I said, so quietly, it could be misinterpreted as talking to myself.

"Yep," Garen said. "She's a piece of fucking work, that one."

I got to my feet and wandered over to the window, staring into the obsidian night, the tops of the trees in Central Park visible only through light bleed, their bare branches buffeted by the stiff breeze. Stuffing my hands in my pockets, I turned around.

"How could she do that to Annie?"

Garen shook his head sadly. "I wish I knew."

I frowned. "But what would stop her from remarrying me, inheriting the money and the title, then simply taking off again?"

"Nothing," Garen said. "And that's the cruelest part of this whole plan. She gets you to fall in love with her again, makes Annie think she's back for good, grabs the money, then runs, leaving the two of you devastated for a second time."

Hot rage at the depths Sara would resort to seared my insides. She'd already wormed her way into Annie's heart, a terrible consequence I'd have to deal with once I'd gotten her out of our lives. But if she'd succeeded in her plan, I couldn't bear to think how much worse it would have been several months, a year, two years down the line.

"What would you do, if you were me?"

"I'd confront her, and then I'd get her the hell away from me and my kid pronto."

My eyes darted around as I planned my approach. "She won't give up without a fight, not with a fortune and a title on the line."

"What's she gonna do? Force you down the aisle?"

"With Sara, it's hard telling. If I back her into a corner, she'll come out fighting."

"Let her," Garen said. "We've got more than enough firepower to take her on."

I nodded, dreading the battle ahead yet knowing I couldn't avoid it. I wished Harlow were beside me. Grabbing my phone, I went to call her, then changed my mind. I needed to fix this shit with Sara first, then win Harlow back. Somehow. I refused to believe it was over between us. She'd asked for space, and I'd granted her that, but as soon as Sara was out of our lives, all my efforts would go into fighting for the woman I loved.

Instead of calling Harlow, I sent a text to Sara.

We need to talk about us. Come over to my place tomorrow morning at ten.

A little cruel as Sara would immediately think I was coming around to the idea of a reconciliation, but that was the point. I wanted her to feel comfortable. I wanted her to think she was going to get everything she wanted, and then I'd cruelly snatch it away.

Her reply came instantaneously.

I'll be there.

She followed that up with another three-word reply, one that was steeped in manipulation and lies.

I love you.

I didn't reply. She wouldn't expect me to.

Turning the screen toward Garen, I showed him our exchange. He rolled his eyes when he reached the end.

"I fucking hate that woman."

I laughed. "I know. You've never made a secret of it."

His eyes twinkled. "You know me, buddy. Shoot from the hip, always."

"Which is why I'm hoping you'll agree to be here tomorrow."

A flash of glee crossed his face, his grin widening. "There's nowhere else I'd rather be."

31

Harlow

Oliver's car slowed to a halt outside his building, and I ducked behind a large oak tree, its wide trunk more than enough to hide me. My chest ached as I watched him appear with Annie, her hand tightly in his as she skipped alongside him. He'd dressed in jeans and sneakers, and a sports jacket that offered little protection against the biting wind. He mustn't be going into the office today.

His driver opened the rear door, and Annie climbed in. Oliver strode around the back of the vehicle and got in the other side. The car moved smoothly away, taking Annie to school. My eyes tracked its movements all the way down the road. It turned a corner, its taillights disappearing from view.

Four days had passed since I'd packed a bag, walked out, and checked into a cheap motel. A far cry from the luxurious penthouse that I'd lived in for almost three months, but beggars most definitely couldn't be choosers.

I'd halfheartedly searched for work, but what I really wanted was to return to the man I loved and his daughter who might not be mine through blood, but nevertheless, felt like mine in every way that counted.

The only problem was that, as far as I knew, nothing had changed on the Sara front. If it had, I was sure he'd have called, but my phone had remained woefully silent save for the odd text from Katie making sure I was okay.

I wasn't okay.

Night after night I'd lain awake wondering if I'd done the right thing by removing myself from the situation. Sara's unexpected and unwelcome—at least by me—return had sent me into a tailspin. My relationship with Oliver was too new to deal with the baggage of an ex hell-bent on worming her way back into his life. Yet my very absence would probably give her the 'in' she craved, and the not knowing was torture.

Which was why I'd decided when I woke long before sunrise this morning that I would reach out to Oliver and talk things over. Get the lay of the land, so to speak. Except, when I'd arrived outside his building thirty minutes ago, I'd lost my nerve. Instead, I hovered across the street like a pathetic stalker.

Removing the plastic lid from my cup of coffee, I blew on the contents and took a sip, screwing up my face when I realized I'd forgotten to add sweetener. If I'd guessed correctly, and he wasn't going into the office today, I'd wait for him to return from Annie's school and approach him then. I couldn't go on like this, heartsick, not sleeping or eating properly, missing listening to his soft breathing as he slept. And Annie, too. I missed her excited chatter when I picked her up from school, the way she bartered so skillfully to stave off her bedtime for "just five more minutes", how her eyes drooped when I read to her, but if I stopped, she'd snap them back open, denying she was tired and begging me to continue.

I estimated it would take Oliver thirty minutes to drive to Annie's school, see her inside, and then have his driver bring him back home. If more time than that passed, then I'd miscalculated his intentions via his casual attire, and I'd head to his office instead. Now that I'd settled on the need to talk with him, I didn't want to put it off for another day.

When Oliver's car appeared, my pulse jolted, and, despite the chilly air, my hands felt clammy. What if he rejected me? What if I'd given him the excuse he'd wanted to break off our relationship by flouncing out and not contacting him since?

The car coasted to a stop, and Oliver climbed out. I tossed the cup in a nearby trash can and buried my hands in my coat pockets. Looking both ways on the busy street, I stepped off the sidewalk.

"Oliver."

My head snapped to the left. I hadn't called his name, so who had?

I got my answer.

Sara.

That she was here was bad enough, but what really crushed me was the friendly smile he greeted her with. And then my heart shattered into a million pieces when he pressed his hand to the small of her back and, together, they walked into his building.

I struggled for breath, my heart racing. I'd once begged Oliver not to hurt me, and I'd believed his earnest vow. I'd thought he was different, but he was just like all the rest. I'd trusted him, given him my fragile heart, and in return he'd lied and cheated. His platitudes about Sara, his supposed unhappiness with her return were nothing more than empty words said for reasons only he could answer.

A sob broke from my throat. The horn from a passing car blared, and only then did I realize I was still standing in the street, my legs frozen in place, my feet glued to the ground. I forced myself to move, stumbling as I stepped back onto the safety of the sidewalk. I reached out a hand to steady myself. A woman passing with a crying child in tow muttered something about disgusting drunks at this time in the morning, but I didn't care to correct her, to plead my case.

I fumbled around in my coat, eventually locating my phone. I found Katie's number and dialed.

"Babes, you okay?" she questioned when she answered, and I didn't respond. "Harlow, are you there?"

"I'm here," I ground out. "I know you're at work, but can I come over?"

"What's happened?"

"Oliver has made his choice. And it isn't me."

∼

"Are you sure?" Katie asked, rubbing my knee as I sat across from her in the hospital restaurant. "Sometimes what we see isn't the truth. Like pictures, our eyes can see things and our brain translates them into a falsehood, but one we readily accept without questioning because we're hurt."

I shrugged. "All I know is that he hasn't contacted me, and then today, I see him with Sara. The way he smiled at her, Katie. That wasn't fake. He was genuinely happy to see her. And then he put his hand on her back." I shivered, but not from cold. "The familiarity of it is what got to me. I can't escape the fact they were married and have a child together. They have a bond that can't be broken, no matter how much she hurt him."

"What bullshit," Katie stated. "I know plenty of women who can't abide their exes and plenty of men who'd happily watch their former wives burn in Hell."

She laughed, her overexaggeration meant to cheer me up. I offered a faint smile, but it didn't hold.

"I don't think I've got any choice but to move back in with my parents," I said, dread circling in my abdomen like a vulture going in for the kill. "I can't afford to stay at the motel for long, and I don't want to waste the little I managed to save these last few months."

"Babes, don't do that yet. You and your dad will clash the second you tell him why you're there. Just give it a few more days. Go and talk to Oliver. Maybe do it on neutral ground. Send him a text and ask him to meet you."

I shook my head. "At least this way, I can hang on to a scrap of hope that he might choose me, that we still have a chance of making it. If we meet up, and he tells me to my face that he and Sara are getting back together, I don't think I could stand it."

"Whether you meet up won't change the outcome in the end," Katie said.

I winced at her bluntness, but I also thanked her for it. Lying to myself, hoping for an outcome I couldn't influence, wouldn't do me any good. If Oliver had decided to give Sara another chance, then it was best I knew. That way I could, in time, move on with my life.

"You're right." I swept a hand over my face. "I will get in touch, but not yet. I need to gather my thoughts so that when I do confront him, I'm prepared for the worst. I don't want to break down in a blubbering mess. If he tells me what I fear he will, I'm determined to walk away with my head up. I refuse to let him see me break."

"Atta girl," Katie said, standing to hug me. "Why don't you come over for dinner tonight? I finish my shift at seven. Stay the night. We can talk things through."

This time I gave her a genuine smile. "That sounds great. I'd love to."

She blew me a kiss and returned to work.

I might have a broken heart, but I counted myself among

the lucky ones to have a friend as good as Katie. Not everyone was as fortunate.

Unable to face another day in that cramped, damp motel room, I jumped back on the subway and headed uptown, disembarking at Lexington and seventy-seventh. A day wandering the Met might just lift my spirits, or at least take my mind off the terrible ache in my chest.

32

Oliver

30 minutes earlier.

I wasn't surprised Sara had arrived earlier than our agreed time of ten a.m. Even as a young woman in college, she'd struggled with being told what to do, where to be, and when to be there. By arriving earlier—or later—than arranged was her way of exerting control. Therefore, when she stopped me after I'd arrived home from taking Annie to school, I greeted her with a welcoming smile, even though it irked me that she still played those childish games.

"Sorry I'm early," she said, lying through her teeth. "Did Annie get off to school okay?"

"She did." I placed my palm in the small of her back and eased her inside.

"I'm so glad you reached out after what happened at the diner yesterday."

"Yeah, bad day," I murmured.

"Anything I can help with?"

I shook my head. "Work stuff. That's all."

I entered the code for my penthouse on the keypad, and the doors closed. The elevator swept us upward. I dropped a quick text to Garen to let him know I had Sara with me. Even though she deserved the upcoming ambush for her lies and deceit, I still had to quell the nervous flutter in my stomach. This wasn't my style.

It was, however, very much Garen's modus operandi. I could imagine him pacing, buzzing, anticipating Sara's reaction when we laid out the truth he'd uncovered. He loved one-upmanship and lived for conflict. Getting one over on Sara would certainly go down as one of his favorite occasions.

Our differences were why we gravitated toward one another. And on a day like today, I felt lucky to have him in my corner. If he sensed a moment of sympathy emanating from me toward Sara, he'd squish it like a bug.

The elevator doors smoothly opened, and I gestured for Sara to go ahead. She confidently strode across the foyer, but I knew the precise moment she set eyes on Garen; she stopped so fast, it was as if she'd hit an invisible wall.

She glanced sharply over her shoulder at me, and her eyes narrowed. "What's *he* doing here?"

I strolled past her, appearing nonchalant even as my insides twisted and swirled. "We need to talk," I said, repeating my text of the previous day.

"And we will, as soon as he leaves."

Garen's top lip curled in a sneer that left Sara in no doubt how he felt about her. "I'm going nowhere."

"Then I'm not staying."

"Sit down!" I barked with more anger than I thought possible.

Sara's eyes widened, then she lowered her chin and stared

at where my fisted hands were shaking as they rested by my sides. "What's going on?"

"I told you. We need to talk."

"I thought you wanted to talk about us?"

"Oh, I do," I snarled. "Y'know, you never fully explained why you suddenly came back after so many years of absence. Let's start there."

She shot a look at Garen. "Don't you think this is a conversation to have when we're alone, Oliver'"

"Why?" I asked. "Are you ashamed of the reason?"

She bowed her head. "No, I'm not ashamed of coming back. I'm ashamed of leaving in the first place."

Garen choked on a laugh. "Fucking hell. Someone call Broadway. We've discovered a new star."

The old saying *If looks could kill* sprang to mind as Sara glared at Garen, venom blasting from her eyes. He held her gaze, a cocky smirk curling his lip on one side.

"Do you love me, Sara?"

She dragged her gaze away from my best friend, returning her focus to me. "You know I do," she said quietly.

"More than anything?"

"Yes."

"What about money? Do you love me more than money?"

A flicker of doubt sparked in her eyes, extinguished immediately when she blinked. "Where is this going, Oliver? Are you asking if I like money? Of course I do. Who doesn't?"

"And what about Annie," I said, switching direction. "Do you love her?"

"Yes. Very much so."

As soon as I mentioned Annie, the rage I'd felt last night came roaring back. Sara deserved everything coming to her and more for the stunt she'd tried to pull. Dear God, I shuddered to think what would have happened had I not already fallen for Harlow. Before I met her, I'd often wondered how I'd feel if, one day, Sara came back. Without Harlow in my life, who knew how easily Sara might have found it to get her hooks into me, and all for money and a stupid title, only to leave me and Annie as soon as she'd gotten her way.

I'd had enough of playing games. It'd been fun while it lasted, but now, I wanted this over with, and Sara out of our lives.

"Do you love me as much as a title, *Countess Sara*," I blurted.

The blood drained from her face, leaving her pale, and a sheen of sweat broke out on her forehead. Her hand fluttered to her neck, and I caught a tremble before she made a fist and pressed it against her sternum.

"Has *he* put you up to this?" She jabbed a finger at Garen, who didn't even attempt to hide his delight. "He's *lying*, Oliver. He never liked me and now he's trying to sabotage our second chance at happiness."

Garen chuckled. "Get it right, sweetheart. It's not that I never liked you, it's that I always *hated* you."

"He isn't lying," I said coldly, striding over to the dining table where the incriminating evidence Garen had uncovered was tucked away in an innocuous beige folder. Last night I'd read every word, memorizing the details. I picked it up, returned to Sara, and thrust it at her. "It's all in here."

She didn't move.

"Read it!" I roared.

She winced and took it from me. Without opening it, she whispered, "I don't need to read it."

"How could you?" I ground out through a jaw that felt fused together. "How could you do this to Annie?"

I thought at the mention of our daughter who, somehow, had inherited all the good things about us both and none of the bad, Sara might show a modicum of regret. Instead, her eyes flashed with hatred, and she slammed the folder into my chest.

"*You* pushed me into having a child. I never wanted kids. I *hate* kids, but you wouldn't let up, so I got pregnant to make you happy. I wanted you, Oliver. Only you. And I thought you felt the same, but as soon as *she* arrived, it was like I didn't exist. Having her was a mistake."

Hearing her call Annie, my wonderful, funny, kooky, bright little girl, a mistake was the final straw. How I stopped myself from throttling her was a testament to my love for my daughter.

"Don't you fucking *dare* call Annie a mistake."

I gripped her upper arm and shunted her in the direction of the foyer. I wanted this woman out of my home and out of my life. I jabbed a finger at the call button, and the doors to the elevator opened.

"Get out, Sara. Get out and don't come back."

She stood her ground. "I want a hundred million dollars, then I'll go."

I laughed at the sheer nerve of the woman. She received ten million as part of the divorce which, at the time, was a fair slice of my wealth, and I didn't intend to pay her another penny. "Not a chance."

"Either pay me what I'm owed, or I'll go for custody of Annie," she spat, the true evil of the woman spilling from her ice-cold core. "I'll get it, too. Judges always lean toward the mother. And then I'll turn her against you. I'll tell her I left because you beat me and abused me. I'll make sure she never wants a damn thing to do with you ever again. I don't give a shit about the kid, but I'll use her to get my way. Bank on it, Oliver. I had you all fooled. It'll be easy to fool a judge. A few tears, a sniff here and there, and you'll lose the person you love the most in the whole world."

Garen took a sharp breath, the air whistling through his teeth at the sheer gall of Sara. I, on the other hand, exuded calm. Sara had played what she thought was her trump card, and in doing so, she'd handed over her power, leaving her defenseless. She'd shown her true colors along with her black heart.

"Go ahead." I used my height advantage to loom over her, a lion protecting my cub, and I would until my dying breath. "Try it. Six years is a long time, Sara, and I'm no longer the man I was. You want a battle? I'll bring a fucking war right to your door. Still want to test me?" I threw my arms out to the side. "Do your worst."

"You'll regret this," she said, standing her ground. "I'll see you in court."

I smiled. "I really don't think you will."

She narrowed her eyes at me. "Misplaced confidence, Oliver. It'll be your downfall."

Reaching into my pocket, I lifted out my cell phone and held it up, screen side toward Sara. "Actually, it's your misplaced confidence that is *your* downfall, Sara. I recorded the entire conversation. Judges don't take kindly to blackmail, or mothers who use their kids as pawns in their fucked-up attempt to extort money from the father who's done nothing but put his daughter first for the past seven years. Now get out of my home and don't come back or I swear, I won't be responsible for my actions."

I caught Garen's stunned expression out of the corner of my eye, but it was nothing compared to Sara's. She opened her mouth then, without uttering a sound, closed it again. Her gaze fell to my phone.

"Try it," I said softly. "Make my day, Sara."

She emitted a frustrated noise and, throwing back her shoulders, gave me a defiant glare and stomped into the elevator. As soon as the doors closed, I reached out a hand and braced myself against the wall, my legs almost refusing to hold me upright.

"Fuckin' A." Garen clapped me on the back. "I'm proud of you. The quiet ones are always the worst."

I turned around slowly. "I need a drink."

"Coming right up."

After three fingers of scotch made their way into my bloodstream, the trembling in my hands abated. I swept a palm over my face, my mind running amok as I thought through how I would break the news to Annie that her mother had left—again.

And then my thoughts turned to Harlow. I cut my gaze to Garen. "Now that that's over, there's something else I need you to do for me."

33

H*ARLOW*

Two days later.

"Where are we going?" I asked Katie as she held out her hand for a passing cab with its lights on. She'd arrived at my motel room an hour ago, insistent I applied a little makeup, brushed my hair, and changed out of the sweatpants I'd started to favor for a knee-length fitted dress. The dress was a little baggy around the waist and over my hips, an indication of the weight I'd lost in the last few days.

"I told you," she replied. "It's a surprise. I figured you needed a little cheering up, and I have just the thing to put a smile on your face."

I groaned. Katie in this mood was a force of nature. I'd learned over the years that it was easier to let her have her moment and simply go along for the ride. Fifteen minutes later, the cab drew to a halt. I peered out of the window and frowned.

"Rockefeller Plaza?" I turned to face her. "What are we doing here?"

She grinned. "Move your butt and you'll find out."

"I am *not* going ice skating," I stated, recalling the last time she'd dragged me to an ice rink, and I'd fallen on my ass so many times, I'd struggled to sit down without wincing for three days straight.

"Or Top of the Rock," I added. "This close to Christmas it'll be crammed with tourists."

Katie rolled her eyes. "My, my, we are in a fine mood this afternoon."

"I just know what you're like," I grumbled. "If I'm feeling down, you always over-compensate."

Handing over the cab fare, she laughed and opened her door. I followed her onto the sidewalk. We entered the iconic building where she ushered me into an elevator along with a small group of excited schoolchildren and two harassed teachers. One of the kids caught my eye and made a funny face. I laughed and did the same back at her.

The elevator stopped on the sixty-fifth floor, and Katie gave me a gentle nudge. "This is us."

I stepped out. Katie linked her arm through mine and set off at a fast pace. I had no clue where we were going. Ahead of us, a guy dressed in a smart suit and tie stood in front of a doorway. He smiled and opened the door. "Welcome, Ms. Winter. Go on in."

I glanced at Katie. "Okay, what's going on?"

She gave me a shove. "Get inside, woman."

I stepped through the door and found myself in the Rainbow Room. I'd never been to this restaurant. The cost of eating here was far too rich for my bank balance. I'd heard of it, though. Who hadn't? The place was iconic.

And empty.

Five o'clock on a Friday afternoon, and the entire restaurant was deserted.

I shot a look over my shoulder. The well-dressed guy had already closed the door, leaving me alone. Despite the confusion swirling through my mind, I found myself drawn to the large windows affording one of the best views of the Empire State Building. With night falling, the entire city lit up, taking my breath away. I'd lived here all my life, yet still New York had the power to astound me.

"Beautiful, isn't it?"

I spun around. Oliver was standing on the other side of the vast space dressed in a full tux, his hair neatly combed, his handsome features clear of any stubble.

"It is," I said quietly, drinking in my fill. Whatever our issues, I still desperately loved him.

"But not as beautiful as you."

My chest tightened, and I made a fist and rubbed it over my sternum. Then I remembered he'd hurt me.

"What are you doing here, Oliver?" I asked, my tone clipped with a hint of irritation. He must have somehow persuaded Katie to assist him in his covert plan. "What am *I* doing here?"

He walked toward me, his steps slow and steady.

I held my breath, slowly releasing it when he stopped right in front of me.

"I'm here to win you back."

"With what? A fancy restaurant and a display of your wealth?" I took a breath, the need to blurt out my pain overwhelming. "I saw you, Oliver. I saw you with Sara on Wednesday morning. I came by to talk to you, to see if we could work things out, and instead, you hurt me all over again."

His jaw flexed, a nerve beating in his cheek. "What do you think you saw, Harlow?"

"You, putting your arm around her. Smiling at her like she

was the best thing you'd ever seen. You told me you weren't in love with her."

"I'm not."

"That's not what it looked like."

He took my hand. "Would you give me ten minutes? That's all I ask for. I have a lot to explain. A lot has happened, and I need you to hear me out."

Desperate to cling to a thread of hope, I reluctantly allowed him to lead me to a table. He pulled out a chair, and I sat. He took the one opposite.

"I found out why Sara came back," he said.

"That's not news," I said. "She told you why. She told *me* why. She made a mistake and wanted you back."

"I found out the *real* reason why. Or I should say Garen discovered her true intentions. When she showed up out of the blue, I asked him to dig around to see what he could unearth. It took him a while, but eventually, he uncovered the truth."

Intrigued, I leaned forward. "Which was?"

I sat, enthralled, as Oliver set his cell phone on the table between us and played a recording. When Sara admitted she didn't want Annie, then threatened to obtain custody through the courts, my blood filled with pure rage. I'd been right to call her an evil witch, because that's exactly what she was.

"Do you think she'll go ahead with her threat, despite you having that recording?" I asked after I'd listened to the rest of it in silence.

"Who knows," Oliver said. "But if she does decide to risk it, I'll make sure every judge right up to the supreme court gets a copy of this recording. We're fortunate that ROGUES hands over huge sums in taxes to this city and, as such, we wield a great deal of influence that I'm not afraid to use if it means securing the safety and happiness of my daughter."

I stared out the window, absorbing the enormity of what I'd heard. What kind of a woman would be so vicious, and all for the sake of money and a stupid title from a foreign country thousands of miles away? Annie was so lucky to have Oliver for a father. Nurture won out over nature in this case.

"I still don't understand why you looked so happy to see her. How you could stand to put your arm around her as if you were a couple when you knew the truth."

"I texted her the night before asking her to come over to talk about us. She thought she'd won. I didn't want her to get suspicious. I had to play the part until we got to my penthouse, and I could present her with the irrefutable evidence of her plan.

"I'm so sorry I hurt you, that despite my repeated denials I felt anything for Sara, I couldn't reassure you enough to trust me. That's on me. But it's you I love. You I want to spend my life with." He reached across the table and captured my hand, bringing my knuckles to his lips. "If you'll still have me."

A lump formed in my throat, and tears pricked the backs of my eyes. I answered instinctively. "Yes, I'll still have you."

Oliver got to his feet and helped me to mine. His hands curved around the back of my neck, and his thumbs brushed my jawline. "We're a team. You, me, and Annie. No one will ever come between us again."

"A team." I nodded, holding my breath as he bent his head and kissed me, the twinkling lights of New York providing the perfect backdrop to a dazzling future.

EPILOGUE

HARLOW

"Annie, stop fidgeting." Oliver took Annie's hand and tugged her to his side. "She'll be here soon."

"I can't wait," Annie said, ignoring Oliver's instruction and bouncing on the balls of her feet. "Has she landed yet?"

Oliver caught my eye and raised his to the ceiling.

I chuckled, then ruffled Annie's hair. "Yes, sweet pea. She's landed. I bet she's waiting for her luggage right this second."

My comment caused further jumping up and down. "Yessss."

Throngs of people appeared, filling up the arrivals hall. Squeals and shouts were followed by hugs as family and friends greeted their loved ones, glad to have them home once more. I kept my eyes peeled for Liv, nerves biting at my stomach. Oliver had told me she was happy about us, but I needed to see it for myself, to look in her eyes and read the truth there.

"There she is," Oliver said. He pointed and waved to catch his mother's attention.

Annie craned her neck. "I can't see her," she wailed.

I bent my knees and picked Annie up, hoisting her onto my hip. "Can you see her now? She's right behind that gentleman in the big hat."

"Nanan!" Annie yelled, her excited scream confirmation that she could now see her grandmother. She wriggled to be put down.

I obliged, but I wasn't quick enough to grab her. She ducked underneath the barrier and took off, pigtails flying, arms outstretched, and flung herself right into Liv's waiting arms.

"Ready to feel surplus to requirements?" Oliver murmured, slinging an arm around my shoulder. "We're way down the popularity list now Mom's home."

I laughed and leaned into him. "I'll live with it. You must be glad she's home."

He didn't have time to respond before Liv made her way over to us, Annie clinging to her side, a beaming smile almost splitting her face in two.

"Darling." Liv hugged Oliver tightly. "Oh, it's good to be home." She released him, then turned to me. Her arms came out, and I found myself enveloped in chiffon and *Chanel No. 5*. "Welcome to the family, darling Harlow."

My nerves floated away on a sea of relief as Liv craned a look over her shoulder and beckoned to the man hovering off to the side while the family reunion took place. He had a receding hairline and a goatee, and a pair of the kindest eyes I'd ever seen. Chocolate brown, crinkles around the edges, a twinkle that alluded to a sense of mischief despite his advancing years.

"Scott, come meet Harlow."

Oliver held out his hand and shook Scott's, then I did the same. "It's very nice to meet you," he said.

"Hope my mother hasn't been too much trouble, Scott,"

Oliver said with a wink. He earned a sharp dig and a glare from his mother in response.

Scott laughed. "We've had an amazing time, haven't we, love?"

"Wonderful." She got a wistful look in her eyes, then blinked two or three times and crouched to hug Annie again. "But I've missed my family, especially this little imp."

"The car is parked in the lot across the street." Oliver grabbed his mother's suitcases. "Scott, can we drop you?"

He shook his head. "I have a car picking me up." He pecked Liv on the cheek. "I'll leave you all to catch up. Call me?"

She nodded, a coy dip to her chin that Oliver caught. He shot me a look, and I grinned.

She's in love.

Liv watched Scott stride across the arrivals hall until he was swallowed up by the crowds. "Right," she said, rubbing her hands together. "Let's go home. I'm sure Annie is dying to open all the presents I've brought her."

Annie's face lit up. "Oh, Nanan. I can't wait."

Annie and Liv chattered the entire journey home, and Liv shared lots of photos of her trip. Once we arrived at Oliver's penthouse, Liv insisted on bathing and reading to Annie, then putting her to bed.

Oliver took her bags up to her room while I pottered about the kitchen, rustling up a light dinner. My eyes locked on Oliver as he came downstairs a short while later and walked over to join me. The last week since we'd reunited had been one of the happiest of my life. I wish I'd trusted him more and avoided breaking up in the first place, but the past had shaped the woman I was, and I'd allowed my demons to take over, believing that Oliver had chosen Sara over me.

He slipped his arms around my waist. "Penny for the thoughts in your head right now," he murmured, nuzzling my neck.

"I was thinking how happy I am," I said.

He turned me and lowered his head to capture my mouth. I melted against him as his lips roved over mine, tasting, exploring, revering.

He withdrew, his eyes traveling over my face. "Mom's moving in with Scott. She just told me."

I nodded and rubbed my lips together. "I'm not surprised. The way she looked at him... How do you feel about that?"

"I feel good about it. More than good. Mom has given up so much of her life for me and for Annie. It's long overdue that she had a life of her own. And Scott's a good man. I couldn't have wished for better."

His gaze moved south, settling on my chest. "She's already insisted that Annie spends a few nights a month with her which means..." He licked his lips. "Sex on the balcony."

I threw back my head and laughed. "You have a one-track mind."

"I don't hear you complaining." He bent his knees and circled his hips, rubbing his erection against me. "I expect Mom will want an early night. How about we follow suit?"

I gasped as he squeezed my nipple through my sweater. "Sold."

～

I woke alone with Oliver's side of the bed cold. He must have been up for a while. I slipped on my robe and used the bathroom, then headed downstairs. Voices floated up toward me. Oliver and his mom. Oliver's tones were quiet, Liv's angry, then incensed. Unwilling to intrude on their private conversation, I paused on the stairs, in two minds as to whether to go back up or carry on down.

And then I heard Sara's name.

Oh heck. Oliver must be telling his mother about her. We'd

spoken a lot about this the past week and made the decision that he'd tell his mother alone once she returned from her vacation. No point spoiling the last few days of her vacation. He must have decided to get it out of the way early. Probably for the best. No doubt Annie would mention her mother at some point. She'd taken Sara's leaving remarkably well, although Oliver kept a hawkish eye on her for signs of distress or abandonment. I didn't blame him. Poor little mite had gone through a lot of change in a short space of time. Kids were resilient, but that didn't mean that they weren't suffering long-term damage.

My mind turned to Patsy, my favorite little girl at the children's home Oliver funded. She still hadn't uttered a single word, but the other day I got a smile out of her. One day I'd break through. I knew it deep in my heart. I'd never give up on that child. She had a lot of love to give. All I had to do was find the key.

I waited until their voices went silent and then I crept the rest of the way downstairs. Oliver's gaze cut to me as I came into view. I mouthed, "Are you okay?" and he nodded. His reaction to me brought Liv's head around. She gave me a wide smile and rose to her feet.

"Morning, darling. Shall I make a start on breakfast?"

"Actually, Mom, we thought we might take Annie to Bubby's this morning."

"Oh, perfect." She came across to me, kissed my cheek, and murmured, "Thank you for slapping that bitch when I couldn't," then swept up the stairs.

I suppressed a chuckle. Oliver must have told her everything.

"What did she say?" he asked, an eyebrow arched in suspicion.

I tapped my nose. "Girl's talk."

He groaned. "Outnumbered again. When we have kids, we're having a boy. I need more testosterone in this house."

My breath hitched. We hadn't discussed having kids, but the fact Oliver wanted them with me sent my heart soaring. I'd always dreamed of having a big family and doing a better goddamn job than my own parents. I'd celebrate my kids for the things they were good at, not the things they weren't. I'd love them unconditionally whether they discovered a new vaccine or emptied the trash. All that mattered to me was that they were good people, and that they found happiness.

"Well, the sex of any baby is up to you, so we'll know who to blame if I end up having four girls in a row."

His eyes widened. "Four?"

I nodded, stood on my tiptoes, and kissed him. "At least."

An hour later, bundled up in coats, hats, and scarves, we made our way to Bubby's. Liv tucked her hand through my arm and pulled me to her for a squeeze. I beamed so wide, I thought that my face might split. At last, I'd found a place I belonged with people who didn't judge me by my SAT score, but for the goodness in my heart.

After we ordered our food, Annie insisted Oliver walk her to the bathroom and wait outside. He obliged with a smile and a ruffle of her hair, which earned him a glower. As soon as they were out of earshot, Liv turned to me.

"How is Annie handling it? Give it to me straight."

"Sara appearing then disappearing, you mean?" When she nodded, I continued. "Surprisingly well. More to the point, how are *you* handling it?"

Liv's lips flattened, and a nerve beat in her jaw. "I promised Oliver I would leave well enough alone, especially as she hasn't shown her treacherous face around here since he and Garen sent her packing, but I won't lie. It's difficult. It's the lioness in me. I want to protect my cubs, to hunt down that bitch and warn her that if she ever comes near my family again, I'll put a bullet in her brain."

I chuckled. "You're fearsome."

The teasing note to my tone brought a smile to her face. She reached for my hand. "I'm so glad Oliver found you. You're the mother Annie deserves and the woman my son does, too. I want you to promise me that if Sara ever comes near my family again, you will tell me. Oliver, like most men, is a stubborn ass, and he won't want to worry me, but I have to know."

"I promise."

Oliver slid into the booth beside me while Annie snuggled up next to her grandmother, putting an end to our conversation. He glided an arm around my shoulder and kissed my temple.

"Daddy loves Harlow," Annie singsonged.

"He does," Oliver said, a promise in his eyes that sent tingles shooting up my spine. "And he always will."

THE END

If I wrote an autobiography about my life right now, I'd call it *Blackmailed by the Billionaire*.

Ruthless, callous, and self-serving are the nicest words to describe the powerful CEO who wants what's mine, and he'll use any method at his disposal to emerge victorious—including coercion.

Too bad. He'll soon learn I'm not like the others he's manipulated to bend to his will. Those bully tactics won't work on me. He has nothing of worth to offer.

Until tragedy strikes and, like a vulture, he swoops in and rips apart my life. Powerless to stop him, I'm forced to stand idly by and watch while he destroys the family business I've spent my whole life building.

But, as I'm about to find out, winning isn't enough for Garen Gauthier.

ACKNOWLEDGMENTS

I owe so much to my wonderful team who cheer me on, encourage me every step of the way, and challenge me to dig deep to make every novel I release the very best it can be.

I love you all - and in no particular order...

To my critique partner, Incy... One sentence. That was all it took to set my mind racing in a different direction and Enraptured is all the richer for it. Thank you from the bottom of my heart.

To my gorgeous, big-hearted, wonderful PA, Loulou. Thank you for always being in my corner. I promise you an asshole next time (and trust me, in Garen, I deliver!)

Emmy - thank you for your brilliant editing as always. I appreciate the heck out of you and am so glad you're my editor.

Katie - you are THE BOMB, lady. I promise you haven't seen the last of Patsy. Thank you for de-Britishing (yep that's a word!) my beloved story, and for your insight and suggestions.

Jean - I'm proud to have given you the tingles. That's an email to keep for years to come! Thank you for proofing for me. I'm so lucky to know you. Roll on November (I hope).

Jacqueline - The continuity queen! Thank you for reading You're awesome.

To my ARC readers. You guys are amazing! You're my final eyes and ears before my baby is released into the world and I appreciate each and every one of you for giving up your time to read —and point out the odd errors that slip through the net!

And last but most certainly not least, to you, the readers. Thank you for being on this journey with me. It still humbles me to think that my words are being read all over the world.

If you have any time to spare, I'd be ever so grateful if you'd leave a short review on Amazon or Goodreads. Reviews not only help readers discover new books, but they also help authors reach new readers. You'd be doing a massive favor for this wonderful bookish community we're all a part of.

ABOUT TRACIE DELANEY

Tracie Delaney realized she was destined to write when, at aged five, she crafted little notes to her parents, each one finished with "The End."

Tracie loves to write steamy contemporary romance books that center around hot men, strong women, and then watch with glee as they battle through real life problems. Of course, there's always a perfect Happy Ever After ending (eventually).

When she isn't writing or sitting around with her head stuck in a book, she can often be found watching The Walking Dead, Game of Thrones or any tennis match involving Roger Federer. Coffee is a regular savior.

You can find Tracie on Facebook, Twitter and Instagram, or, for the latest news, exclusive excerpts and competitions, why not join her reader group.

Tracie currently resides in the North West of England with her amazingly supportive husband and her two crazy Westie puppies, Cooper and Murphy.

Tracie loves to hear from readers. She can be contacted through her website

www.authortraciedelaney.com

Printed in Great Britain
by Amazon